BLOODLUST
CURSE

BOOKS BY LUANNE BENNETT

BLOODLUST CURSE

LUANNE BENNETT

SECOND SKY

Published by Second Sky in 2025

An imprint of Storyfire Ltd.
Carmelite House
50 Victoria Embankment
London EC4Y 0DZ
United Kingdom

www.secondskybooks.com

The authorised representative in the EEA is Hachette Ireland
8 Castlecourt Centre
Dublin 15 D15 XTP3
Ireland
(email: info@hbgi.ie)

ISBN: 978-1-83618-471-3
eBook ISBN: 978-1-83618-470-6

For everyone who's ever felt invisible.
It's never too late to shine.

ONE

Who did the heart belong to? Dog held the organ in his bare hand. I thought I was going to be sick, but Dog seemed unconcerned. Wolves had cast-iron stomachs. Raw flesh, human or otherwise, didn't faze them. My own heart was racing as Samuel declared immediately that it was human, and Dog noted that it was still slightly warm. Whoever it belonged to had been killed very recently.

Dog went back out to the alley and was able to pick up a scent. While he called in the pack to help him track it, I phoned Candy to let her know we were coming. Samuel suspected black magic was involved. Said he could practically smell it, and I couldn't think of a better person to confirm that than Candy. And while I was no expert in the dark arts, finding a human heart in a box on my back step had evil written all over it.

The image of that heart being removed from someone's chest, probably while it was still beating, was vivid in my mind as we left the bar with the special delivery and headed for my truck to drive the two blocks to Candy's shop. It didn't seem right to just stroll down the street carrying the thing. What if we ran into someone?

As I was reaching for the door handle, a patrol car drove up and stopped behind the truck. Murphy was driving, and Rick Carter was riding shotgun.

"Shit," I muttered, looking down at the box in my hand and wondering what the odds were they wouldn't get nosy about what was inside.

Murphy put the car in park but left the engine running as he got out. "Charley." He nodded to me and gave Samuel a quick glance. "Is everything all right here?"

I didn't want to look him in the eye, but that would have made him suspicious, and avoiding suspicion right now was the goal. I pulled it together and gave him my full attention. "Why wouldn't it be?"

He glanced at Samuel again. "Just checking."

The bottom of the box suddenly felt cool against my palm. Almost wet. Then my mind started to race. I'd only gotten a brief look inside the box before Dog pulled that heart out. Was there a pool of blood inside? I couldn't remember, but I had a terrible feeling we were all about to find out, if it was beginning to seep through the cardboard and all over my hand.

Murphy narrowed his eyes. "You look nervous, Charley." Then he glanced down at the box I was suddenly gripping with both hands. "What's in the box?"

A ticket to the penitentiary if he insisted on finding out. Rick Carter was staring at us through the driver's side window like he was about to get out too, and he was even nosier than Murphy.

By the way Samuel was looking at me over the hood of the truck, he must have sensed my heart racing. I was surprised Murphy couldn't hear it beating against my rib cage. "A present from me," Samuel said, leaving it at that.

It was time to end the conversation before I blew it, so I opened the truck door and started to climb in, trying to keep my hand from shaking so I didn't drop the box and spill a human heart on the pavement. "Would you mind moving your car?" He had me blocked in.

Murphy nodded slowly and backed up toward the patrol car, throwing Samuel a wary look. When he started to say something else, I slammed the door shut and prayed he'd get the message and leave. I finally released my pent-up breath when he got back in his car and pulled away.

"Are you all right?" Samuel asked when I sat there and went silent.

I looked at the underside of the box. There was a dark spot the size of a quarter starting to bleed through, but not enough to panic over like I almost did in front of Murphy. My paranoia was working overtime. "I am now," I said, handing it to Samuel. "Remind me again why we didn't call the police the moment we found out what was in that box?"

"Because someone left it for you, Charley. We need to figure out who and why. And for that we need the heart. The police can have it after that."

I let out a weak laugh. "Are we going to just leave it on the sidewalk in front of the police station when we're done with it?"

"One problem at a time," he said when we pulled up to the Cauldron. "Besides, we haven't even determined who or what this heart belongs to yet."

There went my stomach again. "You said it was human?"

He frowned at the box. "Probably, but I'm not entirely convinced now. It's giving off some powerful vibes."

"Great," I muttered, climbing out of the truck.

As we were walking toward the door, Candy came out and glanced at the box in Samuel's hands. "Is that it?"

"Well, it isn't a dozen glazed donuts," I said, heading for the door. She gave me the side-eye as I walked past her. "Sorry."

"I'll let it slide this time," she said, following me inside, "considering."

As Samuel came in and set the box down on the display

case, I got the willies just thinking about looking inside again. "I still think we should leave it somewhere for the police to find." After that encounter with Murphy a few minutes ago, personally handing it over was out of the question.

Candy chuckled. "Those fools can barely trace a fingerprint back to its owner, let alone a heart."

"A body is going to eventually turn up with an empty hole in its chest," I said. "When that happens, even Rick Carter will be able to put two and two together."

The three of us stared at the box, but none of us seemed to be in a hurry to open it.

I looked back and forth between Samuel and Candy. "Who wants to do the honors?"

"I'll do it." Candy let out a sigh and reached for the box. "Just think of it as a chuck roast from the grocery store without all the plastic wrapped around it."

"That's gross, Candy."

She gave me a look. "Well, what do you think you're eating when you bite into a drumstick or a steak? Flesh is flesh, honey. And it's dead, so at least it isn't going to jump out at us." She lifted the folded flap to peer inside the box. "Yep, it's a heart all right. I hope whoever did this had the decency to kill the person before ripping it out."

I cringed as those vivid images resurfaced in my mind, only this time my imagination included a bloodcurdling scream from the victim.

Candy reached inside but hesitated to touch it as a strange look rolled over her face.

Samuel held her gaze for a moment. "You feel it too, don't you?"

She took a step back. "There's definitely something not right about it, but I guess I need to suck it up and lay hands on it to see what we're dealing with here."

Before she could reach into the box again, Dog walked through the front door.

"Did you find anything?" I asked.

He let out a long breath. "The scent led up to the lake."

Candy suddenly lost interest in the box. "Which one?"

There are two lakes in the immediate area around Crimson, and they're known for vastly different things. Snow Lake is named for how the water appears white when the moonlight reflects off its surface. It's a popular fishing spot, and teenagers like to go up there at night on the weekends to do what teenagers do. And then there's Blood Lake on the other side of Crimson, positioned between the town and the mountains. That one isn't so popular, and it gets its name for much darker reasons. More than one body has been found in that water over the years. Several, in fact. Since I was a kid, there's been an urban legend that there's a boneyard at the bottom.

"Blood Lake. The scent led the pack straight to the edge." Dog shook his head. "It's like whoever dropped that box off at the Stag came from and went straight back into the water."

My brows arched. "You mean like a swamp thing?" I was only half joking.

The beams from a set of headlights suddenly filled the shop as the Squad's ancient Buick Riviera pulled up and parked next to my truck. It was black and reminded me of a hearse. Candy must have called them as soon as I hung up with her.

Katherine Belltower got out of the driver's side, and Desiree emerged from the back seat. The passenger side appeared to be empty.

"Desiree doesn't do front seats," Candy said when she saw me squinting at the car. "The pompous crone likes to feel like she's being chauffeured."

The two witches walked into the Cauldron, but the sisters, Mia and Fay Winston, were absent. Katherine's eyes immediately went to Samuel. "Mr. Cain."

"We're past formality," he replied. "Please, call me Samuel."

"Yes, I suppose we are." Her eyes continued around the room and landed on the box on the display case. "Quite an undignified vessel, isn't it? How many of you have touched the heart?"

"Just Dog," I said.

She walked over to him and grabbed his hands, flipping them palm side up. "Fawny would have liked the feel of these." She raised her eyes back up to Dog's. "She liked a man with working hands."

"Who's Fawny?" I said.

Katherine nodded to the box. "The woman that heart belonged to."

Candy's breath hitched. "No! Fawny Goodman?"

Dog tilted his head. "I know her. She lives in that beat-up old house up at Blood Lake."

"Lived," Desiree corrected as a strange grin slid up her face. "We found her this evening, and she was dead as dead can be."

"Or rather she found us," Katherine said.

I was losing patience, and that heart would only stay fresh for so long. "Get to the point. Dead woman, missing heart..."

Katherine threw me a glance and continued. "An owl paid us a visit."

"And it led you to the body," Dog said with a nod. It wasn't a question.

"That's right!" Desiree's eyes practically twinkled.

Her enthusiasm for the macabre was disturbing. I could only imagine what her reaction had been like when she saw the dead woman with a gaping hole in her chest. But I guess we needed people like Desiree Dubois or we wouldn't have undertakers or medical examiners. The cleaners of the world. Vultures and maggots really did have thankless jobs. It actually tempered my opinion of her slightly.

"What does an owl have to do with a dead woman?" I asked.

"Owls are messengers," Dog replied. "Escorts of the dead to take them to the other side."

"Interesting. Remind me to stay clear of owls."

Katherine's expression went cold. "We found her at the edge of the lake. Her face was frozen in a state of terror. The poor thing must have still been alive when it happened." Anger flared in her eyes. "Only a monster could have done this!"

Like that swamp thing I'd jokingly mentioned earlier?

"Why would someone kill a woman I've never even heard of and deliver her heart to me?" I was tired of having a target on my back. Maybe it was time for that vacation I'd been thinking about lately. Time to get out of town for a while.

Katherine shook her head. "I don't know, but Fawny was a witch, so you have that in common."

"Every woman in this room is a witch," I pointed out.

Candy's eyes narrowed. "You don't think...?"

"That Charley's next?" Katherine laughed. "I doubt the killer would warn her."

"I don't know about that," I said, feeling a sudden chill run down my spine. The memory of Keith Barnes's body lying in a heap on my front porch was seared into my mind. "The last time something dead was left on my doorstep, I was caught in a cat and mouse game with a killer vampire. Remember?"

Katherine eyed Dog. "It could have been left for your wolf friend." Then she glanced back at the box. "I don't see a label with a name on it."

She brought up a good point. The Stag was the obvious place to leave something for Dog as well. Most of the wolves lived in houses that comprised a small fortress at the edge of the woods, with Dog's house being the most protected, seeing as how he was the pack leader. It would have been nearly impossible to get past the pack to leave that box at his place. In fact, that heart could have been left for any of my employees.

Candy closed the box. "So, what do we do with it? I've got a client coming in the morning, and this thing is messing with the aura in the shop."

Desiree snatched it from the display case. "What do you think we're going to do with it? We're going to put it back where it belongs."

I felt my face twist up in horror. "You mean you want to put it back inside the dead woman's chest?" I'd suspected that witch wasn't playing with a full deck, but this confirmed it.

"Exactly. If we bury her without it, she'll haunt the lake for eternity. We can't have that, can we?"

I glanced at Candy and then at Katherine, who was supposed to be the voice of reason for the Squad. "Bury her?" I must have heard Desiree wrong. "You mean before the *authorities* bury her?" No one said anything to ease my growing panic. Not even Samuel or Dog. That jail cell I saw in my future was coming closer by the second. "Have you all lost your minds?"

Katherine took a step closer to me. "There's something you need to understand."

"Oh, I think I understand just fine. Everyone in this room is about to commit a felony. Conceal a murder." Like it would be the first time, but this was different. This was a human. "You're talking about burying someone."

"Not just someone, Charley. A witch. There are things that must be done." She glanced at Candy and Desiree. "To all of us when we die, including you. Mia and Fay are already preparing for it back at the house."

A lump started to form in my throat. "Like what?"

"Honey, why don't you have a seat." Candy went to grab one of the folding chairs in the corner.

I found myself taking an involuntary step away from Katherine. "I don't want to sit down."

Desiree huffed. "Just get on with it before the heart starts to stink in that box."

Katherine spelled it out for me. "If you put a witch in the

ground, the magic will seep into the earth where it will be lost forever. We do things differently in Crimson. We harness the magic first, and then the body is left to the forest."

"It's like the boneyard is for the wolves," Dog said.

My eyes shot to his. "How do you know about this?"

"Delia told me. She wanted to make sure I knew her wishes if something happened to her. Or to you, Charley."

My mind started to race. One minute we were talking about a stranger who'd had her heart ripped out, and now we were discussing my mother. "But she was cremated. We had a service for her."

Were they all out of their minds?

"That casket was empty," Candy said. "Her body was taken from the funeral home in the middle of the night so the ritual could be performed." Suddenly she was looking at anything but me. The floor, the wall, the front window. "You wouldn't have understood at the time, Charley."

I didn't understand now. I just stared at her, trying to comprehend what she was saying to me. "Is this a joke?"

"No, honey. It was Delia's wishes. We were afraid you would have tried to stop us."

"So, you just decided not to tell me?" I felt sick to my stomach. Like a fool. Betrayed by the two people I trusted with my life.

Dog could barely look at me either, but there was no apology in Katherine's eyes when I turned back to her. "We're telling you now. Can you honestly say you wouldn't have tried to stop us?"

I probably would have. But right now, all I knew for sure was that the container of ashes on the top shelf in my living room contained nothing but the remains of the coffin they stole my mother from.

Candy reached for me. "Charley..."

"Don't." Anger welled up inside me as I recoiled from her.

"I need to get out of here before I say or do something I'm going to regret."

Dog grabbed my wrist as I headed for the door. "Wait."

A bolt of energy ran down my arm and traveled across his hand. I didn't care. I willed it into him. He stumbled back, hitting the display case hard. The impact cracked one of the panes along the front. A slight gasp left my mouth, but my anger overruled it. To hell with the case. "I'll pay to have it fixed," I said, leveling my gaze on Candy's so she could feel the full weight of the betrayal I felt.

When Dog tried to follow me out of the shop, Samuel stepped in his path. "Let her go."

After getting into my truck, I pulled away from the Cauldron before anyone else could try to stop me, a sob bursting from my mouth the moment I put the truck in drive. Tears streamed down my face as I drove toward the house. I felt like the butt of a bad joke. I'd spoken at my mother's memorial service, and she wasn't even in that box. And all the while, they were planning some ritual that I wasn't even a part of. How could they?

I pulled up to the house a few minutes later and sat there for a moment. When I finally got out and looked up, Rex was perched high in the oak tree. Instead of swooping down to follow me inside, he stayed put, his small black silhouette standing out against the brightness of the moon. Maybe he sensed my mood and thought it wise to keep his distance.

As I went up the steps and stuck my key in the lock, Samuel appeared on the porch behind me.

"Charley..." He wrapped his arms around me from behind. "What can I do?"

I just shook my head, turning around to bury my face in his chest as the dam burst again. It was like a purge of toxins that had built up over weeks. Months. Nearly two years since my mom walked out the door and never came home. Add the betrayal from the people I trusted most, and it was Armageddon inside me.

Without saying another word, Samuel held me and stroked his hand down my back as I got it out of my system.

When I finally came up for air, I gazed up at his face and sighed. "Sorry about that." I wasn't much of a crier, but tonight warranted a good one.

He brushed a strand of wet hair out of my eyes. "Sorry for what?"

I glanced at the wet spot on his chest. "For soaking your shirt." I finally managed a smile. "It was just a lot to take in."

"They had their reasons, Charley. You know that."

"I guess. I'm just so angry right now. Why didn't they just tell me?"

Before he could offer more consoling words, there was a scratching at the door followed by a bark that sounded more like a dinosaur's roar.

"Oh, shit! I forgot about Diablo!" No wonder Rex didn't follow me inside. I'd rescued Victor Steele's hellhound from the Beast last night. After we'd killed the vampire, the poor dog cowered under a table, so I took mercy on him and brought him home with me. By now, he'd probably shredded my house and left a pile on my living room floor.

As soon as I pushed the door open, he barreled past me and ran down the steps to lift his leg against the nearest bush. Then he disappeared around the corner to do the rest of his business.

When Samuel and I went inside, I left the door open for Diablo. I didn't smell anything bad and my couch was intact, so the dog must have had a strong bladder and some training. Then my eyes landed on the bookcase against the wall. And the nondescript nine-by-six box on the top shelf. Tears threatened to flow again, but there were none left. I was all dried up.

I'd never ordered an urn because I'd planned to spread her ashes immediately. My mother was a free spirit. She would have hated to sit on a shelf for eternity. But finding the perfect spot had been more difficult than I'd ever imagined. How do you dust a loved one to the wind without knowing in your gut you've chosen the right spot? Weeks of searching for that perfect place to deposit her ashes had turned into months and now nearly two years, and that box was still up there.

"I have to look at that thing all night," I said, nodding to the shelf. "I can't bring myself to throw it out, even knowing she's not in there."

"Then stay at my place." Samuel held up a set of keys. "I'm officially a resident of Crimson now."

I stared at them for a moment as the words *my place* sank in. I still had no idea where he'd been staying since he got to town. It was like some big secret, and I was beginning to wonder if he was hiding something. But now that we'd taken our relationship to the next level, I intended to find out. "You rented a place?"

"A house at the end of Moon Street." A grin spread across his face. "With a name like that, how could I resist?"

There was only one vacant house at the end of that street. "You mean the old Pullman place?" It had been empty for years. Ever since Clifford Pullman died. He was a vampire whose demise was a cruel twist of fate. His car had flipped when he ran off the road one night and ended up in a ravine, pinning him underneath. It nearly severed his head, but not enough to turn him to dust. When morning rolled around, the sun did him in though. They found him a day later, reduced to a pile of ash under the wreckage. If it hadn't been for his clothes on the ground, we may have never known if he'd died in the crash or just vanished.

"When did you do this?" I asked.

"A few days ago, but it's not a rental. The heirs were eager to sell, since the place has just been collecting dust for years. I got it for a good price and paid cash."

So, Samuel was here to stay. I was elated, but I also needed a moment to let it sink in.

He pinned me with his blue eyes. "You seem nervous."

Diablo came trotting back into the house, interrupting the moment in the nick of time. He hopped up on the couch and made himself comfortable, hanging his massive paws over the edge before resting his head between them.

"Make yourself at home," I said to him.

Samuel took my chin and turned my eyes back to his. "You didn't answer my question."

I wasn't nervous, but I was a little overwhelmed by feelings I'd never had before. I was no stranger to lust and attraction, but I'd never felt anything that came close to what I'd experienced with Samuel over the past couple of weeks. There was no running from it now though. No hiding from the way my heart was beating from the way he was looking at me at that moment. We weren't just having fun anymore, and now he was here to stay.

Samuel's eyes wandered down to my chest. "Your heart is beating dangerously fast." Then he brought them back up to mine. "Will you let me calm you down?"

"Yes," I said, my voice barely a whisper. But then Diablo raised his head to look at us. "What about him?"

Samuel glanced at the dog. "He's not invited."

I smiled as he led me toward the bedroom, my fear of commitment fading with each step. By dawn, I knew that any shred of it would be gone, and Samuel Cain would have to beg me to leave him.

TWO

I rolled over to face Samuel. "Were you serious about me staying at your place?" I knew that Candy would give me some time to calm down, but Dog would eventually show up here, to try and mend the fence he'd just demolished. I wasn't ready to talk to either of them yet.

I'd texted Patrick after Samuel and I went to the bedroom and asked him if he could handle the co-op deliveries solo in the morning, and God bless him, he agreed. I think he sensed the fatigue in my voice.

"It would just be for the night." It was after midnight, so technically it was morning. But I was wide awake now and wanted to see Samuel's place. "I still have to take care of Diablo until I can convince Beau to take him."

"You think that's a good idea with Beau's predicament?"

Samuel was convinced Beau was changing. Changing into what was still a mystery. Victor Steele had attacked him. Bitten him. But something had gone wrong. Instead of turning, Beau was stuck somewhere in the middle. A *halfling*, Samuel had called him.

"He needs that dog now more than ever," I said. "If something is happening to him, he'll be vulnerable. Maybe Diablo can protect him."

Samuel chuckled. "If you say so. And of course you can stay at my place. For as long as you'd like. You can even claim a closet and leave a toothbrush in the bathroom. And the refrigerator is all yours."

There was that strange feeling again. That nervous pang in the pit of my stomach. I welcomed it though. Anything to take my mind off the bombshell that had just been dropped on me back at the Cauldron.

"Let me just grab a few things and feed the dog."

Samuel gave me a strange look. "It's the middle of the night. How often does he eat?"

"Have you noticed the size of that dog? Unless you want me to take him with us so I can feed him first thing in the morning?"

"No, thank you." He got up and grabbed his pants off the floor. "I don't think Sebastian would approve."

As I got up to get dressed, he pulled me against him. "I mean it, Charley. You can stay at my house for as long as necessary. Move in if you'd like." Seeing the look on my face, he kissed me on the forehead and resumed the search for the rest of his clothes. "Don't look so terrified."

"I'm not terrified."

He shot me a grin and headed for the bedroom door. "Good. Now, go feed the dog. I'll meet you outside at the truck."

The first thing I did was put my mother's ring on. It seemed appropriate to wear it, now that I had someone sending me body parts possibly laced with dark magic. Then I stuffed a few things in a duffel bag and sat on the edge of the bed for a moment staring at the sapphire.

After pulling myself together, I went into the kitchen to whip up some breakfast for Diablo. "You're lucky I have a spare carton," I said as he sat there licking his chops while I cracked half a dozen eggs into a skillet. After scrambling them, I refilled his water bowl and set it on the floor along with his breakfast. "Be good, and please don't eat my couch while I'm gone."

On my way out, I grabbed my bag and some cereal from the top of the refrigerator. After locking up, I opened the box and set it on the porch for Rex before heading down the steps.

Samuel was leaning against the truck. "I was wondering if you'd changed your mind."

"Sorry. I had to break out the frying pan." I needed to pick up a huge bag of dog food on my way home in the morning. Maybe even two: a starter bag for Beau and enough to hold me over until I could convince him to take the dog.

"No problem. Your friend has been keeping me company." He nodded to Rex who had flown down from the top of the tree and was perched on the lowest branch hanging over the truck. "I think he brought you a gift."

"Oh yeah?" I tossed my bag in the bed of the truck. "What kind of gift?"

Samuel opened his hand and revealed a silver pendant and chain. "Crows like shiny things, but I doubt he brought it for me. The stone is missing," he said as he handed it over, "but it's the thought that counts."

I looked at my ring and realized it matched the setting of the necklace I was holding, minus the sapphire in the center. "Rex brought this to you?"

"He dropped it from the tree. Why? Is something wrong?"

I shook my head. "I think this was my mother's. She must have lost it somewhere in the yard." Still stunned at what I was holding, I looked at Rex on the tree limb. He stared back at me briefly with his shiny black eyes and then cawed and flew away.

* * *

We turned onto Moon Street, passing some of Crimson's finest houses. Or at least they used to be. Most of them were in need of major repairs or full renovations, but the people who lived in them or inherited them didn't have the money to keep them up. Folks around here could barely pay their property taxes, let alone sink money into their homes. It was a shame to see such beautiful houses fall into disrepair. To see some of Crimson's history slowly crumble.

The Pullman place was the last one on the left. It sat on a good two acres, which was unusual. Most of the houses within the town limits were built on half an acre at most, and many sat on postage-stamp-size lots. But Clifford Pullman was one of Crimson's wealthier residents. A reclusive vampire who'd made his fortune in investments, from what I'd been told.

As we pulled into the driveway, my headlights lit up the front of the house, revealing an even worse paint job than I recalled. In fact, the whole place seemed only a fraction as charming as I remembered it. But it had been a long time since I'd been down Moon Street. Probably years.

I got out and looked up at the place, seeing past the bad paint as the charm I remembered came rushing back. "It's a colonial, right?"

"Colonial with classical elements. I grew up in a house like this."

I was terribly curious about his past. I didn't even know how old he was. Vampires stopped aging the moment they were turned, so there was no telling. I had a lot of questions for Samuel tonight.

"It's nice," I said with a deep sigh. "But I hope you got it for a *really* good price because it's going to need a lot of sprucing up."

He grinned slyly. "Cash is king when you're trying to unload a house that's been empty for years."

Down in Atlanta, there'd have been a bidding war on a place like this. But up here in the boondocks, the market wasn't nearly as strong, although the house still couldn't have been cheap. But I had enough manners not to ask.

When we got to the front door, Samuel pulled out a key. "I'd like you to have this. A spare."

I stared at it for a few seconds, not knowing how to respond. My person was offering me a key to his house, but it was way too early for that. "Oh, I don't know, Samuel."

"It's just a key, Charley. For emergencies," he quickly added with a shrug. "I might need a plant watered now and then."

"Well, when you put it like that." I took the key and stuck it in the lock. The door yawned as it opened. The moment I stepped inside, a musty odor hit my nose, reminding me that the place had been empty for years. A dozen open windows and a solid cleaning would help, but odors like these went with old houses. Mine was a fraction of the size and still had that ancient farmhouse smell. But I preferred it over the sterile scent of new construction any day.

"Wow. Pretty impressive." Just inside the entrance was a staircase leading to the second floor, butting up against the living room wall on the right. The floors were dull, but I knew there were beautiful original hardwoods under all that dust and grime. "The place is huge."

"It's probably too much space for me, but it was a bargain."

I followed him into the living room and looked around at the period furnishings. "I guess the furniture came with it?"

"Drab, isn't it? It'll do until I can replace it with something a little more colorful."

Something was definitely missing though. "Where's Sebastian?" I expected him to come running into the living room when he heard my voice. In fact, I hadn't seen the cat in a while.

Samuel's brow furrowed. "He took off the day I bought the place. Sniffed around the kitchen for a while and then disappeared. He'll show up when he gets hungry. He always does."

"He's probably catting around making more little Sebastians," I said. "You really should get him fixed." It was the responsible thing for a pet owner to do, and I intended to make it my mission to see that Samuel did.

He snickered. "Tell that to Sebastian. That cat isn't what you think he is, so don't worry about him spreading his seed."

I squinted at him. "What is he?"

"*That* is a very good question. I've been trying to figure that out for decades, but you'll be the first to know when I do."

"Decades?"

When he didn't elaborate and started rummaging through a desk against the wall, I decided to move on to another question. But I intended to return to the subject of Sebastian later. I didn't want to be rude and dive right into Samuel's financial situation, so I started with an easy one. "What will you do now? As far as a job, I mean?"

He picked up a paperweight with some kind of flower encased in the glass and absently fiddled with it. "You mean for money? I have plenty of that."

Okay. We were getting somewhere.

He set it back down and looked over his shoulder at me. "Family money, but I do intend to work."

"You mean you intend to keep hunting?"

"I've been a hunter for a very long time, Charley. It's who I am."

I understood that. I knew now what I was, and there was no taking it out of me. Rough around the edges or not, the witch was here to stay. "Does that mean you'll be spending a lot of time away from Crimson?"

"I hope not, but my work will take me out of town occasionally."

Samuel was free to come and go as he pleased. There'd be none of that joined-at-the-hip stuff. But I'd be lying if I said his absence wouldn't bother me. Wouldn't make me count the hours until he returned.

He came closer, his fingers grazing my cheek. "But I won't be going anywhere for a while. Not until I find out who left that heart at your back door."

"That box might not have even been meant for me."

"Don't be naive, Charley."

I knew he was probably right, especially after finding out who that heart belonged to. But why would someone be targeting witches in Crimson? We were the least of people's worries around here.

Samuel's eyes had turned grave when he looked back at me. "What concerns me most is the way that heart was taken. Post-mortem, it's nothing but a trophy. But when it's removed while the victim is still breathing, it's for use in dark magic. And Katherine Belltower seemed convinced that the witch was very much alive when it was ripped from her chest." His brows lifted. "You're in danger."

There was no arguing with that. But it wasn't the first time, and it wouldn't be the last.

"I really do think you should move in here for a while." He motioned around the room. "I have enough space to start a boarding house." A grin slid up his face. "And you'll only have to tolerate me at night."

"Tempting, but I'll pass. I guess you'll just have to spend more time at my place."

He came closer and stared down at me with an intense gaze. "You're a stubborn woman."

"So I've been told by just about anyone who's ever met me." I also liked my freedom, and I wasn't about to get myself locked up in this musty old house.

It was time to change the subject, so I went back into the entryway and looked at the top of the staircase. "Mind if I take a tour?"

"You have a key to the place, so explore away."

I took the steps up to the second floor, wandering into each room briefly to inspect it. It was just the way I thought it would look. Like a time capsule since Cliff Pullman walked out the door years ago and never returned. It had been sitting empty ever since, collecting dust as Samuel had said and probably its share of mice in the attic. It was going to take some serious elbow grease to make it livable, at least by my standards. And we'd start by getting rid of all the sheets on the beds.

The bedroom at the end of the hallway must have been the master. It was grander than the others and had thick blackout drapes covering the large windows. It was a lot cleaner than the others too. There wasn't a trace of dust on the dresser when I ran my finger along the top, and the floor was bright and shiny. Someone had done some cleaning in the room.

"The linens on this bed are fresh," Samuel said from the doorway.

He was leaning against the frame watching me when I turned around. "You should know better by now than to sneak up on me like that. My power hand is still unpredictable."

We locked eyes as he walked toward me. Gripping my right wrist, he backed me up slowly toward the bed. "You mean this hand?"

When he pressed his lips to my palm, my legs went weak. "Yeah, that one." It was like my bones had gone soft.

The edge of the mattress stopped me. I sat down, raising my arms as Samuel lifted my shirt over my head. I fisted the silky sheets in my hands as he tilted my chin up to kiss me, sending shivers through my body when he stepped back to get undressed.

I was on my feet a moment later, shedding the rest of my clothes before climbing back onto the bed. On my knees, I beckoned him toward me. Before I could catch my breath, he was on top of me, moving my legs apart to settle deeply inside me. No foreplay. Just raw need as we christened the bed, the room, the whole damn house tirelessly for the next few hours.

* * *

I lay halfway on top of Samuel as I stroked my fingers over his chest. The thought of staying in that bed for days was tempting. With the blackout drapes, I couldn't tell if it was dawn yet, but I could see faint light beyond the bedroom door starting to stream into the hallway.

"You need to cover the hallway window," I said as I got up and walked across the room.

He sat up and pushed his hair out of his face. "Are you leaving?"

I shut the bedroom door and climbed back into bed, easing him against the pillows so I could lie on top of him and rest my cheek against his chest. "Not unless you want me to."

He gripped me tighter. "I'd tie you up and keep you here if I thought I'd get away with it."

I'd been bottling up a lot of questions since I realized Samuel was going to be a part of my life for as long as he'd have me, and I couldn't think of a better time to ask them. "You know everything about me, but I know nothing about you other than you're sexy as hell and like cats. Tell me something about your life, Samuel."

His body stiffened slightly beneath me. "You know who my maker was, and that's not a small thing."

It was kind of hard not to know who his maker was, considering that Victor Steele had been an existential threat to this entire town. He was avoiding the question.

"I want to know about *you*, Samuel. Where you're from. Who your family was." I glanced up at him. "Do you still have family? I don't even know how old you are." I was coming up with questions I hadn't even thought about until that moment.

He groaned but finally relented. "My father was British, and my mother was from Boston. That's where I grew up."

I smiled. "So that's why you're so proper."

"Proper?" He laughed quietly. "My father would be appalled if he could hear me now. He was quite the snob, but I guess some of him could have rubbed off on me."

"You were a rich kid, weren't you?" He said he had family money.

"So that's why you're sleeping with me. You're a gold digger."

I looked up at him again. "Is it that obvious? Damn!"

We both laughed for a moment before he started to open up.

"My father was an industrialist, although these days I guess you would call him an entrepreneur. Textiles. I wouldn't say we were Boston Brahmins, but we reeked of money. In the nineteenth century, a young man fresh out of college with a family like mine didn't explore his own path. My path was handed to me."

My eyes shot wide at hearing the words *nineteenth century*. But I didn't want him to shut down on me now, so I kept my face pressed against his chest to hide my surprise.

He flipped his hand dismissively. "There was none of this free-spirited, I-need-to-find-myself nonsense. No living in your parents' basement while you figured out what you wanted to do with your life. I was told what to do with mine. The first option was to join the family business."

"What was the second option?" I asked when he went quiet.

"Law school, of course. Harvard."

I rolled off him and propped myself up on my elbows. "Shut up! You're a lawyer?" I could have used his services when Beau got railroaded for the attacks in town.

"Not on your life." His eyes darkened to a deep sapphire blue. They were nearly black. "I did what was expected of me. Took the first option and went to work for my father and spent the next twelve years exporting wool and cotton, and I despised every second of it. I was about to tell my father I was done. I was leaving Boston and the company when..."

"When you were turned?" I asked when he hesitated. We were just getting to the good part.

"When I met Shane. I had one foot out the door when Shane Ronan came into my life and destroyed it."

THREE

"I thought Victor Steele destroyed your life," I said. Steele was his maker.

Samuel sat up and ran his hand over his face. "He did. They both did."

He went quiet after that and refused to speak another word about this Shane Ronan guy. Just saying the name had clearly hit a nerve, and I knew better than to push him for more information. When Samuel was ready, he'd tell me. But at least I knew a little more about him now than before the conversation came to an abrupt halt. Like the fact that he didn't have to worry about money, and he was old enough to be my great-great-grandfather.

Okay, I needed to push that thought out of my head.

"Will you stay with me for another hour?" I rolled onto my back and sank into the pillows. It may have been morning, but I still needed to get some sleep. I wasn't going to make it through a busy Saturday night at the Stag if I didn't.

Samuel climbed off the bed. "There's nothing I would rather do, but those drapes can only block out so much light." He gazed at me for a moment as if reconsidering, but then he looked away. "I need to get some rest, and I can't do that without complete darkness."

My brow tightened. "You stayed in bed with me all day yesterday with only blankets covering my bedroom windows. It wasn't even as dark as it is in here."

"And I'm already feeling it, Charley. I need to be sharp, especially now with what's happened. If I don't get some rest in my chamber, I'll grow weak."

Chamber?

I sat back up. "What kind of chamber?"

"The kind that's dark and quiet. It's necessary for vampires like me who are highly sensitive to even the smallest hints of daylight."

That was something else I'd always been curious about but never thought to ask until I met Samuel. "Why is it that some vampires..." Like Ian Masterson. "...can go out at dawn and dusk, but others can't even tolerate that?"

"It's an inherited trait from one's maker," Samuel said, drifting off in thought. "The darker the maker, the darker the progeny. And Victor Steele was as dark as they come."

It was hard to believe that Ian Masterson wasn't turned by a vampire just as dark as Steele.

"Anyway," he said, "it's small and drab, but it serves its purpose."

"I'll go with you to your... chamber."

He stared at me for a few seconds, his lips tightening slightly. "No."

"Well, all right." The rejection stung.

Reading the look on my face, he sat on the edge of the bed and ran his hand up and down my thigh. "Charley, my chamber is no place for you. For any human. I would stay with you up here if I could."

As I lay back down, it started to sink in. Dog had said it. Loving a vampire came with tradeoffs. Was I really in love with

Samuel? I'd never been in love with anyone before, so I had nothing to compare it to. But as I lay there looking at him, it was undeniable that I'd never felt anything like this before. Not even close.

He reached over and kissed me. "I'll come by the Stag tonight." Then he headed for a door on the other side of the room.

"Your chamber is in the closet?" I said.

"There's a staircase that leads to the cellar. The chamber is below it. Pullman was a vampire, so the house came with benefits. Another reason it was a perfect fit for me." He slipped through the door, leaving me alone in the bedroom. I'd accept it for now, but one of these days I was planning to make my way down those stairs. With Samuel's approval of course. I could sleep in a dark chamber. How bad could it be?

I'd fallen asleep and didn't so much as stir for the next three hours. I'd been running on fumes for the past week and needed the rest, but I also had a dog at the house that needed tending to.

So much for taking a shower.

After jumping out of bed and getting dressed, I went downstairs to check out the kitchen. The place felt enormous as I walked down the long hallway, the only sounds the creaking of the wood floors and other miscellaneous noises old houses make. I stopped and listened for a moment as if I might hear Samuel stirring somewhere below the cellar. Of course I didn't, but it was comforting to know he was somewhere in the place.

The kitchen was at the end of the hall on the back side of the house. It was big with the usual refrigerator and stove, but the countertops were bare. No microwave or toaster. No pots and pans hanging from the rack suspended from the tall ceiling. But the previous owner was a vampire, and vampires weren't known for their cooking skills. Most never bothered with human food, except maybe to entertain their human guests.

The second I walked inside, I detected a glorious smell in the air and spotted a programmable coffee maker in the corner near the refrigerator. There was a freshly brewed pot waiting for me with a small box and a note next to it.

A LITTLE CAFFEINE AND SUGAR TO HOLD YOU OVER.
SEE YOU TONIGHT.

The box was filled with donuts. He must have picked them up yesterday in anticipation of me waking up here this morning.

"A foregone conclusion, am I?" I smiled and set the letter down to pour myself a cup. That coffee had been sitting there for a while, but it was still warm. Besides, caffeine was caffeine, and I would have been grateful for even an ice-cold cup.

After taking a few gulps and stuffing a donut in my mouth, I grabbed my phone and keys. Diablo's bladder must have been ready to burst, if it hadn't already. Then I locked up and climbed in my truck.

Before heading out of town, I stopped at the feedstore to pick up the biggest bag of dog food they had. The owner, Pete, was coming out of the back room when I walked inside.

"Hey, Pete."

"Charley." He nodded to me before dumping a sack of chicken feed on the floor. "What can I do for you?"

I glanced around the store at all the bags stacked up against the walls. "I need some dog food." I could hear barking coming from behind the shop where he kept his prized hunting dogs in a fenced yard during the day when the shop was open. "I'm guessing you have some."

"Got you a dog, huh?"

"Yep." I didn't have time to explain the hellhound. "Got me a dog."

"Any particular brand?"

"Whatever you feed your own dogs will do." Pete treated his dogs like his children, so I figured he fed them the best he had.

He went in the back and returned with a bag big enough to last Diablo a few days at best.

"I'm going to need something bigger than that."

"What kind of dog did you get?"

"A big one. Do you have any fifty-pound bags?"

"Forty is the biggest I carry."

His dogs kept yapping while he went to fetch the bag. "What's with the dogs?" I asked when he came back out. Hunting dogs tended to be loud in general, but I'd never heard them like this before.

"Yeah, something's been getting 'em all riled up for the past few days." He dropped the bag of food on the counter. "Probably some vampires up to no good, like the ones who broke into my store a while back. My dogs don't like vamps."

Ian Masterson and his crew had paid a visit to the feedstore the evening before the break-in, so it was assumed that they were responsible. But I never believed that. All they did was intimidate a few customers, and they had nothing to gain by trashing the place. Ian wouldn't have wasted his time.

"Vampires make up half this town," I reminded him.

Pete glanced up from the register. "Well, there's something out there."

There was no denying that, but I doubted whoever delivered that package to the bar was in the market for chicken or hog feed.

I paid for the dog food and hauled it out to my truck, despite Pete's protests about not letting him carry it out for me. I'd carried heavier.

I took a quick detour past Webers' Thrift Shop on my way home to see if Mag's bike was parked out front. Not that I was being nosy. Well, I guess I was. But I was happy for Tucker.

After everything that had happened with Victor Steele, she deserved some happiness, and Mag Ryan had made his intentions clear. That wolf was smitten.

As I suspected, his bike was there. It was comforting to know there was another wolf in town who had both mine and Tucker's backs, even if he and Dog still needed to work out their differences. At least they *were* working them out.

I continued out of town, making a note to myself to offer to help Tucker find a better place. That apartment she was living in was a dump. And for the rent she was paying, she could do a lot better.

When I neared the house a few minutes later, I thought my eyes were playing tricks on me. From a distance, it looked like a ring of black around my property. But the closer I got, the more I realized I was seeing just fine. All I could do was stare at the small figures standing on the grass. There must have been hundreds of crows forming a circle around the perimeter.

They flew into the air all at once as I pulled into the driveway, like a black halo rising up to settle in the trees. It was eerily beautiful and slightly terrifying at the same time. In my experience, a murder of crows this large only appeared at the worst of times. When danger wasn't far off.

I got out of my truck and was looking up at the roof over the porch when I heard a loud caw. Rex flapped his wings, his single white feather distinguishing him from the rest of the army.

"What are you trying to tell me, Rex," I whispered to myself, debating whether I should get back in my truck and leave. But I had a hellhound in the house, so there was that. It was also high noon, so no vampires were out. Threats didn't always come with a set of fangs though.

I cautiously started walking toward the house, keeping an eye on Rex for signs that I should stop and turn around. He just sat up there looking down at me, and when he started preening himself, I knew I was overreacting. Who doesn't find a few hundred crows lining their yard every now and then?

When I stepped inside and didn't encounter anything out of the ordinary, I finally relaxed—until Diablo practically knocked me over and ran down the steps to do his business. Then he came running back up to the porch to greet me. I swear that dog smiled.

"Hey, boy. Did you keep the monsters away today?" There were definite benefits to having a massive dog with a questionable pedigree. Even a vampire would think twice about tangling with him. As soon as we went inside, he headed straight for the kitchen and sat down next to the stove. "I guess you're hungry. Well, I got you something. You're probably not going to like it as much as those omelets I've been feeding you, but you're a dog."

I went back outside to get the bag of food but caught movement from the corner of my eye as I was about to haul it out of the bed of the truck. "What in the hell?" There was a ruckus on the side of the house toward the backyard. It looked like a couple of animals were going at each other.

Dropping the bag, I went over to see what it was, glancing up at the crows in the trees. There were three dogs in a frenzy about thirty feet from the house, but they weren't fighting—they were digging. I didn't recognize the dogs as belonging to any of my neighbors, so they probably came from one of the farms in the area. And they were destroying my yard.

"Go on! Get out of here!" There was a lot of growling going on. They were focused on a single spot, tearing up the grass and spraying red clay all over the place. Careful not to get too close, I waved my arms at them. "Go home!"

One of them stopped and turned, snarling with saliva dripping from its mouth. When it lowered its head and fixed its eyes on me, I started to slowly back up. I doubted I'd make it to the house if it charged, but I had no choice but to try.

I turned and ran, stumbling over my own feet before hitting

the ground. I rolled onto my back just in time to see a swarm of crows descending from the trees. But before they could reach the dog, I threw my hand out in front of me and willed my magic to flow. My palm lit up like a torch, and a ball of light shot toward the dog and slammed into it. The animal flew about ten feet back and dropped to the ground, shaking it off before charging at me again.

As I summoned another round of magic, I looked back up. The crows had dispersed, as if repelled by the light. And then a second dog came from behind me and wrapped its jaws around my forearm, twisting it until the beam of light shot into the ground. I screamed from the pain as I felt its teeth crunch down on my bone.

The sound of glass shattering distracted the dog long enough for me to yank my arm free. As I climbed to my feet, a large black figure with glowing red eyes barreled toward me. I jumped out of the way as Diablo lunged, taking two of the dogs down at once, the third hightailing it toward the woods with the crows on its heels.

I stumbled toward the house with blood running down my arm, the horrific sounds of snapping and snarling filling my ears. As I climbed the steps up to the porch and turned around, I heard a high-pitched squeal as a second dog retreated toward the woods and Diablo continued to shake the remaining one like a rag doll.

"Diablo!" I yelled. "No!" I don't know why I tried to stop him. I just couldn't bear the thought of having to bury that other dog. I just couldn't.

He went still but refused to let go of the dog, his eyes glowing brighter than ever.

"Release!" The command must have been familiar because he finally dropped his prey and trotted back toward me. "Good boy."

The injured dog climbed to its feet, stumbling and shaking

blood from its fur before charging again. Diablo turned and met the dog halfway across the yard, his muscular body going rigid as he came to a stop and warned the intruder with a deep growl. The dog halted and did an about-face, disappearing into the woods after the others.

I sat down on the top step, catching my breath as Diablo came up to sit next to me. There wasn't a mark on him, and his eyes were still glowing like rubies. "What are you?" I ran my hand down his back, feeling a rigid line along the top of his fur. It softened under my touch, and his eyes started to fade as he licked the bite wounds on my arm. To my shock, they began to heal before my eyes. "Whatever you are, thanks."

Rex appeared and flew down to the porch, landing on the railing within snapping distance of Diablo's massive jaws. But the dog didn't so much as move.

"Diablo, meet Rex."

The two stared at each other for a moment before Rex took off toward the woods where the others had flown. All I could say was that Beau was getting more than just a dog—he was getting a partner. If my life wasn't so hectic, I might have kept him all for myself. But it wasn't fair to Diablo. He deserved better. I foresaw a lot of bring-your-dog-to-work days at the Stag. Maybe he could be the mascot for the bar.

I stood up and looked at the broken glass on the porch. It was a small price to pay for my life. I didn't have a clue what had gotten into those three dogs or why they were digging in my yard, but I was going to find out who they belonged to. Then the owner was going to get a talking-to and a bill for that front window.

I motioned for Diablo to follow me inside. "Come on. To hell with the dog food. Let's go make an omelet."

FOUR

I'd called Beau to assess his mood. To gauge whether today was the right day to introduce him to Diablo. He seemed cheerful enough, so I asked him to meet me at the Stag later that afternoon. Mentioning the dog upfront was risky. It was better to spring it on him *after* I had him cornered in a room, so I tempted him with a surprise. The promise that I was about to check off something on his bucket list. That something was wanting a very large dog.

After boarding up my window with some old planks I found in the garage, I drove to the Stag.

Dog was already there when I pulled around back and went in through the alley.

"Have you gotten over it?" he asked when I walked inside, "or do I need to grovel?"

"How'd you expect me to react?" Staying angry at him would only cause tension at work. And Dog was family, so we were stuck with each other. "I'm not mad at you. I'm just disappointed." And I was hurt. "We'll talk about it later."

He looked at Diablo and started to chuckle.

"What are you laughing at?" I said.

"I'm just looking forward to seeing Beau's face when you try to pass that thing off on him."

Diablo sat obediently and cocked his head.

"Piece of cake. And he's not a *thing*. He saved my life today." I didn't think those dogs would have killed me, especially if the crows had gotten to them, but they could have done some serious damage if Diablo hadn't broken through the living room window.

Dog lost his grin. "Saved you? What happened?"

"A pack of mutts showed up at my place this afternoon and went crazy. They were digging like there was prime rib buried in my yard."

"They attacked you?" He had a skeptical look on his face. "You sure they weren't wolves?"

I deadpanned him. "One of them looked like a Golden Retriever. Trust me, they weren't wolves."

"Come on, Charley. You must have done something to provoke them."

The memory of that dog snarling at me gave me the chills. "I tried to scare them off by yelling because they were tearing up my yard, but it wasn't like I threw rocks at them. When one of them came at me, I used my magic on it. Then another one clamped down on my arm and put an end to that." I thought about that dog twisting my arm. "It was like that dog knew what he was doing. Like it knew which one to grab."

Dog looked at me sideways. "I think you're giving a dog too much credit, Charley. That animal got lucky."

"All I can say is Diablo saved me. He crashed through the living room window and tore into them. They took off into the woods like a bunch of scared puppies." I started to mention how those crows had been circling the house before it happened, but I heard Beau come into the bar up front.

"Watch Diablo for a minute," I said. "I want to see for myself how Beau is doing before bringing him back here." I shrugged. "You know. Ease him into the introduction."

Dog glanced at the hound. "Sure, I don't have anything else to do."

Beau was wearing a pair of sunglasses when I walked out to the bar. They were different than the ones he'd been sporting for the past few days. Bigger, and the wide lenses had a rainbow sheen to them.

"Hey, boss. What's this big surprise you have for me?" His hair was messed up, which was unusual, and he was still kind of pale.

"Take those glasses off." I was relieved to see his eyes were back to their usual green when he removed them. His pupils were back to normal too. The way they looked last night was downright creepy. "Your eyes look fine to me, so what's with the sunglasses?"

"They're still sensitive to sunlight, and the glasses help. Is that okay with you?" He grumbled something under his breath and gave me a pointed look. "Well? I don't have all day. I have to be back here in a few hours, so what is it?"

Testy. I got on with it before his attitude worsened. "There's someone I want you to meet."

A grin edged up his face. "Oh yeah?"

"It's not a woman." Jeez.

His grin flattened as he put his sunglasses back on and followed me down the hallway. When he entered the room and saw Diablo sitting next to the desk, he came to a halt. "Whoa! What the hell is that?"

"Your new roommate." I called Diablo over and patted his massive side as he leaned against me. "Isn't he gorgeous?"

Beau huffed and looked back at me. Seeing my dead-serious expression, his face went slack. "What?"

Dog let out a wheezing laugh and headed for the door. "I'll be in the kitchen if you need me."

"Thanks for the backup," I said as he disappeared into the hallway. Then I looked back at Beau and continued with the convincing. "Before you decide anything, let me explain."

"Decide?"

His eyes were hidden behind those glasses, but I was pretty sure they were flaring, which wasn't the reaction I was going for. "Calm down, Beau."

"Charley, that ain't no dog—that's a moose!"

I bent down to hug Diablo's neck and plant a kiss on his huge head. He looked up at me at the same time and butted his skull against my mouth, nearly knocking out a tooth. "Ow!"

"See? That thing is dangerous."

I couldn't argue with that, because he was dangerous, but only to the enemy. I had no doubt that dog was harmless unless provoked. That was true for most protective breeds. A Rottweiler wouldn't behave any differently. I wouldn't have even considered handing him off to Beau if I thought otherwise.

He took a closer look at Diablo. "Where'd you get him?"

I was hoping to avoid that conversation until after I'd convinced Beau to take him. "Uh... the Beast?"

"Is that a question?" He shook his head. "That ain't no ordinary dog."

"You're right, he isn't ordinary. He's better than ordinary." I took a deep breath and confessed. "He belonged to Victor Steele. Now that he's dead, the dog is homeless. And we couldn't just leave him down at the Beast with those vampires. They probably would have killed him."

Beau put his hands on his hips. "You mean the vampire who bit me. Are you nuts?"

"I'm sane as can be. Now, take those ridiculous glasses off. You look like a human fly."

The moment he removed them, the dog's eyes flared up like shiny rubies. Beau stumbled back, his jaw dropping.

"It's okay, Diablo. He isn't going to hurt you."

"Hurt *him*?" Beau shook his head. "Hell no! That name fits him. That thing's a devil dog."

This wasn't going well, so I needed to do some damage control fast. "He's just being protective." And I was pretty sure he'd been mistreated by vampires. He could probably sense Victor Steele all over Beau. I hadn't even thought about that. "You've got to trust me on this. He's a great dog. He's just a little different. And you're always talking about how much you want a big dog."

He calmed down a little and rubbed his forehead. "Do you even know what he is?"

I shrugged. "I'm not exactly sure, but I think you two would be a good fit for each other. He needs someone who can handle him, and I think that's you."

Beau's brow creased. "I don't know, Charley. He's looking at me funny."

Diablo was staring at Beau intensely with drool brimming his pendulous jowls.

"You're kinda looking at him the same way," I said. "I think he's just curious about you." When Diablo's head cocked slightly, I knew it was nothing more than that. A half-dozen scrambled eggs, and Beau would have a new best friend. "Look, you can have the night off. Just take him home and see how it goes."

"It's Saturday. I need the tips."

I'd anticipated that. "You can switch shifts with Tucker tomorrow night, and I'll pay you the difference in tips." They'd be about half as much on a Sunday night, but it was a small price to pay. "Just give it one night. If it doesn't work out, I'll take him back."

He let out a heavy sigh. "Fine." When he looked at Diablo,

his worried expression softened. "He is kinda cool looking. I just hope he doesn't eat me."

Speaking of which. "I've got a forty-pound bag of dog food in the bed of the truck. That should hold you over for a while." My anxiety was starting to ease a little because I was sure Beau would fall in love with him once they got to know each other. "You might as well introduce yourself and pet him."

His hesitant look returned. "Uh... sure." Then he bent down at eye level with the dog and got a goofy expression on his face. "Come to Daddy."

Diablo refused to budge, and I started to wonder if this was a stupid idea. If Diablo sensed Victor Steele on Beau, it would either comfort him or trigger him. The latter could spark disaster.

I was about to call it off when Dog walked up behind Beau and handed him a plate. "Why don't you try this. I'll go cook him some fries just in case."

Brilliant.

Beau grabbed the hamburger patty and held it out. That did the trick. Diablo took it from his hand and swallowed it whole. Then he shoved his massive jowls in Beau's face and gave him a good sniff before licking him in the mouth.

"Aww... that's a good boy." Beau was a goner.

I let out my pent-up breath. "I think the ice has been broken. Why don't you take him home and show him his new yard. Just go slow with him tonight."

Beau smiled at the dog and ruffled his short pointy ears. "What do you say, buddy? You want to go home and have a beer?"

"I hope you're kidding," I said.

He stood up and grinned at me. "Maybe just a sip."

I was relieved that it was finally going well. It was also some-thing to take Beau's mind off his strange transformation. At least until we could figure out what was happening to him. But for now, he appeared to be stable.

"Don't forget to grab the dog food from my truck parked out back," I said as he was walking Diablo into the hallway. "But if you really want to bond with him tonight, cook him an omelet. He loves those." That dog was about to become a pampered pooch, something I'm sure he'd never experienced before. "I'll call you later to see how he's doing."

They made it almost to the end of the hallway when Dog stepped out of the kitchen and cut them off. "Better go out the back door. Murphy just pulled up."

"Good idea," I said. I wasn't interested in explaining the hellhound. And if Diablo sensed Murphy's inner asshole emerging and decided to flash his glowing red eyes, I wouldn't put it past the cop to try to shoot him.

Beau quickly went out through the back door as Murphy walked into the bar. "Something I can help you with, Tom?"

"I didn't see your truck out front," he said.

"I parked in the back. Why? What's going on?"

He glanced at Dog. "I came to talk to you, but since Charley's here..."

"Since I'm here what?"

"I just heard that Samuel Cain bought the old Pullman place. I figured Dog might know something about it."

Here we go again.

Dog looked at me curiously. "I wasn't aware of that."

"I just found out myself last night," I said to Murphy. "Is there a problem with that?" A lecture was coming on. I could feel it. "Just say what's on your mind, Tom, so we can bitch at each other and get it over with. I have things to do."

His face went cold. "All right. What was your car doing parked outside his house at three a.m.?"

I let out a curt laugh. "You're spying on me now?"

"Answer the question, Charley."

"All right. I was sleeping with him. Happy? And I'll probably do it again tonight." I backed up and gave him a warning look. "Stay out of my business, Tom." Like that was going to happen.

He took a deep breath and gritted his next words out between clenched teeth. "We still have a killer on the loose, and we know nothing about this vampire."

"Who? Samuel?" Murphy still had no idea that the killer he'd been searching for was Victor Steele. Or that Steele was dead. I wasn't sure how to break it to him though.

Dog did it for me. "There won't be any more murders."

Murphy's eyes narrowed at him. "What's that supposed to mean?"

"It means it's been taken care of," I said. "The killer was the new owner of the Beast. A guy named Victor Steele up from Atlanta. He was also responsible for the female vampires disappearing in Little Crimson, not that you cops gave a shit about them." The story was so much more complicated than that, but that's all he was getting from me.

Murphy's cold gaze leveled on mine. "You need to come down to the station and make a formal statement about what happened."

"She doesn't have to do anything," Dog said. "What happens in Reaperstown is out of your jurisdiction. Out of everyone's jurisdiction. You know that. So, call it justice and move on."

Murphy looked back and forth between us but didn't say anything. Crime within the city limits of Crimson was one thing, but there were certain things outside of those limits that even nearby law enforcement kept their nose out of. Certain pack business for instance.

He pointed his finger at me as he backed up toward the door. "You're playing with fire, Charley."

I shook my head. "Nope. I'm just a concerned citizen who

helped clean up a mess around here, and there's nothing you can do about it. Let it go, Tom."

Without another word, he walked out the door and got into his patrol car.

"You think he'll let that lie?" I said.

Dog snickered. "Not a chance."

FIVE

I'd been on edge all day thinking about that heart and everything else that had happened over the past twenty-four hours. Every time I opened the back door, I expected to find another body part. Or God forbid, an entire body. It had been quiet all day though. But you know what they say about the calm before the storm. It was just the beginning. Dark magic had found its way into this town, and until we identified who brought it here, who murdered Fawny Goodman, there'd be no peace.

I tried to shake off my dark mood because I was working the bar, helping Tucker for a couple hours. Lucy had agreed to cover for Beau at the last minute but couldn't get here until eight because she was watching her brother's kids.

When I looked up, I spotted Mag walking into the Stag. Like usual, his eyes roamed around the room before landing on Tucker behind the bar. It was like he was surveying the place for competition, but I don't think he had any at this point. He and Tucker were a solid thing, so she was out of luck if she got any ideas about leaving that wolf. By the way she looked at him, I doubted that was going to happen.

As he sat down at the end of the bar, I went up to the order window where Dog was looking out. "Are you okay with him being in here?"

Dog nodded and kept his eyes on his former packmate. "We're hashing it out."

I glanced up at a small chalkboard hanging over the window. "I see you hung a menu." We'd never needed one before because we only served a handful of things, and customers knew what they were.

"People are getting tired of burgers, so I added a couple of options. I figured it was enough to justify a menu."

He'd added a tuna melt and patty melt to the bar's offerings. Everything came with fries, so that hadn't changed. "And what's with the TV?" The last one we had mounted up in the corner near the ceiling died months ago, and I hadn't bothered to replace it. At least the volume was down. I was kind of glad when the old one broke so I didn't have to listen to it all night.

He shrugged. "I got a new one, so the old one either ended up in the landfill or in the bar. Besides, I'm sick of listening to customers complain. I set up streaming service too, so you'll be getting a bill for it."

"Great. Just what I need. Another bill."

He pointed his thumb up at the menu. "The patty melts will pay for it."

Dog got back to work, and I walked down the bar to where Tucker was getting lost in her wolf's eyes. "How's the hand?" I asked Mag, glancing down at the one I'd nearly fried during our takedown of Victor Steele the other night. While he was restrained to a wall, I'd used my magic to turn the shackle into molten metal long enough for him to get his hand free. It must have been excruciating.

He held it up. "Good as new."

"Glad to hear it." I glanced at Tucker and then at the guy a few stools down waving his empty glass at her.

"Oh, sorry." She pulled her eyes away from Mag and went to get her customer another drink.

"You need to quit distracting my bartender," I said to him, only half joking. Her head was in the clouds every time he walked in here.

"Yes ma'am," he said with a salute.

As I was walking away, I heard a stool hit the floor. Mag was on his feet and towering over the customer Tucker was waiting on.

A growl came from his mouth. "Say something like that to her again, and I'll rip your head off and shove it up your ass so far you'll be staring at your own heart."

"Hey!" I yelled. But before I could make it back down to them, Dog was out of the kitchen and had the wolf backed up against the bar.

An even deeper growl snaked up Dog's throat. "I said I'd tolerate you as long as you acted like a civilized wolf." Dog's muscles were tensed so tight they threatened to rip through his shirt, his wolf itching to come out. He glanced at the customer who looked like he was about to piss his pants. "That ain't civilized."

"She's mine!" Mag spat through gritted teeth. "That asshole was coming on to her. You know I can't ignore that."

"I don't care if he got her fucking number." He brought his face closer to Mag's and flashed his amber eyes. "This isn't the woods. This is Charley's place. You got that?"

Mag lowered his head and averted his eyes. "Yeah, I got it." He might have gone astray from the pack, but it was clear he still knew who the Alpha was.

Dog finally backed off but kept his eyes on the wolf for a few more seconds. "Now, get out of here."

Mag looked at me. "You heard Dog," I said. "This is your last warning. One more incident and you're banned for good." If it had been anyone else, there wouldn't be a next time. But I had a soft spot for Mag, just like my mother had, and I didn't even know why. Maybe it was because I knew deep down he wasn't a bad wolf. He just had issues.

Dog shook his head and muttered under his breath, shooting me an I-told-you-so look on his way back to the kitchen.

After Tucker walked Mag out, she came up to me behind the bar with a timid smile. "I'm really sorry about that, Charley. I don't know what got into him."

"*You* got into him. That's what. I hope you know what you're doing with Mag." She'd been claimed by a wolf, and not just any wolf. One with a wicked temper.

She started wringing her hands. "I guess I need to have a talk with him."

"Mag's had enough of that from Dog. It's like talking to a brick wall." I looked up when the front door opened. "Lucy just got here. Go ahead and take your break so I can get out of here when you get back."

As Tucker headed down the hallway, Lucy came around the bar. "I swear to God, I'm getting my tubes tied ASAP."

"Rough day with the kids?" I could only imagine. Her brother's kids were miniature terrorists.

Her face scrunched up. "I don't know how Richie and Krystal have managed to stay out of jail for child abuse."

"I'm guessing you're not the maternal type." Actually, she'd probably be a good mother. Not like parents these days who let their children run all over them.

"Are you kidding me? Those little rats are evil."

I chuckled at the thought of her chasing them around a room. "Well, they invented wine for a reason."

She glanced at the chalkboard above the order window. "What the hell is that?"

"Dog put it up. We have some new menu items, so point it out to customers."

"Tuna melt," she muttered as she stuffed her bag under the bar.

Giving into my nervous curiosity, I pulled out my phone. "Can you handle the bar for five minutes while I call Beau?"

Lucy looked at the growing crowd and let out an exasperated breath. "Well, hurry up. We're about to get slammed."

"Yes ma'am." I walked into the hallway and dialed his number. He picked up on the second ring. "Is everything going okay with you two?" I said without a greeting. I could hear the TV on in the background.

"Why wouldn't it be?"

I pulled the phone away from my ear for a second and stared at it. "Oh, I don't know. Because you're spending your first night with a hellhound." I cringed the moment I said it, but it seemed to fly right over his head.

"Everything's fine. D and me are watching the game and getting to know each other."

"D?"

"Yeah. I don't like his name. People are going to think he's vicious."

I hated to break it to him, but people were going to draw conclusions about that dog just from looking at him. "Then why don't you give him a whole new name?"

He huffed into the phone. "You can't just change a dog's name. He won't know who he is."

I closed my eyes and shook my head. "Look, I just called to check in on you, but I need to get back up front. I'll talk to you tomorrow."

As soon as I went back behind the bar, I heard a burst of laughter. There was a guy I didn't recognize sitting at the other end, and he must have said something funny because all the customers around him were laughing. When I looked closer, I saw a deck of cards in his hand.

I motioned to Dog through the order window. "Who's that?"

He leaned through it and looked down the bar. "I've never seen him before."

"Whoever he is, he makes friends fast."

Dog straightened up to get back to work. "Push the patty melt on him."

"What's going on down there?" I asked Lucy when she walked up to the tap to pour a beer.

She looked back at the stranger. "Just some guy doing card tricks."

I walked over to him as he was shuffling them. "Are you new in town?"

Instead of answering the question, he fanned the deck out in front of me. "Pick one."

Okay, I'd play along. I pulled one of the cards out and looked at it. It was the ace of spades, and it had a creepy skull in the middle of it. "That's an interesting deck you have there."

"It should be. It's one of a kind."

"Really?" I'd never heard of a custom-made deck. He must have really loved his card tricks.

He motioned for me to stick the card back in the deck. Then he shuffled them again and spread them out on the bar face down, his fingers walking over the pile before landing on one. Glancing back at me, he flipped it over. "Is this it?"

It was the ten of clubs. "Nope. Not even close." Maybe that fancy deck wasn't such a good investment for him after all.

He held my gaze for a moment, making the hair on the back of my neck bristle slightly. "Well, I'm not always right." Then he stuck his hand out. "Decker. I'm new to the area."

"Decker? Is that some kind of card joke?" When I shook his hand, an ever so slight current traveled through my fingers. I wasn't sure if it was coming from me or him.

He smiled. "Something like that."

I didn't ask for a last name when he didn't offer one, and I detected a slight accent that I couldn't place. But he definitely wasn't a Southerner.

Lucy came up behind me and looked at Decker. "Make sure you lock your doors at night and stay out of Reaperstown, and you might survive till Christmas."

"Lucy!" Who was I to scold her? She was giving him sound advice, considering all the trouble around town lately. Not to mention someone ripping hearts out of people's chests.

She set a beer down in front of him. "It's the truth." Then she continued over to another customer.

"Don't mind my bartender. She doesn't have a filter." Decker's eyes settled on mine, making me uneasy again. "Let me know if you need anything else."

"A menu?" he said as I was walking away.

I pointed to the board above the window. "Most people go for the burger." Since he was a new customer, I thought it wise to recommend something tried and true.

"I'll have the tuna melt."

"Coming right up."

Tucker came back from her break as I was walking toward the window, so I went into the kitchen to place the order. "The guy wants a tuna melt."

"Really? I didn't think anyone would want one of those things."

"Then why did you put it on the menu?"

Dog shrugged. "You never know."

While he dropped the fries into the oil and started the sandwich, he brought up the elephant in the kitchen. "Any more news about what happened?"

I shook my head. "I haven't talked to Candy since I left the Cauldron last night."

He nodded his head with a grunt. "You need to forgive her, Charley. What happened with Delia wasn't her decision."

"It wasn't yours either, but one of you should have told me."

The truth was, I wasn't one of those people who got attached to an urn full of ashes or a gravesite with a headstone. When someone died, they were gone. The fact that my mother's body wasn't in that box wasn't what was upsetting me. It was the lie.

He set the sandwich on the griddle. "We're telling you now. Jesus, Charley, you didn't have a clue what you were at the time. How the hell were you going to understand what they were doing? You would have thrown a fit."

I was a wreck when my mother died, so he was probably right. I wouldn't have understood. I knew she was a witch, but I probably would have thought they'd all lost their minds if they told me they were planning to leave her body in the woods. "All right. I get it now. Just let me have my anger for a moment."

He flipped the sandwich onto a plate and dumped the fries next to it. "Order up."

When I walked out of the kitchen and down the bar, Decker was gone. "Where did he go?" I asked Lucy. She pointed to the front door as it was closing behind him. "Well, damn. If he comes back in here, make sure he pays for this food he ordered before you serve him anything else."

I took the plate back into the kitchen and set it on the counter.

Dog glanced at it. "That bad, huh?"

"He left before I even served it to him. The deadbeat." I rubbed my face and went back toward the door. "I'll be working in the office if you need me."

As I walked into the back room, a hand slipped around my waist and caressed my stomach. "Never sneak up on a witch," I said, turning and splaying my fingers against Samuel's chest. "Feel that?"

He had me against the wall a moment later, kissing me as a gentle flow of magic continued to travel from my hand into his body. "I feel something all right," he whispered against my lips.

"I'm serious, Samuel. Can you feel it?" I focused and willed it even stronger. "I'm getting better at controlling it now."

He glanced down at my hand. "Yes, you are."

"I can even control the intensity." A playful smile slid up my face. "Maybe I can use it for pain *or* pleasure."

He gripped my wrist and pulled it away from his chest. "I think the latter is going to need a little more practice."

"Oh! Sorry." I let up on the energy and dropped my hand.

His brows lifted. "You've been practicing since you left this morning?"

"Sort of. I had to use it on a pack of dogs this afternoon."

"Dogs? What are you talking about?"

I shook my head to brush it off. To make it seem less dramatic than it actually was. "There were some dogs digging up my yard when I got home, that's all. They got a little aggressive, so I zapped them with this." I waved my hand around. "It felt so natural. Like second nature." I rolled a shoulder. "Well, Diablo helped. He finished the job and sent them running into the woods."

"Sounds like that dog is earning his keep. Maybe you should reconsider handing him off to Beau."

"Too late. He's already in his new home. It wasn't exactly love at first sight, but they're growing on each other." A grin spread across my face. "That means you can stay at my place tonight."

Samuel frowned. "You're already getting tired of my new house?"

"I just feel like sleeping in my own bed tonight." At least until we got his place dusted and spruced up. And I was a bit of a homebody. And then there was Rex to look after, whether he needed me to or not. "I mean, *if* you want to come over. No pressure." We were spending so much time together. I didn't want him to think I expected it.

He leaned closer. "Oh, I want."

After a brief kiss, he was out the door, making it very difficult to focus on work with his lingering scent filling the room. His vampire pheromones stuck to me like cologne. But before I did anything, I needed to call Candy. The rift between us must have been eating away at her, and it was eating at me too. It was time to call a truce and let her know I planned to stop by tomorrow so we could talk. I was just dying to tell her about Samuel buying the old Pullman place.

As I was reaching for my phone, I felt something next to it in my pocket. I pulled the object out. "What are you up to, Decker?" I said, staring at the playing card, the ace of spades, and wondering what the odds were that it was a coincidence that the stranger showed up in town just as the shit was hitting the fan.

SIX

My eyes flew open when I heard a sound coming from somewhere in the house. Something falling. Samuel was gone, but it was still dark outside. He'd waited until I'd fallen asleep to go back to his place. To his mysterious chamber.

I sat up and reached for my phone on the nightstand. It was 3:33 a.m. "Perfect." Nothing good ever happened during the witching hour.

I got out of bed and threw my robe on and then slipped quietly into the hallway, listening for that sound again. But the house was dead quiet. After looking in the spare bedroom and seeing nothing out of the ordinary, I continued down the hallway to check my mother's room. The door to the adjoining room was ajar. It was the small space where her books and magical things were stored.

I didn't recall leaving it open, so I stepped quietly toward the door and listened for any movement inside. Something was definitely in there. My hand started to tingle, the energy building in my palm as I peered through the gap. Something flew past me, a wing grazing my cheek as Rex sailed toward an open window. A window I knew damn well *I* hadn't opened.

After shutting it and making sure it was locked, I went back to the small room and flipped on the light to see what kind of mess he'd made. There was a box and its contents scattered on the floor. Pictures and letters had spilled out, along with a few drawings I made for my mother in grade school. I couldn't believe she'd kept them.

I got down on my hands and knees to gather everything. After tucking it all back in the box, I noticed an envelope that had slipped under the bookcase and fished it out. My mother's name was handwritten across the front, and it had a broken wax seal on the back. It was the letter W with a smaller H and A embossed on the sides. A monogram. Inside the envelope was a folded note that simply said, THE DEED IS DONE. It was signed HESTER.

"Who's Hester?" I muttered, turning the envelope over to look for a return address or something, but there wasn't one.

Another sound came from somewhere in the house. I stuck the envelope inside the box and put it on the bottom shelf. Then I climbed to my feet and went back into the hallway, a faint shuffling drawing me toward the kitchen.

I stopped at the edge of the doorway and pressed my back to the wall, listening for it again. But all I could hear was the hum of the refrigerator. The icemaker dropping cubes into the bin. A pipe clanking in the basement. Then I flinched when something moved in the living room. It was the slightest shadow, but I caught it from the corner of my eye.

With adrenaline practically creeping up my throat, I pumped my fist to build energy and stepped from the hallway. "Show yourself!"

A figure emerged from the dark corner, and the ball of light whirling in my hand sailed across the living room. Ian Masterson dodged it, his eyes darting to the wall behind him as the magic slammed into it, leaving a smoldering hole where he'd just been standing.

He turned his gaze back to me. "Hostile."

"Ian Masterson, you need to get out of my house."

Wagging his finger, he came closer with a cocky grin on his face. "I'm afraid that won't work anymore. Su casa es mi casa."

I shook my head. "What?"

His smile flattened. "No hablas español?"

"How about English? Get! Out!"

"As long as my blood is inside you, I can come and go from the house as I please."

Smug vampire. I knew there was a catch to drinking his blood at the Beast the other night. But it was the only way to convince Victor Steele that Ian had claimed me. Samuel said he'd find a way to wash it out of me eventually, but apparently it was still flowing strong.

"Why are you here, Ian?"

"Can't I just drop by to see a friend?" His chin lowered as he looked down at my robe. Then he glanced around the room. "Where's the hellhound?"

I pulled my robe tighter, suddenly missing that dog. "None of your business."

He nodded to the boarded-up window. "Did you and your boyfriend have a fight?"

Refusing to dignify the remark with an answer, I crossed my arms and waited for him to make the next move.

After strolling around the room for what seemed like days, he made himself comfortable on the couch and patted the cushion next to him. "Let's have a chat, shall we?"

I refused to budge. "What do you want, Ian?"

"As I said. Just checking in on a friend."

"We aren't friends," I reminded him. "And you don't do anything unless there's something in it for you, so cut the bull-shit and tell me why you're here."

He was on his feet and standing in front of me so fast I barely saw him move. "What do you know about what happened up at the lake? About the witch who was slaughtered the other night?"

The word *slaughtered* gave me the chills. "How do you know about that?"

"Because I have eyes everywhere." He hesitated. "And she works—worked—for me."

"What do you mean? Why would a witch work for a vampire?"

"Well... *work* is probably not the right term. We were colleagues. Fawny wasn't just a witch. She was a powerful conjure woman. A blood witch. Blood was integral to her magic. To her clients. She funneled a lot of business my way, and now she's dead."

I shrugged. "Dealing in vampire blood can be a dangerous business. Things happen."

"Are you telling me you and that bunch of hocus pocus clowns know nothing about it? Because I'm not buying that."

He'd find his mouth sewn shut if the Squad got wind of what he'd just called them.

"Not only do I know about it, Fawny Goodman's heart was delivered to my doorstep after it happened. In a plain brown box," I added. Why I told him anything, I don't know. It would only prolong me getting him out of my house.

He was in my face a second later. "Where is it?"

"The box?"

"The heart!" Now he was practically on top of me.

"I took it to the Cauldron. The Squad picked it up and said they were going to put it back where it belonged. Back into Fawny's chest before giving her a proper witch burial." Not exactly a burial, but I wasn't about to get into the details with him.

He gave me some breathing room and scowled. "Fuck!"

"What's going on, Ian? Why do you care about that heart?"

"Because Fawny Goodman had eyes in the back of her

head. No one would have gotten close enough to kill her without using dark magic to do it. And if that heart is laced with it, it might be the only thing that can lead us back to her killer."

Why did Ian Masterson care about a dead witch anyway? "The Squad is dealing with it. Why are you so worried?"

"Because black magic is nothing to fuck with." A snide laugh came from his mouth. "You think things have been bad around here lately? Wait until that kind of trouble weaves itself into Crimson. It'll be Reaperstown next, and I happen to like my life right now. I just got my hands on the Beast, and I intend to enjoy my reign without having to worry about some ambitious sorceress or demon." He pushed his hair out of his face and settled down. "Did you touch it?"

"The heart? God no!"

"Good. I'm sure whoever sent it to you assumed you would. It's a very effective way of getting dark magic inside of one's target."

Now he had me worried about Dog because he did touch it. He picked it up and held it like something he'd gotten from the butcher shop.

"You're a vampire," I said. "How do you know so much about black magic?"

"Let's just say I've slept with my share of witches. One of them was proficient at the dark arts and taught me a thing or two." A roguish grin slid up his face. "She was quite talented with magic in many ways."

"For Christ's sake, Ian. I'm not interested in hearing about your sex life."

His brows hiked. "No?"

The front door suddenly flew open, and Samuel stepped inside. "Well, well. What do we have here?" He glanced at my robe and back at Ian. "I'd suggest you start explaining, Masterson."

A Cheshire Cat grin worked its way up Ian's face. "Charley and I were just having a chat."

"Your blood isn't an invitation to walk into her house whenever you feel like it."

Ian chuckled. "I disagree. But don't worry, I prefer brunettes. For now," he added under his breath.

Samuel's eyes darkened, and Ian egged him on with a crook of his index finger.

I decided to end it before all hell broke loose in my house. "If you two want to start something, take it outside." I didn't need rescuing. Then I headed for the kitchen. "I'm making coffee."

By the time the pot finished brewing and I walked back out with a cup, the two of them were sitting opposite each other in the living room. There was no blood on either of them, so apparently they'd made their peace.

"Ian was just expressing his concerns about black magic," Samuel said. "I hate to agree with him, but he's right. We don't know what we're dealing with."

I sat down and took a sip of my coffee. "Candy and the Squad will figure it out."

After a tense moment of silence in the room, Ian glanced at the window and back at Samuel. "It'll be dawn soon. Better be on your way back to your hidey-hole." He was just gloating because he was more tolerant of the sun than Samuel was, but it was time for him to leave too.

Samuel shot him a cold smile. "Predators first."

I got up and headed for the hallway. "I'm going to take a shower and get dressed. You should both leave while you still can. Lock the door on the way out." It was more for Samuel's benefit than Ian's.

They were both gone when I came back out a few minutes later. Then I went to the bedroom to grab my phone to check the time. It rang as I was reaching for it. Candy's name appeared, but it was way too early for her to be calling me unless something was wrong.

"Morning," I said. "Is everything okay?" I could hear her shudder out a breath on the other end. "Candy? What's wrong?"

"You need to get over to the Cauldron to pick me up. We need to take a ride."

Something in her voice set off alarms in my head. "A ride where?"

"Out to the Squad's house. Something bad has happened."

"You're scaring me, Candy. What happened?"

There was a pause on the other end of the line. "Just get over here as soon as you can."

After hanging up, I grabbed my keys and headed for the truck. Something was seriously wrong, and not knowing was killing me. I drove to town so fast I was surprised I didn't get pulled over.

Candy was waiting for me outside when I pulled up to the Cauldron. When she climbed in, I could feel her energy running haywire. It took a lot to mess with Candy like that, but something had done it.

I put the truck in park. "Are you going to tell me what's going on?"

She finally looked at me. "Mia Winston was attacked."

"Attacked? By who?"

"You mean by what."

I just stared at her for a moment as the worst ran through my mind. "Is she dead?"

Candy sighed. "She's still breathing, but she isn't talking. That's all I know, so just drive."

As we headed out of town, my imagination started to run wild with all kinds of images of what could have attacked one of the Squad. Maybe it was that beast I'd encountered in the woods during that messed-up test they'd put me through. The one I wasn't sure had even been real. By the time we reached the turnoff to the road leading up to the house, I'd killed Mia Winston off in my mind by any number of culprits, including vampires. Lord knew we had some bad ones around here.

The house was as eerie as I remembered it, but at least there wasn't a strange man looking down at us from the octagon-shaped room on the top floor like the first time I was here. "Candy, you don't think that guy up there...?"

She followed my eyes up to the window. "No, honey, I do not."

Desiree opened the front door as we walked up the steps. "You're late."

"I don't recall being given a specific time to arrive," Candy said as she brushed past her. "Where's Katherine?"

The witch led us down the hallway and up the stairs to the second floor. I glanced inside each of the rooms as we continued down to the last one on the left. They were just as drab as the rest of the house, with oversized dark furnishings that made the place feel like it was trapped in a Victorian time warp. And there was a distinct possibility it was. I couldn't get the smell of linseed oil out of my nose from all the polished wood.

When we walked into the room, Katherine Belltower was standing vigil over the bed. "This is war," she said without turning around.

"Hold your horses," Candy said as she walked over to the bed and looked at Mia's unconscious form. "Back up and tell us what's going on before you start declaring war."

And explain why I need to be here, I wanted to say. Candy could have driven herself out to the house.

"What happened to her?" I asked.

Fay Winston walked into the room carrying a tray. "They broke her!"

"Broke her how?" Candy said.

Fay set the tray down on the nightstand and took a shuddering breath. "We were preparing Fawny in the parlor, and Mia went to get some fresh rosemary from the garden. When she didn't return, I went to see what was taking so long." Her voice cracked. "That's when I found her, face down in the mugwort with a caterpillar crawling along her back. A caterpillar! When I ran back into the house to get my phone, Fawny was gone."

"So much for a proper burial," Candy said.

That was the least of my concerns. "What about her power?" It wasn't clear to me if harnessing Fawny's energy was part of the body preparation or the ritual in the forest.

Katherine released a heavy sigh. "Whoever did this already took most of it when they murdered her up at the lake."

"But not all of it," Candy said. "The stakes just went up."

I walked up to the bed to get a better look at Mia. She was flat on her back and out cold. "Shouldn't she be in a hospital?"

Katherine bent over and lifted one of the witch's eyelids. Her pupil was nearly as wide as her iris. "She's in a trance. I'm afraid a doctor can't help her. This is dark magic."

Ian's words filled my head as I glanced back and forth between Candy and Katherine. "You think another witch did this?"

Katherine straightened back up. "A witch. A warlock. It could have been either."

"Aren't they basically the same?" Every one of them shot me an incredulous look. "I guess not," I muttered.

"Don't look at me," Candy said when Katherine glared at her. "I didn't teach her that."

"A warlock is most certainly not a witch," Katherine said. "They're nothing but rats without tails. I'm sure Delia would have taught you better had her time not been cut so tragically short."

Well, that stung.

"But I suppose it could have been something else," she

continued. "Whatever it is, it's powerful. It either got past the wards around the property, or the magic itself did." She shook her head. "If I wasn't seeing this with my own two eyes, I would have said it was impossible."

After everything I'd seen lately, nothing seemed impossible to me anymore. "How can we help her?"

Fay sat on the edge of the bed and grabbed a cup from the tray. She placed it to her sister's lips and slowly poured a small amount of the liquid into her mouth. "We wait."

"For what?" I asked.

"For whoever did this to tell us what they want," Katherine said. "Magic like this is never random. A demand will be made." Her eyes grew more intense. "But I'm afraid they picked the wrong group of witches to fuck with. A price will be paid."

I was starting to feel uneasy being thrown in the middle of all this. "Why am I here?" I asked Candy, finally getting around to the question. "You didn't need me to drive you."

She smiled at me weakly. "Because you're one of us, honey."

"That's right," Katherine said. "You're an Underwood, and Underwood witch blood runs deep in Crimson. What happens to one of us happens to all of us." She walked over to the window and scanned the yard before looking over her shoulder at me. "You're a crow, Charley. Let the war begin."

SEVEN

It was six o'clock by the time I got to the Stag. Candy had made us lunch after we got back to the Cauldron so we could talk about what had happened after my mother died. About the ritual, and why she never told me. She didn't beg me to forgive her or anything like that, and I wouldn't have let her. As far as I was concerned, Candy was family. And while it wasn't water under the bridge yet, eventually it would be.

"Has anyone heard from Beau?" I asked. He should have shown up by five o'clock at the latest.

Lucy continued to prep the bar. "Nope. Maybe that big dog ate him."

I started to laugh but suddenly got an uncomfortable feeling. "Did you try calling him?"

"He ain't answering his phone."

Dog had a strange expression on his face when he looked at me through the order window. "We've got the bar if you want to run over there to see what's going on with him."

He looked a little pale.

"Are you okay?"

"I'm fine." He kept rubbing his rib cage with his palm. "It's just a little heartburn."

If he wasn't a wolf, I would have asked if he was having chest pains. But wolves didn't have heart attacks like humans. They were healthy as horses, and it took a lot to take one down. Usually an attack by another wolf.

"Are you sure?"

"I said I'm fine!"

"Okay. Got it." There was nothing wrong with his temper though.

I dialed Beau's number, but it went to voicemail after several rings. "I think I will drive over there. I'll be back as soon as possible." It was Sunday, so at least it was one of our slowest nights.

After climbing in my truck, I dialed his number again. This time I left a message when it went to voicemail. "Where are you, Beau? Call me."

On the ride out to his place, the worst kept running through my mind. I'd left him with a dog capable of God knew what, and now he was MIA. But I kept telling myself I was being ridiculous. Diablo hadn't shown any aggressive behavior unless he was provoked. But what if I was wrong? What if being provoked was something as simple as saying a trigger word or giving off the scent of his previous owner? With every minute that passed, I started to panic.

Beau's car was parked in the driveway when I pulled up. Nothing seemed out of the ordinary other than the garage door being open, so I got out and walked toward the stairs that led up to the apartment above. Halfway up, I heard something behind me. A panting sound.

I turned as Diablo bounded up the steps. He barreled past me, nearly knocking me down the flight of stairs, and stopped at the door with his ears perked.

"What are you doing out here?" I scanned the yard,

expecting to see Beau coming out of the surrounding woods with a story about how he took the dog for a hike, forgot his phone, and lost track of time. But he was nowhere in sight. He'd put that dog outside—alone. If he wasn't injured or dead inside his apartment, I was going to kill him.

When I got to the top of the stairs, I tried the door. It was unlocked. "Beau?" I called as I pushed it open slowly and went inside. Diablo ran toward the bedroom and let out a deep bark. "Are you in there?"

The tiny apartment was dead quiet. But then Diablo stuck his nose to the bedroom door and started to growl. The muscles in his body stiffened and his hackles rose. For the first time since rescuing that dog, I was nervous about approaching him. He was too riled up.

"Come here, boy." I patted my thigh, trying to get him to come to me instead and away from the door. Then I heard Beau's voice coming from the bedroom. I couldn't make out what he said, but Diablo went nuts. The dog lunged at the door and snarled like the first time I'd seen him in that basement at the Beast. When Victor Steele was controlling him.

I stumbled, my hand pumping with adrenaline as I prepared to use it on Diablo if necessary. Something had gotten into him. He was determined to get to Beau in the bedroom, so I backed up toward the open front door and stepped out onto the landing. "Diablo, come!" It took him a moment, but he finally obeyed. He gave the bedroom door another sniff and then trotted outside to where I was standing. I quickly pulled the door shut and led him down the stairs. "Good boy," I said, leading him into the garage. "I'll be back for you in a few minutes."

After locking him in, I went back up to the apartment and put my ear to the bedroom door. "Beau? What the hell is going on?" It was quiet at first, but then I heard a strange sound coming from the other side. The sound of scratching.

A healthy dose of fear hit me in the chest. "You're scaring me, Beau." I tried the knob, but the door was locked. "If you don't open this door, I'll open it myself." My hand started to glow. If I had to, I'd incinerate the damn thing. "I mean it. You've got five seconds."

"Is Diablo gone?" His voice was deeper than usual. Darker.

"I put him in the garage. You can come out now."

When the knob started to turn, I stepped back. The room was dark inside. All I could see was the outline of Beau's back standing in the far corner of the room. "You need to take me to see my father," he said.

I swallowed hard. "Your father? Why?"

He slowly turned, giving me a look at his eyes. They were glowing amber. Then he raised his hands to look at them. At the claws protruding from his fingers. "So he can tell me what I am."

* * *

"Damn it, Beau! Would you quit waving those claws in my face!" We weren't going to make it to Daniel Henry's house alive if I wrapped my truck around a tree.

"I can't help it!" There he went again. Motioning around like a wolverine on caffeine. "I'm freakin' out here!"

I needed to de-escalate the situation. It was bad enough that Diablo almost broke down the garage door as we scurried past it into the truck, but now my beast of a bartender was having a meltdown in my passenger seat.

"Just think calming thoughts," I said, taking a few exaggerated breaths like we were in a Lamaze class.

Beau let out a sarcastic laugh. "Yeah, right."

"Is this the first time this has happened to you?" I nodded to his hands. "I mean the claws?" His eyes had been doing strange things ever since Victor Steele had bitten him, but this took it to a whole new level of strange. And to think he was worried about becoming a vampire.

His brows were pulled tight as he cocked his head at me. "What do you think?"

"Lose the attitude, or I'll hit the brakes and let you walk the rest of the way."

He gave me a limp smile. "Sorry."

"Jesus!" I swerved when I saw the tips of a set of fangs sticking out from his upper lip.

"What?" He twisted the rearview mirror to take a look at himself. "Fuck!"

I got a grip and focused on the road instead of what was happening in the seat next to me. My cook was a wolf, and I was sleeping with a vampire, so I could handle my bartender turning into something in between. Not to mention my own unique heritage. Beau would fit in just fine at the Stag.

Samuel had been dead-on when he said Beau was a halfling. The fangs explained the vampire half. I had no idea what the other half might be. But there'd been rumors going around town for years that his father was hiding something, other than being a major asshole to his kid. It was starting to look like those rumors were about to be substantiated. I was still on the fence though about walking into that big house where Beau grew up. I hadn't been there since we were teenagers, and I never thought I'd be back, especially not under these circumstances. To see Beau confront his father about a set of claws at the end of his fingers.

The house was outside of town on a large property at the edge of the woods. The place was old and grand and sat on a hill, with ancient oak trees on each side. Back in the day, Beau used to sneak out at night by climbing down the one next to his bedroom window.

I could feel Beau's nerves as we turned onto the long drive-way. His skin had gone pale, and it wasn't the vampire coming out—he was terrified. His father had always had that effect on him, but he never talked about it candidly. I knew Dan Henry had been rough on Beau when he was growing up, but I also knew I wasn't getting the whole story. Considering the situation, I think I was finally starting to understand why. The big Henry family secret was sitting right next to me, but I had a feeling Beau's current predicament was only the half of it.

I hit the brakes before we reached the house. "Are you ready?"

"I don't think I have a choice."

We continued up the drive, the corner of the place coming into view as we rounded a stand of trees that served as a barrier between the road and the house. And a spectacular house it was. Two stories of neoclassical charm for a man who had none.

"Maybe you should have called him to let him know you were coming." Beau's fear was traveling over the seat into me. At least his fangs and claws had retracted. But his eyes were still unsettling to look at.

He stared straight ahead at the house and shook his head. "He knows I'm here. He always knows when I come home. Always did."

"Except now you're a grown man. He doesn't have any control over you anymore, Beau."

He laughed nervously. "Tell him that."

I was starting to feel like a third wheel. "Just go in there and demand the truth. I'll be right out here when you're done."

"What?" He looked at me like I'd just told him he had a month to live. "I ain't going in there by myself. You're coming with me."

"Beau, I don't think that's a good idea. Your father isn't going to tell you the truth if I'm standing there."

"Hell yeah, he will. He owes me."

I let out a long breath. "All right. But don't blame me if we leave here with nothing."

We got out and walked up the brick walkway toward a porch supported by a set of two-story columns. The house was painted white but still managed to feel very dark.

"Where'd you say your family got their money from?" I didn't think he'd ever told me.

"It's family money." He shrugged. "My grandfather left it to him."

"Does that mean this will all be yours one day?"

He never took his eyes off the house. "I don't think he's ever going to die."

There was a light on in the living room, but the rest of the house was dark. As soon as my foot hit the top step leading up to the porch, a light came on in the foyer, but I couldn't see anyone through the glass panes on either side of the door. Then it opened and a man motioned us in.

The moment I stepped inside, I was fifteen again. The place left an impression, good or bad. I recognized the man from the last time I was here. The Henrys' butler or manservant. Whatever you called them.

"Hey, Edward," Beau said in a low voice. "Still working here, huh?"

The man gazed at Beau's amber eyes for a moment. "It's good to see you, Beau."

"Yeah, you too. I'm here to see my father, but I guess that's kinda obvious."

"Of course. Your father is expecting you."

Expecting him? I guess Beau was right.

Beau nodded to me. "You remember Charley. We went to high school together."

Edward smiled briefly but didn't seem as excited to see me. I didn't take it personal. I'm sure it had everything to do with how Beau's father would react to seeing that his son had brought company for the big family reveal.

"Edward!" Dan Henry's voice echoed through the large

entryway. "Don't bother showing my son in. I'm sure he still knows the way."

Edward's expression softened. Seemed almost sympathetic. "He's in the study." Then he disappeared down the hallway, leaving us to maneuver our way through the big house.

As we walked through the living room toward the study, the smell of gardenias filled my nose. I noticed several vases of the white flowers positioned on tables around the palatial room.

"They were my mother's favorite," Beau said when he saw me looking at them. "I guess he can't let go of her."

The woman had been dead for years.

Beau came to an abrupt halt when he entered the study. I followed his gaze as I walked in behind him. His father was standing next to the window, his eyes the same amber color as Beau's. The moment he saw me, they faded to green.

"You didn't mention you were bringing a friend."

Beau's face twisted. "I didn't even tell you I was coming."

Mr. Henry laughed quietly. "Yes, you did. You just didn't realize it." He glanced at me again. "Does she know?"

"Neither of us know," Beau said. "That's why I'm here. To get answers. What am I?" He squinted at his father's eyes. "And what the hell are you?"

"Don't raise your voice to me, boy."

Beau finally got the nerve to stand his ground. "Do I look like a boy to you? I came here to find out what I am. Tell me the truth, and you'll never have to lay eyes on me again. And whatever it is, you can say it in front of Charley," he added when his father looked at me again.

"You know what you are. You just haven't accepted it yet." Something between a smile and a sneer crossed his face as he walked toward his son. "You've been watching it happen your entire life."

Beau flinched. It was a slight flinch, but I caught it. It was like an invisible hand had slapped him in the face. I wanted to grab his arm and take him out of that house, but his hands had started to tremble, and claws were breaking through the tips of his fingers again. It triggered my urge to run.

Dan Henry's eyes came around to mine as if he could smell my fear. "Don't you dare move. You wanted to see this, so see it."

Suddenly Beau's entire body started to shake. "What's happening to me?" It was that same voice I'd heard back at his house, but now it was even deeper. He raised his hands in the air and watched his claws lengthen, the hair on his arms growing longer. He was vibrating so fast he became a blur.

As if mimicking his son, Dan Henry started to vibrate as well. His body twisted unnaturally, like his bones were disjointing under his skin. The sound of them cracking filled the room as he dropped down on all fours, leaving a pile of clothes on the floor, and settled into some kind of beast. It looked like a cross between a bear and a wolf.

I turned to run but collided with Edward who was standing in the doorway.

"I'm very sorry, Ms. Underwood. I can't let you leave just yet."

When he wouldn't let me pass, I grabbed his arm and sent a shock through his body. He howled and stumbled back, leaving the exit wide open. But instead of going through it, I got a hold of myself and turned around as the huge beast began to stalk toward Beau.

But Beau didn't cower. He stood there, half like his father and half like himself. His fangs had descended, but the tips barely peeked past his lips. They were more like overgrown incisors. Like they were just as stuck in the middle as he was.

Dan Henry suddenly shifted and stood naked in the middle of the study. Like Dog and the rest of the wolves, it didn't seem to bother him that he had an audience. He stared at his son, but his curious gaze quickly turned harsh. "What are those?"

"What do they look like?" I blurted out. "They're fangs." I couldn't help it. The man infuriated me.

As if suddenly embarrassed by the whole thing, Beau covered his mouth with his hand. "I got bit." The fur on his body started to disappear, and before I could blink, he was back to normal. Back to being as confused as when we arrived.

"By a vampire? So, now you've tainted the bloodline." His father's lips turned upside down like he'd eaten something rancid. "You really are a disappointment."

I was itching to hurl a ball of light at the bastard. "He didn't taint anything. He was a victim." I grabbed Beau's arm. "Let's get out of here."

Beau pulled it out of my grip. "Not until he tells me what I am."

I guess he needed to hear his father say it. To give it a name.

Dan Henry stepped closer to his son with a scowl. "You were born a Hollerwolf, but now you're nothing but a failure. Looks like the bloodline dies with me."

Beau stood there staring at his father for a moment. Then he followed me out of the room without another word. This time no one tried to stop either of us.

As we were leaving, Edward came through the front door after us. "I'm sorry, Beau," he said as we walked away from the house. "But you should know your mother was always proud of you."

There was an audible hitch in Beau's throat as he turned around to look at the man. "See you around, Edward."

Then we climbed in the truck and drove away from the house, probably for the last time.

EIGHT

Beau had shut down for the entire drive back to his house. He refused to speak, and after what had just happened, I didn't push him. But by the time we pulled into his driveway, I was done with it.

I shut the engine off and sat there for a moment waiting for a peep out of him. "Was your father right?" I finally said when he continued with the silent treatment. "Did you know all this time?"

He looked out the window at the garage. "Know what? That I came from a family of freaks?"

"Stop it, Beau. You're talking to a woman who can shoot light from her hands." And who sleeps with a vampire and hangs out with witches and wolves. "We're all a bunch of freaks in this town. I wouldn't have it any other way." But I still didn't know exactly what he was. "What's a Hollerwolf?"

He refused to look at me and kept his eyes on the garage where his new hellhound was being sequestered. "Some kind of shifter, but I didn't have a name for it until now. That's all I know."

"I can't believe you never told me." We were thick as thieves in high school. At least I thought we were.

"I didn't know anything for sure." He held his hands up and looked at his fingers, which were back to normal. "And none of this has ever happened to me before, until that damn vampire bit me. But I saw and heard things in that house when I was growing up."

"Things like what?" He had me really curious now.

"Like my father coming out of the woods late at night. I'd see him through the window, and sometimes I'd swear he looked like... like he did tonight. And I walked in on him once eating a piece of venison from a deer he'd hunted that season."

"There's nothing strange about that," I said.

He turned to look at me. "It was raw."

"Okay, that's strange."

"And then there were all those weird noises always coming from my parents' bedroom. Grunts and groans."

"Beau, they were probably just... you know..."

His face flushed. "Having sex? Jesus, Charley. Thanks for putting that image in my head."

"Let's just move on. I think maybe your father was right. You've seen things all your life, but you blocked it out. Normalized it so you didn't have to accept what you are."

You would have thought I'd slapped him by the way he looked at me. "So now you're a shrink?"

"Look, Beau. Why don't you take the night off. I think you need it, and half the night is over with already."

He got out and walked toward the garage, shaking his head. "No way. That bastard ain't winning tonight. I'm going to take my dog upstairs and feed him, and then I'll come into work for a couple of hours."

I didn't argue with him. He suddenly seemed so confident, even though I knew he would probably get home after his shift tonight and crumble. Fall apart. But if he needed to come to work to be around his real family, who was I to stop him.

Before leaving, I waited to make sure Diablo didn't try to rip Beau's face off. His Hollerwolf had retreated, but that dog could obviously smell it on him. It was going to take a slow and careful introduction to Beau's beast for those two to co-exist.

When Beau opened the garage door and Diablo bounded out without so much as a growl, I figured it was safe to leave. After the two of them went upstairs to the apartment, I drove back to town.

When I pulled up to the back of the Stag ten minutes later, I flinched when Samuel appeared next to the truck door as I started to open it. "Damn it, Samuel! Give a girl a warning. You scared the hell out of me."

He looked me up and down. "What happened to you tonight?"

"Nothing." I got out and headed for the back door, but he stopped me before I could walk up the steps. "I'm fine, Samuel."

"Dog said you drove out to Beau's place. Something happened out there. I felt it."

And he gave me my space and didn't crash the party, which I appreciated.

"Talk to me, Charley."

It wasn't my place to out Beau, but it was just a matter of time before the whole bar figured it out. He'd been slowly outing himself right in front of everyone. "You said Beau is a halfling. Well, I met his other half tonight. We went out to his father's house to get some answers about his family history, and his father shifted right in front of us."

Samuel raised his brows. "Really?"

"And it wasn't pretty," I said, recalling the beast I saw in that study. "Beau comes from a line of something called Hollerwolves."

His curiosity turned to disdain. "Christ. Not those things."

"Have you met one before?"

"More than I'd like. They're shifters from the hollows of Appalachia, and they can be nasty." He shrugged. "But at least they're not as bad as werewolves."

Not something to be compared with the pack. Someone had once called Dog a werewolf, and he nearly took their head off—literally. There was a huge difference between someone who was forced to violently transform into a wolf-like creature at the mercy of the moon and someone in full control of their inner beast because they were born that way.

"And you were also right about Beau being stuck somewhere in the middle. He started to shift at his father's house, but then his fangs came out and he just stopped. It was like he couldn't go any further." I laughed and pushed the door open. "Should have seen the look on his father's face when he saw them."

"You should keep your distance from him."

I looked over my shoulder at him. "You mean Beau? He works for me, Samuel."

"Not Beau, his father."

That was easy. "I don't think either one of us will be spending any time with Dan Henry in the future. He practically disowned Beau when he realized his son had *tainted* the family bloodline with vampire. No offense."

"None taken, but I wouldn't bet on it. Hollerwolves and the like don't walk away from their kin that easily. Tell Beau to watch his back."

"I'll do that. Are you coming in for a drink?"

He gave me a bare smile. "A raincheck?"

Raincheck?

We had been seeing a lot of each other lately, so I guess he needed some time to himself. But I couldn't swallow the uncomfortable lump forming in my throat. Before it showed all over my face, I smiled back at him. "Well, have a good night."

"Hey," he said, grabbing my arm before I could go inside. "I just have some business to take care of. That's all." Then he kissed me and stepped down into the alley. "I'll see later tonight?"

"Of course." We gazed at each other for a moment before I finally broke eye contact. "I better get in there before Dog sends the pack out looking for me." I should have been back long before now, so I was surprised he hadn't.

Halfway down the hallway, I heard a ruckus in the bar. When I went up front, Dog was escorting a customer to the door.

Lucy planted her hands on her hips and glared at me. "Where the hell have you been?"

"Putting out a fire. Is that okay with you?" Last time I checked, I was the boss and didn't answer to her. "What's going on here?"

"What do you think?" she said with another heavy dose of attitude. "Dog happened. You've been gone so long, he had to help me out, and that wolf is a walking disaster behind the bar." She glanced over my shoulder. "Where's Beau?"

"He'll be here in a few minutes. I'll fill in until he gets here."

Dog came back over and looked at all the customers who were avoiding eye contact with him. "Anyone else want to open their mouth about how I mix a drink?"

"Dog!"

"What?" he barked at me.

My foot caught something slippery on the floor, and before I could grab the edge of the bar I was going down. Dog caught me with one hand and yanked me back to my feet. "Get out of my way," he said, "so I can clean up this mess."

The floor was covered with liquid, and it wasn't water. "What happened?" This was why I avoided letting Dog fill in behind the bar. It usually ended up costing me.

He rubbed his forehead. "I'm a little shaky tonight. I dropped a few drinks, that's all."

Shaky my ass. He couldn't bartend to save his life. And then he got into it with someone over a bad drink? Dog usually didn't start shit with customers. He was the one who broke shit up.

"It's your fault," Lucy said as she stuck a mop in my hand. "I ain't cleaning up this mess."

"You're right. I shouldn't have been gone so long." I glanced at Dog who was rubbing the bridge of his nose in frustration. "Go back to the kitchen. I'll take care of this." He went to grab the mop from my hand, but I held it out of reach. "Kitchen, Dog!"

"All right. Chill." He threw his hands up and backed away.

"Sometimes I feel like I'm surrounded by toddlers," I muttered while I mopped.

As I was finishing up the floor, Patrick walked in and took a seat at the bar. I leaned the mop against the wall and went over to him. "Thanks again for taking care of things this morning."

He pulled his sunglasses off and hooked them on his shirt. "Anything to keep you from shriveling up from that dry spell you've been having for years."

I snorted. "I wouldn't say it's been years."

"Mmhmm."

"Shut up." I wasn't having any more of this conversation about my *dry spell*. "You want a gin and tonic or something?"

"Sure. I'll take a G and T. So, how are things going with that vampire boyfriend of yours?"

I thought about it while I grabbed a bottle of gin. "How would you interpret a guy asking you for a raincheck when you invite him in for a drink?"

Patrick groaned. "And here I thought you'd finally figured out how to tame a snake."

"What's that supposed to—" I slid his drink toward him so hard I nearly sent it into his lap. "That's disgusting."

"Oh, but it feels so good."

I looked over at the front door when Beau walked in. He'd lost the sunglasses, and his eyes were brighter than ever. Amber like a shot of bourbon, with slightly elongated pupils. It was like he was showing them off proudly, which was a far cry from where his head was at when I left him back at his place. His shirt was unbuttoned halfway down his chest too.

Patrick followed my gaze and saw Beau's strange eyes. "What the hell happened to him?"

"We need to have a talk about your *vadar*," I said. "You failed miserably the other day when you said he wasn't turning into a vampire." In fact, Patrick was adamant that Beau was overreacting to getting bitten by Victor Steele in that jail cell.

Patrick cocked his head and pointed his thumb over his shoulder. "That ain't no vampire."

"You're right. It's worse. Looks like Lucy isn't my only bartender with family secrets." Although the Wyatt family made no attempt to hide theirs. The men were wolves, and the women were just half-crazy. I leaned closer to him. "Ever hear of something called a Hollerwolf?"

Patrick took a sip of his drink. "It's about time he came out of the closet."

"Wait a minute. You knew?"

He shrugged. "Rumors have been going around for years about what goes on in that big old house." He leaned closer. "Parties, if you know what I mean. Your golden boy isn't as squeaky clean as you think he is."

"That's crazy. Beau didn't even know what was happening to him until we went to see his father tonight. Although Dan Henry did point out that this has all been happening around Beau for years. I guess denial is a powerful thing."

Patrick snickered. "And that boy is in some *serious* denial."

"Not anymore," I said as Beau came around the bar.

"I'm back," Beau said, flipping a glass in the air and catching it. "Better than ever. This is the new me."

Patrick nearly fell off his stool when Beau grinned and revealed a set of micro fangs. "Holy shit!" They weren't really long enough to be called proper fangs, but they were still fangs.

"That's the other part I didn't tell you about," I said to Patrick.

"You can tell the whole damn world if you want," Beau said, not the slightest bit annoyed that I'd outed him. "I ain't hiding anymore." He threw his arms wide. "This is who I am. Beau Henry, halfling."

Patrick eyed him like he had a screw loose. "A whatling?"

"Half vampire and half Hollerwolf," I muttered. "We'll talk about it later."

Patrick put his sunglasses back on and looked at me over the top of the lenses. "I guess there's a first time for everything."

"That's right." Beau patted him on the shoulder. "I guess we got something in common now. Maybe we can sit down and have a beer sometime. You know. You can show me the ropes." He straightened up and got a sour look on his face. "Wait. Am I gonna have to drink blood now? Because I don't think I can do that."

"Whoa," I said to Beau. "I think you're getting ahead of yourself." Other than sprouting a set of baby fangs, he'd shown no signs of becoming a full-fledged vampire. I was certainly no expert, but surely if he was a vampire he would have needed to feed by now. On the other hand, I had no idea what a Hollerwolf ate.

Patrick downed his drink and stood up. "I got to get out of this asylum. I'll call you tomorrow." He stared at Beau for a moment through his dark sunglasses. "And you got a whole bar full of vampires who can *show you the ropes*. I ain't nobody's teacher."

"I'd love to come with you," I said to Patrick, "but as you can see, I have to babysit my bartender so he doesn't do something stupid."

"Well, good luck with that." He blew me a kiss and headed for the door.

After he climbed into his MINI Cooper and drove off, I heard a crash behind me. Beau and I looked at each other and ran into the kitchen. Dog was sprawled out on the floor, gripping his chef's knife in one hand and a potato in the other.

"Dog?" I dropped down next to him and looked into his eyes that were fixed up at the ceiling. "What's wrong?" His mouth was moving, but there was no sound coming out. When I tried to get the knife out of his hand, he gripped it tighter. Then he started to tremble.

"We need to call an ambulance," Beau said, his amber eyes growing brighter.

"N-no!" Dog managed to gurgle out.

What we needed was the pack, so I pulled out my phone to call Loki. "He's a wolf. They can't help him in a hospital." Loki picked up on the first ring. "Dog just went down. Get over to the Stag, now!"

Lucy came running into the kitchen a few seconds later. "Is he okay?"

"Find me something I can use as a pillow." Then I looked at Beau. "Go clear the place out."

While Beau went to get rid of the customers, I called Candy and told her to get over to the bar.

"Here." Lucy dropped a small sack of potatoes on the floor next to me.

I stared at it for a second. "Are you kidding me?"

The kitchen door flew open as I was about to bark at her to use her brain. Loki and Lux ran through it, buck naked, and pushed me aside to examine Dog.

"What the hell happened to him?" Loki said.

I shook my head. "I don't know. He was acting kind of funny a little while ago, and then we heard him hit the floor."

"Charley!" Candy called out from the bar.

"We're in the kitchen!"

Dog suddenly went still, his blank gaze still fixed on the ceiling. My heart felt like it was about to break as I wondered if we were too late.

Candy ran into the kitchen a moment later and looked down at him. "Is he...?"

"Fuck no, he's not dead!" Loki growled, grabbing Dog under his armpits while Lux took him by the ankles. "We have to get him to the pack."

"He won't make it," Candy said. "Get him into Charley's truck and take him to my shop. The wolves can meet us there." She glanced at their naked bodies. "And find some clothes. It's going to get crowded at the Cauldron tonight."

NINE

Katherine and Desiree arrived at the Cauldron thirty minutes after we got Dog settled into the spare bedroom upstairs. It was more than unnerving to see a wolf as powerful as Dog lying motionless and barely breathing, but Loki had assured us that the shallow breathing was normal. Under extreme physical duress, wolves shut their bodies down to the bare minimum to conserve energy for healing.

"What took you so long?" Loki said when the witches walked into the room.

Katherine met his harsh gaze. "Take that tone with us again, and you'll be chasing your tail for the next week."

I got an image of him spinning in circles for hours without a clue as to why.

He growled under his breath. "No offense, ladies. I'm just a little concerned about my pack leader right now."

I understood why he was on edge, but if he didn't get that sarcasm out of his voice, Katherine was going to make good on that threat.

"How's Mia?" I asked for Loki's sake.

Katherine sighed. "The same, but at least she's stable. We'll get her through this."

She breezed past Loki and over to the bed, placing her hand on his forehead. "His temperature is high, but his color looks good."

Dog's color had started to return, but until he opened his eyes and told us what had happened to him tonight, I wouldn't rest.

As if he'd read my mind, his eyes fluttered open. He fussed with the comforter we'd put over him and struggled to sit up.

"Take it easy, Dog," I said. "You're not out of the woods yet."

Loki was at the side of the bed a second later. "What happened?"

Ignoring my advice, Dog managed to prop himself up against the headboard. "Fuck if I know." He threw the covers back and started rubbing his ribs like he had earlier that evening. "I felt jumpy all day. Off. Like my skin was crawling, or I ate some poison." Dog would know because he'd been poisoned before. During a territory war a few years back with another pack up in the hills. "Last thing I remember was feeling like someone was twisting my heart."

"May I?" Katherine asked him, extending her hand.

"Be my guest," he grumbled. Dog wasn't the best patient. He'd had a moment of lucidity when we got him in the bed and turned combative, but Candy threatened to kill him herself if he didn't settle down. That's when he passed out again.

Katherine flattened her hand over his chest and moved it back and forth. As he was starting to get impatient, she lowered it to his stomach. To the spot just above his navel. Then she spread her fingers. "This may hurt a little."

"Just get it over w—" His growl went up an octave as she dug her fingers into his skin, wrapping them around something underneath it. It looked like a lump of hard flesh or a tumor that she'd managed to grab a hold of, and it was moving.

"What is that?" I said.

Katherine released it, and the mass settled under his skin. "Something that doesn't belong in there." Her forehead was deeply creased. "Have you eaten anything unusual recently?"

"Define unusual," Dog said.

"An animal acting strangely, for instance."

Well, he was a wolf.

"You mean something rabid?" He huffed. "I don't mean to be rude, but I ain't stupid, lady."

He lost his patience and attempted to climb out of the bed.

Katherine's eyes focused on the floor as she fell into thought. "You said you touched the heart?"

Dog went still. "The one in the box?"

"Is there another?"

"He picked it up," I said, recalling the sick feeling I'd gotten from seeing it in his hand. Then I remembered what Ian had told me when he showed up at my house that morning. *It's a very effective way of getting dark magic inside of one's target.*

"So sue me," Dog said. "I'm a wolf. I don't get squeamish."

Desiree tsked. "You foolish man."

"Candy almost reached into that box too," I said, coming to his defense. "So don't judge."

Candy put her hand on her hip and smirked at me. "But I didn't, did I? I could feel the bad juju all over that heart."

Loki looked back and forth at us. "What the hell are you talking about?" I guess Dog hadn't briefed him yet.

"The woman who lived in that run-down house up at Blood Lake was murdered," Candy said. "Whoever did it ripped her heart out and sent it to Charley. In a neat little box. Probably hoping she'd stick her hand inside."

"We don't know for sure if it was meant for me," I reminded them. But I was being naive.

Loki shook his head at Dog. "And you touched it? Jesus, Dog, you know better."

He rubbed his chest again. "I do now."

"Where is this heart?" Loki asked.

Desiree dismissed him with a look. "Where it belongs."

"I placed it back inside Fawny's chest myself," Katherine said.

Did I hear her right? She touched it too? "Why didn't it have any effect on you?"

"Because I took precautions before laying hands on an organ laced with dark magic." Then she looked at Dog. "You'll be fine. You're obviously strong enough to withstand whatever magic was infused in that heart, which confirms that it wasn't intended for you." Her eyes met mine. "Someone is out to get you, Charley. You're in danger."

What else was new? "Don't worry. I won't be opening any more boxes left on my doorstep."

"Or the mail or daily deliveries," Dog said, wincing as he stood up. "I'll handle that until we can figure out who's behind this."

Lux had been quietly listening from the corner of the room. "We should have a look at that heart. There's another conjure woman in the mountains who dabbles on the dark side. Maybe she can tell us what kind of magic we're dealing with."

"That's not going to happen," Katherine said. "Fawny's body was stolen."

Loki huffed. "Stolen? By who?"

"Who do you think? By whoever killed her."

"You're lying," he said, narrowing his eyes at the witch.

Katherine shot him a withering look. "Why would I lie? And it's none of your business regardless."

Loki snarled. "Our pack leader was attacked. That makes it wolf business."

"Back off," Dog said to his second-in-command. "Katherine's right. It's not our place."

The idea of the perpetrator being able to breach the Squad's fortress and then get the better of Dog was making me nervous. That back room downstairs in the shop had a lot of nasty things bottled up on the shelves, including the essence of Atticus Devereaux, a particularly nasty demon who'd almost destroyed this town not too long ago. A bottle of black magic sitting next to him in there would be a disaster waiting to happen.

Still a little shaky but stable, Dog headed for the door, motioning for Lux and Loki to follow him. "Let's get out of here."

"You can stay as long as you need to," Candy said. "You never know when a residual wave might hit you."

"I appreciate that, but I'm sleeping in my own bed tonight."

I walked them out of the shop and gave Dog a commiserative smile. "Sorry about dragging you into this. Are you sure you're okay?"

"I'm fine. It's you I'm worried about." He glanced down at my hand. "Keep that trigger finger handy."

"Locked and loaded."

Relief washed over me when wolves emerged from the shadows and followed them down the street. No one was getting to Dog tonight.

Candy and the others came downstairs as I walked back inside. "By the way," I said. "Ian Masterson showed up at my house at four o'clock this morning asking about that heart."

Desiree's lips curled back. "The vampire?"

"He was working with Fawny, and he knew she'd been killed."

"Why would Fawny Goodman be working with a vampire?" Candy asked.

"Because she specialized in conjure," Katherine said. "Blood magic, to be specific. Fawny may have been one of us, but there was a darker side to her work. Nothing evil," she quickly added, predicting the next question out of Candy's mouth. "But there can be no light without darkness. The same is true for magic."

My mother used to say that. Usually when teaching me about tolerance. "Ian said Fawny had eyes in the back of her head. That no one could have gotten close enough to kill her without using black magic. And he seemed awfully nervous about it."

"He should be," Desiree said. "We should all be nervous."

No argument there. "I told him about the heart, and he demanded to know what I did with it." I shrugged. "So I told him."

Candy's eyes took on a wicked look. "If that vampire shows up again *demanding* anything, you send him my way. I'll set him straight."

Ian wasn't much of a threat to me these days, on account of how we'd been beneficial to each other lately. And because I could put him in his place with my magic. So I wasn't worried about him anymore. He was more of an annoyance.

"I need to get back to the Stag." We'd shut the bar down abruptly and left Beau and Lucy to clean up, and I needed to help. Dog wasn't the tidiest cook, so the kitchen was probably a mess.

On my way out, I nodded to the door leading to the back room. "Are you sure it's wise to keep the goodies in that closet back there?" I used to think nothing could get into the Cauldron without Candy's blessing, but now I wasn't so sure.

"Let's hope so, honey."

Let's hope so? I felt much better now.

I left the Cauldron and drove to the bar. When I walked inside, there was no sign of either of my bartenders, and the place was still a mess. "Beau?" It was dead quiet. Too quiet.

But then Lucy's voice came from the kitchen. "We're in

here." And it wasn't her usual loud and brash tone. She sounded kind of shaky.

When I walked into the kitchen, Lucy was to my left, pressed against the wall and staring straight ahead. Never taking her eyes off what she was looking at, she raised her hand and pointed. When I followed her gaze, I spotted Dog on the other side of the room. He'd shifted, and there were broken dishes all over the floor. In the corner opposite him was something I couldn't put a label on. It was just as big as Dog's wolf, but it stood upright and had black fur and long claws half the length of its paws. It was only when it turned to look at me that I realized what it was. Or who.

"Beau?"

Before I could stop Dog, he lunged, taking down the beast and a tall shelf against the wall along with him. The room filled with snarls and other ungodly sounds as they collided head-on. The two of them were nothing but a ball of whirling fur and fangs.

I grabbed Lucy's arm and pulled her with me as I ran out of the kitchen, barely escaping a tornado of glass shards kicking up from the floor from the brawl.

Lucy fought to catch her breath when we made it to the back room. "What the hell was that thing?"

"What do you think? It's Beau!"

Her jaw practically hit the floor. "Shut up!"

Just when I thought I'd have to invest in a complete kitchen renovation, I heard the sound of wolves up front.

"Wait here." I ran down the hallway and stepped in Loki's path before he made it into the kitchen. "That's my bartender Dog is fighting with in there. It's Beau." The wolf cocked its head. "Don't you dare hurt him."

Conflicted about whether I was handing Beau a death sentence, I stepped aside. Loki charged, nearly knocking the door off its hinges with Lux right behind him. Four people in that kitchen was tight enough. Three wolves and a Hollerwolf was pushing it.

Minutes passed before the commotion finally stopped. When I couldn't hear sounds beyond the door, I dared to push it open to look inside. The wolves were standing in the middle of the kitchen with their hackles raised, and they were looming over Beau. He was back in human form and lay motionless on the floor.

Dog shifted and looked at me, his face blank as he stumbled and crashed into the refrigerator behind him, obviously still weak from the dark magic. He looked stunned.

"Tell me you didn't kill him." I gazed down at Beau's bloodied body. "Say something!" I demanded when Loki and Lux shifted and just stared back at me.

"He's still breathing," Loki said, "but we need to get him help."

"Help?" My mind was racing. Beau was torn up bad. I knew nothing about Hollerwolves, but I was pretty sure a little R & R wasn't going to fix him.

Lux looked down at Beau and then back up at me. "He needs vampire blood. Fast!"

For someone who supplied vampire blood to the community, I was awfully confused about how to get my hand on some at that moment. I ran over to the freezer where I usually kept a spare vial for emergencies, but there was none. I'd never replaced the last emergency vial I'd used. "We don't have any."

"Well, *find* some," Loki barked, "or he's dead."

If we'd still been open, we would have had volunteers lined up at the bar. But I was standing in a vampire watering hole that doubled as a blood co-op, and I had nothing. The irony was tragic.

I pulled out my phone and called Patrick, but it went straight to voicemail. And then I heard someone walk into the bar.

"Charley?" Samuel called out.

My heart started to flutter. "In the kitchen. Hurry!"

I didn't have to say a word when Samuel walked in. He went into autopilot when he saw Beau on the ground and bit into his wrist with his fangs. Then he fell to his knees and held it to Beau's lips, forcing blood into his mouth.

Beau stirred, and I finally remembered to breathe. "Thank God!"

Samuel looked up at us. "What happened?"

I was about to explain when Beau's eyes popped open. His tongue flicked at the blood. Then he began to suck, a set of small fangs descending as he dug them into Samuel's wrist.

When Loki spotted them, he stepped back. "What the fuck?"

"It's a long story," I said.

When it was clear that Beau was stable, I went to check on Dog. He was on the floor with his back pressed against the refrigerator, so I sat down next to him. "What are you doing here? You were supposed to be on your way home." I was so relieved that he was okay, I wanted to cry. One close call was enough, but two in one night?

"I didn't feel right about leaving the kitchen mess for someone else to clean up." He glanced over my shoulder at Beau, who was sitting up now. "Why didn't you tell me about Beau?" He knew Beau was dealing with something strange. His eyes made that obvious. But I hadn't told anyone at the Stag what had happened at Dan Henry's house. I was hoping Beau would do that, and I guess he just did.

"I just found out myself," I said. "Hell, Beau just found out when we went to his father's house tonight. But why did you attack him?"

Dog frowned. "I didn't. He attacked me."

That made no sense. "Did you do something to threaten him?"

He let out a weak laugh. "Yeah, I did something. I got dizzy when I walked into the kitchen. I was about to hit the floor again, so I shifted to break my fall. Next thing I know, that beast comes busting through the kitchen door gunning for my ass. He must have smelled the wolf and saw me as a threat." He shook his head. "I had no idea it was Beau. Jesus, Charley, Beau's fucked."

No more than Dog or the rest of the pack were. From what I could see, they had a lot in common. They were all shifters. Beau was just different. But these two were co-workers, and that meant they had to tolerate each other. It was just a matter of introducing them and letting the wolf and the Hollerwolf get a noseful of each other.

I climbed back to my feet. "Can you stand up?"

"I think I can manage."

"Good, because you two need to call a truce. You can start by going over there and helping Beau off the floor." I glanced around at the colossal mess. "Then you've got a kitchen to clean up."

TEN

Samuel set a plate down in front of me and grinned. "Bon appétit."

It looked delicious. Far too good for a late-night snack. More like a two a.m. snack, with me in my robe and Samuel very naked in my kitchen. As usual, I hadn't eaten in a while, and baked chicken with a decadent olive sauce hit the spot. The way he'd whipped it up with the slim pickings in my kitchen was a mystery.

"How does a vampire know how to cook like this?" I took a bite and laid my fork down. "You don't even eat food."

He leaned over the kitchen counter and grabbed an olive from my plate, popping it between his lips to chew it slowly. "I like a salty olive now and then." Then he straightened back up. "I haven't always been a vampire. I used to cook all the time." His smile faded as a thought seemed to fill his mind. "Maybe I would have been a chef in another life."

Some information at last. It was just a hint of who he really was. The man behind the dark and mysterious exterior. But little by little I was extracting morsels of his past, each one worth its weight in gold. Being born over a century ago, there was a lot to learn about Samuel Cain, and I could listen to him for days if he would just let down his walls and talk to me.

"I love this," I said.

"The chicken?"

I smiled. "Getting glimpses of who you are. Who you were. I don't think you realize how much this means to me, Samuel."

"Trust me, Charley. I've done things you wouldn't approve of. Or find very attractive."

"We all have secrets, Samuel." I know I did. Nothing terrible, but I'd done some embarrassing things back in the day.

"I wish my past was as innocent."

I cocked my head at him. "Don't tell me you used to rob banks." When he stared at me with a straight face, my stomach sank. "Did you?"

"Not quite." He took the fork I'd laid down and held it out to me. "Eat."

After taking a few more bites, I moved the chicken around my plate as a question stirred in my mind. A question I'd had since he'd given me that key to his house. Hesitantly, I asked, "Do you think we're moving too fast?"

His brow tightened. "Because I cooked for you?"

I looked up from my plate. "You know what I mean."

"No, I don't. When I find something I want, I take it." His eyes locked on mine for a moment. "I've learned the hard way that if you walk away from something special, it will disappear." He reached over the counter and lifted my chin, running his thumb gently over my bottom lip. "And I want you, Charley. I knew it the moment I walked into your bar."

"That's not how I remember our first meeting." He was kind of rude when he walked into the Stag for the first time. Had the nerve to diss Dog too.

"Are you saying I didn't win you over immediately with my charm?" He got serious and pinned me with his sapphire eyes.

"Taking a vampire as a lover isn't for every human. There are sacrifices, so I had to be patient. Let it be your choice."

As I opened my mouth to respond, he beckoned me to follow him.

"Come. I need to get dressed."

"You're leaving?" And we were just making progress.

"I have business to take care of, and you need to get some sleep."

I climbed back into bed as he grabbed his clothes. I liked watching him get dressed. The way he slipped into his pants. The movement of his muscles as he pulled his shirt over his shoulders. And the way his eyes met mine while his fingers manipulated his buttons. Simple pleasures I couldn't get enough of.

After putting on his shoes, he bent over the mattress to kiss me. "Sleep. I need you strong and healthy. I'll see you tomorrow."

Rolling over on my stomach, I watched him walk out, wondering about this business of his at night. He was a vampire, though. And a hunter. This was Samuel's equivalent of my daytime job. One of the sacrifices he'd mentioned.

I curled up and tried to drift off, fantasizing about what it would be like if I were a vampire. What life would be like if we were creatures of the night together. But for now, I was human, and fatigue won, lulling me into a deep sleep.

* * *

I glanced up at the moon as it shined brightly in the night sky, illuminating the yard. My naked body. As I looked down, my mind became laser focused on the grass under my feet and an overwhelming urge to dig.

Dig!

It was like I was caught in a strange dream, and all I could think about was the spot of earth beneath me. I scanned the ground for something sharp to penetrate the hard Georgia clay anchoring the grass and spotted a stick a few feet away. I grabbed it and dropped to my knees, plunging the end into the ground over and over until it broke in two.

My heart started to speed up as the need to break through the dirt grew more intense. I plunged my fingers into the grass, my nails scratching at the unrelenting clay. My very existence depended on me digging deeper.

Dig! Dig! Dig!

"Charley?"

Samuel was standing behind me, but I ignored him and kept working.

He rested his hand on my shoulder. "What are you doing?"

When I shrugged it off, he grabbed me and pulled me to my feet. I turned and shoved him, delivering a shot of blue light to his chest, sending him crashing to the ground a few yards away.

As he climbed to his feet, his bewildered look was replaced by determination. A second later, I was pinned to a tree under his full weight. A flash of ruby came from his eyes when he grabbed my hand and looked at my bloody fingers. Then I went limp against him.

When I woke up, I was on the couch and Samuel was handing me my robe. He sat down next to me and helped me gently work the sleeves over my shredded fingertips. "Ow!"

"What the hell was that all about out there?" he asked.

I glanced down at my hands and back up at him. "I... I don't know."

His head cocked as he studied my face. Then he lifted my chin to examine my eyes. "I think you were walking in your sleep."

"Walking in my—" Then I realized I had no idea of how I'd ended up on my couch, naked. Or why my fingers were caked with dirt and blood. And they hurt like a mother. "What happened?"

"That's what I'd like to know." He led me into the kitchen toward the sink and turned on the faucet. "This is going to hurt."

"Jesus!" I winced as he held my hands under the cool water. A few of my nails had been torn halfway off.

Samuel let go of my hands and bit into his wrist, holding his arm out to me. "Go on."

The pain was getting worse by the second, so I latched onto his arm and drank, the relief immediate as his blood slid down my throat.

"That's enough, Charley." He pulled his wrist away when I wouldn't let go.

It was hard to stop, and I understood the allure of vampire blood for those who were suffering. Samuel's blood being exceptionally powerful made it even harder.

"My hands feel better now," I said, licking a drop from the corner of my mouth. "Thank you."

"Good. They're already healing."

When we went back into the living room, Samuel asked the obvious question. "Why were you digging in your yard at three a.m.? With your bare hands?"

I shook my head. "I have no idea."

"You remember nothing until I showed up and carried you inside?"

"I remember you cooking for me and then leaving. I must have fallen asleep after that." But some of it was starting to come back to me. "Wait. I remember looking up and seeing the moon. Then I think I got this weird urge to dig." It made no sense to me, but it explained my hands. "I guess you're right. I must have been sleepwalking."

"Is that something you do often?"

"Not that I'm aware of. But when you live alone, it's hard to tell." For all I knew, I did it on a regular basis, which was a frightening thought. He'd know better than me, since we were sleeping together.

Samuel glanced out the window at the yard. "You said there were dogs digging out there the other day. Where?"

I met him at the window and looked at the spot where those dogs had torn up the grass. "Well, that's strange."

"What's strange?"

"I filled in the hole the dogs made, but part of it is dug up again."

Samuel gave me a funny look. "You did that, Charley. That's where you were digging when I got here."

I shook my head. "I couldn't have done all that."

He grabbed my hand, which still had traces of dirt and blood caked on it. "Yes, you did." He glanced at the hole. "Maybe we should find a shovel and see what's down there."

"What? Like a body?"

"Would it really be that unusual in Crimson?"

I think I would have noticed a freshly dug grave in my yard. "No one's digging up any more of my yard." At least not tonight. "And why are you here? I thought you had business to take care of."

"I forgot something." He went into the bedroom and came back out with his keys in his hand. "They must have slipped out of my pocket earlier tonight."

He didn't fool me. A lock on the door wasn't enough to keep Samuel Cain from getting into his house. He sensed something was wrong. The question was what?

* * *

The next morning, I went into town early to see Candy. As I drove past the Stag heading for the Cauldron, a familiar face caught my eye across the street in the square. It was Bob Flanders sitting on one of the benches. I was surprised to see him home so soon, let alone up and walking around, considering he'd been in ICU in Adlersville less than a week ago.

I parked in front of the bar and went over to say hello and to see how he was doing. I was feeling guilty for not going to the hospital to visit him.

I tried not to startle him when I walked up behind him. "Bob?" When he turned around, I was shocked at how good he looked. For an elderly man who'd been attacked by a vicious vampire, he looked great. Even his hair was combed neatly.

"Charley." His face lit up with a smile as he patted the spot on the bench next to him. "Have a seat."

I had a few minutes to kill. And besides finding out how he was doing, I wanted to ask him a few questions. "I was sorry to hear about what happened to you."

He chuckled quietly. "So was I."

"You look great." I was still shocked to see him up and about so quickly.

Noticing my surprise, he satisfied my curiosity. "I had a little help with my recovery. Candy came to see me at the hospital and brought me some medicine." He leaned closer. "Unsanctioned by my doctors."

"Vampire blood?"

He cleared his throat loudly and winked at me. "Did I say that?"

My first thought was that she didn't mention she'd gone to see Bob at the hospital. My second thought was, where did she get her hands on vampire blood? But Candy was capable of getting a hold of things that were a lot more difficult to procure than that. The woman had access to zombie blood and had a mummified penis in her display case.

"Well, I'm glad it worked. And if it makes you feel any better, we caught the vampire who attacked you. He's been taken care of."

His smile softened. "That's good to hear. Best if you killed him."

I was shocked. A man of the law suggesting such a thing? But Victor Steele wasn't your average perpetrator—he was a monster. And the only way to stop a non-human monster is to kill it. I glanced at the rubble across the street that still haunted the spot where the last monster that blew into Crimson had done all his dirty work. The remains of Morceau, the restaurant that Atticus Devereaux built.

"How's Beau doing?" he asked.

That was a loaded question. "He's doing good. Turns out he had an alibi after all."

"You mean being in jail when I was attacked."

I nodded. "Ironically."

The conversation hit a lull as I hesitated to ask a delicate question. Bob had lived in Crimson for a long time, so he was no stranger to the diverse inhabitants of this town, but I still felt the need to tread lightly. "How well do you know Dan Henry?" Bob's comments when he was trying to help me get Beau out of jail indicated that he was familiar with Beau's father.

He thought about it for a moment. "I know what he is, if that's what you're getting at."

"Then you know what Beau is?"

A deep sigh escaped him. "I didn't know for sure, but I guess you just confirmed it. Sometimes it skips a generation."

Sort of like Lucy and the other women in her family dodging the wolf gene.

"Is he dangerous?" I asked.

"Who? Beau?"

"His father." I never got a chance to see Dan Henry's temperament firsthand when we were growing up because Beau rarely brought friends to his house. Now I knew why.

Bob took a deep breath and let it back out slowly. "That

depends on which side of him you're on. Stay off Dan Henry's bad side and you'll be just fine."

"It's not me I'm worried about. It's Beau. He just found out what he is, and his father confirmed it." I didn't want to get into what had happened to Beau in that jail cell. That Victor Steele had bitten him and triggered his change. "Let's just say Dan Henry isn't thrilled with how Beau turned out. He called him a disappointment, and I doubt he wants anything to do with his son. I guess I'm just wondering if that means he's out of Beau's life forever."

Bob got a knowing look on his face. "Dan Henry never gives up his property, so tell that boy to watch his back."

"Property? We're talking about his son."

"Exactly. And Alice was his wife. But that didn't stop him from keeping her prisoner in that big house. She would have left him years ago, if she could have."

It sounded like he knew Beau's mother awfully well. "You two were friends?"

"Yes, we were, but that's all." He slowly shook his head. "She stayed for Beau's sake more than anything. You asked me if Dan Henry is dangerous." He turned to look at me, his eyes as serious as I'd ever seen them. "The answer is yes."

ELEVEN

Candy was nowhere in sight when I walked into the Cauldron. The door to the back room was open, so I figured she was probably in the middle of a session with a client and forgot to shut it, which wasn't like her. Especially with the front door to the shop being unlocked.

"Candy?" There was no reply, so I called out again louder. I was about to walk back there, praying I didn't get an eyeful, when she came through the door.

A smile flashed across her face as she brushed a stray lock of hair out of her eyes. "Charley?"

"What are you doing back there?" I asked. She seemed flushed. "Running a marathon?"

Her forced grin grew wider as she put a hand on her hip and propped the other one against the doorframe, trying to block my view. And her voice was too breathy. "Just some housekeeping. Dusting and such."

Baloney.

"Who's back there?" I tried to look past her, but she was doing a good job of filling up the doorway.

"No one."

Normally I wouldn't dare intrude on her side business, but she was hiding something from me. We'd barely mended fences over the last secret she'd kept, and I wasn't sure how much more our relationship could take.

We were at a standstill, so she let out a groan and stepped aside. "Go on. See for yourself."

The back room was empty, but the door to her secret closet was open. The one where she kept all the bad things. The worst of the worst. Vessels containing things that no decent, law-abiding human being should ever come into contact with.

She leaned against the doorframe, crossing her arms. "As you can see, no one's back here. Are you satisfied?" The heel of her shoe kept tapping nervously against the hardwood floor.

"Not even close."

She grumbled and dropped her arms. "Someone broke into the shop last night."

"Are you serious?"

"Why would I joke about something like that?"

The last time someone vandalized her shop, they shattered the front window. Candy warded the place heavily after that. "I didn't see any broken glass or damage to the front door. Did they come in through the alley?"

"That's the part that doesn't make sense. There's no forced entry."

I glanced around the undisturbed room. "Then what makes you think someone broke in?"

She hesitated and then looked at the closet. "Because something's missing, and some mouse didn't run off with it."

"You mean something from in there?" I pointed to the open door as a sick feeling came over me. "Please tell me it wasn't—"

"No! That devil is still sitting on that shelf where he belongs."

I sagged with relief. Just the thought of someone setting

Atticus Devereaux free was enough to make me want to throw
up. But that left another question. "Then what did they take?"

"Something just as bad."

"What could be as bad as that devil?"

She hesitated again. "A necromancer's charm."

I stared at her for a moment. Nothing remotely connected
to the word *necromancer* could be good. Although it shouldn't
have surprised me as much as it did. Candy was the keeper of
all kinds of dangerous things in that small room, but I'd never
asked her what was in the rest of those bottles, jars, and boxes. I
guess I should have asked though, because if something ever
happened to Candy—God forbid—someone needed to know
what we were dealing with on those shelves.

"Do I even want to know what a necromancer's charm is?" I
said.

She sighed. I could see that she was worried, which made
me worry. "Do you remember when your mama and me took
that day trip down to Savannah to pick up a painting she bought
online?"

"Yeah?" I remembered that ugly thing. It was a cheap land-
scape that looked like a paint by numbers. And my mother had
better taste than that.

"Well, we went to pick something up, but it wasn't that
painting."

The surprises kept coming. "Then what was that thing
hanging up at the Stag?" She'd eventually trashed it, but not
before letting it take up wall space at the bar for several months.

"Delia didn't want you to think we were hiding something
from you, so we stopped at a garage sale on the way back and
bought it for a couple bucks."

"But you *were* hiding something," I said, hoping she'd speed
it up.

"A gentleman in Savannah was referred to me. He'd been

dabbling in the dark arts and procured an item that ended up being more than he could handle. A bone."

"And?"

"Turned out to be stolen, and the necromancer it belonged to wanted it back. You see, it wasn't just any old bone. It was a bone from her own rib cage. The fool cut it out herself. A necromancer's charm doesn't get any more powerful than that."

I shuddered to think. "Why didn't he just give it back to her?"

She looked at me like I was naive. "You don't just hand a necromancer her stolen property back and apologize for the inconvenience—you get rid of the evidence." She shrugged. "You call an expert to take it off your hands. Quietly. And I am the queen of incarcerated objects." She glanced at the closet as a sly grin played across her lips. "And believe me, it was risky. He paid me a lot of money to do it." Then her grin quickly vanished. "And now it's gone."

"Jesus, Candy. What else is in that room?"

"We can discuss that later." She went back into the hallway and returned with a bunch of small towels and a box. "Start packing."

"Packing what?" I didn't even want to speculate, but when she walked into the closet and came back out with two bottles in her hands, it became obvious.

She handed me one. "Handle this like it's dynamite. And wrap it up good before putting it in the box."

I was speechless as I took it and stared at the black object floating inside. I recognized the other bottle in her hand. It was the one containing Atticus Devereux's evil essence. "Why are we doing this?"

"Because they're not safe in here," she said, suddenly looking unsure of herself. And Candy never looked unsure of anything. "Whoever broke in here knew how to manipulate my wards. And since that charm is the only thing they took, you can bet they knew what it was."

"You're giving me a bad case of nerves," I said as she went to get more vessels. "I've got enough of those already."

She stepped back through the closet doorway with a determined look in her eyes. "Now, you listen to me. Everything's going to be fine. We're going to walk out of here with that box with our heads up and tits out like the bosses we are. You got that?"

"Yes ma'am."

"Good. We're just taking the most dangerous ones over to the Squad's house temporarily until we find out who did this. Breaking into my shop," she muttered. "I'll break something when I get my hands on the bastard."

I almost pitied the culprit because Candy didn't make idle threats.

We packed up the last item and walked outside, with me looking over both shoulders on the way to the truck. After Candy climbed in, I carefully handed her the box containing five vessels that were arguably equivalent to ticking bombs.

As we drove out of town, I kept glancing at it. "Are you sure those things are stable in there?" As I said it, I hit a pothole, sending the box lurching forward.

Candy caught it before it ended up on the floorboard. "Pay attention to the road."

I slowed down, praying Crimson PD didn't pull me over for driving well under the speed limit. All we needed was for Carter or Murphy to get nosy again like they did when I was carrying that box with the heart in it the other night.

"I saw Bob Flanders in the square this morning," I said to take my mind off it. "He looked awfully good for a man that was in ICU less than a week ago. He said you gave him some vampire blood."

She pulled her eyes away from the window. "I did."

"Where'd you get it?"

"Where do you think? A vampire."

"Very funny. Seriously, Candy. Why didn't you just ask me?" I didn't know why I didn't think about it myself.

She stared at me like I was dense. "I think you've got enough to deal with right now. Besides, anyone can get their hands on vampire blood in this town."

That was true, but the co-op was the only place where you could get clean blood that was guaranteed not to be infected with pathogens. You never knew who a vampire was feeding on, and there were a lot of questionable donors around here. A bad dose could have done more harm than good. "I hope it was from a reliable source."

She didn't dignify the comment with a response.

"Hold onto that box," I said when we finally turned onto the bumpy dirt road leading up to the Squad's house. The three-minute drive seemed to take forever, and I held my breath until we parked and got out.

The front door opened as we reached the porch, and Desiree Dubois motioned us in.

"Take it into the kitchen," she said, giving us a wide berth as we brushed past her and continued down the long hallway. When we entered the room, Candy set the box on the table but kept her hand on it.

Katherine came through the doorway and looked at it. "Is that all of them?"

"Just the ones I'm most concerned about," Candy said. "The others aren't as dangerous. More of an annoyance if they get set free."

After staring at the box for a moment, Katherine headed across the room. "Come with me."

Candy grabbed the box, and we followed her toward the staircase at the back of the kitchen. The one that led from the top floor all the way to the basement. We took the steps down, into the bowels of the old Victorian house, where the smell of mildew mixed with some other intense scent assaulted my nose.

"What is that smell?" I asked.

"Probably patchouli," Katherine said. "I don't even notice it anymore."

When we made it to the bottom of the steps, a cold draft rushed over my skin like an Arctic breeze. "What do they do down here?" I whispered to Candy. "Store bodies?"

"Not anymore," Katherine said without the slightest hint of a smile.

We continued into the basement with nothing but a dim light overhead to illuminate what seemed like an endless space. The room went on forever. I could barely see the floor below my feet, and I had excellent eyesight. But I couldn't speak for Candy's vision, and it wasn't the best scenario for someone carrying a box of evil objects.

Katherine came to a stop in front of us and looked down. "Here."

I could barely make out a round shape on the floor. A shadow. "What is that?"

"A place where no one would dare to go without an invitation." Katherine looked at Candy. "Drop it in."

"You mean the whole box?" I said, looking back at the dark circle inches from my feet. "Is that... a hole?" I bent down to take a closer look, and a blaze of light licked at my face. It was more like a flame.

"Stand back," Candy said to me as she approached the edge.

Had she lost her mind? "You're not going to toss the whole thing in there, are you?"

Without acknowledging my question, the box slipped from her hands and disappeared into what looked like a portal to hell. The light flared up again, consuming the box and all the vessels inside. I could have sworn I heard a tiny scream come from it as it vanished into the floor.

Katherine let out a satisfied sigh and smiled. "Let's go upstairs and have a cup of tea, shall we?"

"Sounds divine," Candy said, following her back toward the stairs.

I stood there for a moment in disbelief. The light had disappeared, and all I could see was that dark shadow on the floor, my foot itching to test if it was real.

"I wouldn't do that if I were you," Katherine said without looking back at me as I was about to slip my foot over the edge to find out.

I took her sage advice and caught up to them. That basement gave me the creeps.

When we got back up to the kitchen, Desiree was waiting with a tray in her hands. We followed her into the living room, and I was shocked to see Mia sitting in a chair with Fay standing next to her. Mia stared straight ahead and didn't so much as blink when we walked in.

"She's better?" I whispered to Candy.

"Define better," she muttered back.

Desiree set the tray down on the table and poured herself a cup of tea. "Help yourselves."

Candy reached for the tray. "You want a cup?" she asked me.

"No way." The last time I drank tea in this house, I found myself hallucinating in the forest. At least that's what I told myself. You never knew what was real when you entered this house or the surrounding woods.

Candy put on a smile. "How's she doing?"

"Still not talking, but she's alive," Fay said, patting her sister on the shoulder.

I flinched when I looked back at Mia and realized her eyes were fixed on me. It was eerie the way they seemed so lifeless yet focused. And there was a slight twitch of her lips.

"What's that?" Fay lowered her ear to her sister's mouth.

"What did she say?" Candy asked.

Fay shook her head. "Nothing. She wants to communicate, but the words won't come out."

"She's been like this since this morning," Katherine said. "Awake, but trapped inside a sleeping body."

That was an interesting way of putting it, but I was glad to see that she'd come around. "She hasn't been able to tell you what happened to her?"

Katherine shook her head. "Not yet."

"Some belladonna would be beneficial," Desiree said as she sipped her tea with her pinky fully extended. "It might jump-start her mind."

"Isn't that dangerous?" I said. Belladonna was called deadly nightshade for a reason.

A strange smile appeared over the edge of her cup. "Not if used correctly."

"There will be no experimenting," Katherine said. "Especially given your track record with botany."

Candy set her teacup on the coffee table. "Can we discuss business please? Someone just stole something dangerous from the Cauldron, and I'll be the first to admit that it scares the hell out of me to think about why." She reached into her pocket and pulled out a folded piece of paper. "I found this on the shelf where the box had been." She read the note. "'Retribution is coming.'"

"Retribution for what?" I asked.

Candy tossed the note on the table. "Who the hell knows." Then she looked at Katherine. "You better be sure those vessels are safe in that basement."

"Basement?" Katherine laughed. "You know as well as I do how safe they are."

I couldn't keep quiet about that hole in the floor any longer. "I won't be able to sleep at night until I know what it was that I just saw down there. Until I know we didn't just unleash Atticus Devereaux on the world again."

Katherine stood up and walked across the room. She stopped next to the ostentatious portrait of Victoria Wilderbrandt, the first witch to arrive in Crimson well over a hundred years ago. "Nothing is leaving that basement unless Victoria allows it." She waved her hand around the room. "This is her house. She's alive in the walls. And to answer your question, Charley. That *hole* isn't just a shadow on the floor—it's the womb of this house."

I suddenly felt small in the room, like Victoria's eyes were bearing down on me. Judging me for even questioning the sanctity of her home. "Got it," I said, sinking deeper into the chair cushion. "The... womb." Whatever that meant.

"The break-in was no coincidence," Candy said. "I think whoever did this is the same person attacking witches around here. The person who sent that heart to Charley."

Katherine thought about it for a moment. "I guess it is likely."

"Likely?" Candy snickered. "We'd be fools to think otherwise."

Desiree scoffed. "Speak for yourself."

That witch rubbed me the wrong way, but I kept my mouth shut because I wanted to leave here in one piece.

Katherine looked at me curiously. "Has anything else strange happened? Any more *gifts* left on your doorstep?"

"Something strange happened in the middle of the night. That's why I stopped by the Cauldron this morning."

Candy gave me a surprised look. "Why didn't you say so?"

"Because we had more important things to worry about. The break-in." I was probably making a big deal out of nothing anyway. "You're probably all going to think I'm crazy, but I was sleepwalking early this morning and ended up in my yard."

Candy reached over and patted me on the thigh. "That ain't

crazy, honey. That's just good old-fashioned stress. You've been under a lot of it lately."

"I was digging up the yard with my bare hands."

"Well," Desiree said, taking a sip of her tea, "that is crazy."

Candy shot her a withering look to shut her up. "Go on, Charley. Tell us what happened."

"Like I said, I must have been sleepwalking." I stared at the floor trying to recall everything. "I remember having this stupid urge to dig. Then Samuel found me scratching at the dirt until my hands were bloody." I held them up. "If he hadn't given me some of his blood, half my fingernails would be missing right now. The strangest part is I was digging in the same spot where those dogs were the other day."

"What dogs?" Candy asked.

I guess I forgot to mention them. "I got home Saturday afternoon and found three dogs digging up my yard. I don't know who they belong to, but when I tried to scare them off, they attacked me. If it wasn't for Diablo, I might not be here right now."

Desiree's eyes narrowed. "Who's Diablo?"

"A dog I rescued. It's a long story."

"Get back to the other dogs," Katherine said. "What were they digging for?"

"How am I supposed to know? Maybe they lost a bone."

Katherine locked eyes with Desiree for a moment. Then she looked at Candy. "Yes, that was probably it. Where exactly was this spot?"

"Where I was digging? On the side of the house toward the backyard. Why?"

"No reason." Katherine finally pulled her eyes away from Candy and brought them to mine. "No reason at all."

TWELVE

Beau called and said he was running late, which had become a habit lately, so I found myself behind the bar again helping Lucy out. At least it took my mind off other things temporarily. Like the way Katherine Belltower kept staring at me out at the Squad's house. Something had been on her mind, but she wasn't talking. Neither was Candy. When I asked her about it on the drive back to town, she got irritated with me and told me to worry about the road. But the conversation wasn't over.

I stuck my head through the order window. "Are you doing okay in there, Dog?"

"Same as I was ten minutes ago when you asked me. And the ten minutes before that." He grumbled and grabbed a head of lettuce from the refrigerator. "Just worry about the bar."

"Excuse me for caring."

He set the lettuce down on the cutting board and rubbed the bridge of his nose. "I didn't mean to bark at you. I'm just not used to feeling like this."

That dark magic had really blindsided him. I could count on one hand how many times I'd seen Dog even remotely sick. "It's okay. I've been barked at before."

Candy was convinced that the attacks and the break-in were all connected, but the worst part was that she also believed whoever stole that charm knew exactly what they were taking. They intended to use it.

"Let me know if you need any help with the dishes or the trash or—"

"Charley..."

I decided to back off before I really irritated him. When I turned around and headed down the bar, I saw the guy who was doing card tricks the other night sitting at the other end. If he planned to stiff me again, he was in for a rude awakening.

"Is it Dexter?" I asked as I walked up to him.

A grin that didn't sit right with me slid up his face. "Decker."

"Right. Decker. You know you owe me for that food the other night."

"My apologies. Put it on my tab."

The nerve of this guy. "As long as you close it out before you leave."

His eyes zeroed in on mine. "Of course."

The room suddenly got warmer. I felt lightheaded like I'd stood up too fast or my blood sugar had dropped.

When I swayed and leaned against the bar to steady myself, he reached over and grabbed me. "Are you okay?" he asked, tightening his fingers around my arm.

"I'm fine." After locking eyes with him again, I pulled my arm away as a strange vibration traveled across my skin. "What are you drinking?"

He glanced at the wall behind me. "Whiskey."

"What kind?"

His grin vanished. "Surprise me."

I usually hated when customers said that to me, but at that moment, I just wanted to end the conversation. I grabbed the closest bottle and poured him a drink. "That was an interesting card trick the other night," I said as I set his glass down in front of him.

"You liked it, did you?"

Without another word, I headed down the bar to where Lucy was standing. I couldn't get away from the guy fast enough, and I didn't even know why. "Make sure he pays his tab before he leaves. Tell Beau too." If he ever got his ass to work tonight.

She glanced past me toward the front door. "What the hell?"

I looked over my shoulder as Rico Suave himself walked into the Stag. "You've got to be kidding me," I said to myself as my tardy bartender strolled toward me. A series of hoots and whistles came from customers, but it didn't seem to bother him. Based on his wide grin, he seemed to be enjoying the attention.

Lucy was staring, and Beau gave her a dismissive glance. "What are you looking at?"

"You, idiot." She turned and went back down the bar, flipping him off.

It was going to be a fun night keeping them from harassing each other.

Beau had on a pair of skinny black jeans with a silky black shirt to match, unbuttoned halfway down his chest. To top off his new look, he was wearing a single gold earring. His hair was darker than usual, probably from all the product in it, and it was slicked back with a thin strand dangling down the side of his forehead. I doubted that was an accident.

"Is that a spray tan?" I asked, giving him a good sniff. He was wearing cologne, and it was obnoxious. Beau was a pretty boy, but he usually just smelled like soap. Customers were going to have a field day with him tonight.

He rolled his shoulders as he straightened his shirt. "Yeah. This is the new me."

"The new you what?"

His eyes flashed amber. "The new Beau Henry."

Looked like I wasn't the only one starting to get a grip on my special talents. "You can control it now?"

He leaned closer to give me another look at his golden-brown eyes. "Pretty cool, huh? From now on, I'm living my life. I'm not hiding a damn thing."

"Well, tone it down. You're going to freak out the customers."

He huffed. "Hell, half of them are freaks themselves." Then he turned around and glanced up and down the bar, giving everyone a good look. "Anyone got a problem with this?" he asked, pointing at his glowing eyes.

There were a few grumbles in the bar, but no one got up to leave. Not even the new guy, Decker, who was watching Beau curiously. And Beau was right. The place was filled with vampires and probably a few other things. I just hoped his new wardrobe wore off quickly.

Dog looked at Beau through the order window and shook his head. "Christ." Then he got back to cooking without further commentary.

"I don't care what you wear to work," I said to Beau, "but no more cologne. It's giving me a headache."

When I looked back down the bar, Decker was finishing his drink and getting up to leave. This time I was going to make sure he paid his tab, so I headed for him. He placed a bill on the bar and practically ran toward the entrance before I reached him. It was a fifty. Almost double what he owed.

"Decker," I called as he walked out. We encouraged tips at the Stag, but I didn't take advantage of people, and that was way too much.

Lucy snatched it from the bar. "I'll split the tip with you," she said as she continued toward the register.

When I went to grab his empty glass, there was something

underneath it. "Are you kidding me?" It was a card. The ace of spades.

I stuffed it in my pocket, I don't know why, and looked at the door again. "I'll be in the back," I said to Lucy. "Make sure Beau doesn't do anything stupid tonight."

"Like what? Hump someone's leg?"

"He's a Hollerwolf, not a dog." Although there was a canine resemblance.

She slapped half the tip on the bar in front of me. "I ain't his babysitter."

"You are tonight. Keep the tip."

I went to the back and pulled the card out of my pocket, tossing it on the desk. As I was staring at it, I heard scratching at the door leading to the alley. Sebastian strolled inside when I opened it.

"Where have you been?" His fur was a mess, like he hadn't groomed himself lately. He looked straggly. Samuel said he'd been gone for days, but it must have been a week by now. "Are you hungry?"

I went to get him a can of tuna, but as I was about to push the kitchen door open, I saw Samuel walk into the bar.

"Did you see Candy today?" he asked when I walked up front.

"I stopped by the shop this morning." I decided to get the pleasantries over with before springing the latest bad news on him about the break-in. "You want something to drink?"

"No. What's wrong?" he asked, easily reading me.

I shrugged. "Just another day at the asylum." When he didn't seem to find my humor amusing, I cut to the chase. "Someone broke into the Cauldron last night. They got inside Candy's back room."

"You mean the room where she keeps her special items?"

They were special all right. "Yes, that one. They stole something called a necromancer's charm."

Samuel stared at me for a moment like he was trying to process what I'd just said. "A necromancer's charm? How did Candy get her hands on one of those?"

"So, I guess I don't have to explain what it is. How she got it is a long story, but it's gone now."

"I think I'll have that drink," he said.

He took a seat at the bar while I went to pour him a glass of his favorite. As I was setting his drink down, Beau walked by.

"What's up with him?" Samuel said.

I glanced at Beau's ridiculous outfit. "He's embracing his inner beast."

"He looks like a gigolo."

"Don't tell him that," I said. "You might give him ideas."

I continued with Candy's theory. "Candy thinks whoever broke into the shop is the same person who killed Fawny Goodman and sent me her heart."

He stared at his drink for a moment. "Speaking of which, I've been doing some tracking."

"So that's why you've been leaving me at night. I was starting to get a complex. Any luck?" The pack had traced the heart back to Blood Lake, but that's where the trail ended. Right to where Fawny had been killed.

"Before I came back and found you sleepwalking last night, I was at the lake. I needed to see for myself what happened up there."

When he hesitated, I got uneasy. "Don't stop now, Samuel. What did you find up there?"

"There was a significant amount of blood on the ground. It was everywhere."

"Of course there was. The poor woman had her heart ripped out."

He shook his head. "Not just hers. There were traces of someone else's blood as well. Around a fire pit near the house she lived in."

I didn't expect to hear that. "How do you know it was someone else's blood?"

"I'm a vampire, Charley. Everyone's blood has its own unique fingerprint, and it definitely didn't all come from Fawny Goodman."

"Really?" Who would have thought blood had a fingerprint?

"*Really.* Most of the time we don't notice the difference unless there's something very special about a particular person's blood. Something that draws us to it. Then it's nearly impossible not to notice." He lowered his chin slightly. "I could pick yours out in a sea of blood."

My heart started to race from the way he was looking at me, and I wondered if he could sense it. I shook it off and got back to the conversation. "So did you recognize it? The other blood?"

"Not exactly."

"What does that mean?"

He hesitated before changing the subject. "I think Fawny knew her killer."

Ian Masterson did say Fawny had eyes in the back of her head. That it would have been nearly impossible to get close enough to kill her unless magic was involved—or she knew her killer and never saw it coming. "Based on what Ian said the other night, you're probably right."

"I think it's more than probable. Masterson said Fawny was a blood witch. I think she was performing some kind of ritual that involved this person's blood, and he killed her afterward."

"Or *she*," I said. "Don't underestimate us."

Samuel got a puzzled look. "There was something else I detected near that fire pit. I picked up on a vampire, and he or *she* had been there recently."

"You were probably sensing Ian. He did business with her, so it makes sense that he'd been up there more than once. Recently."

Samuel shook his head slowly. "I know what Masterson smells like, and it wasn't him."

Lucy wandered over and started wiping down the bar a few feet away. She inched closer, like I wouldn't notice.

"A little privacy," I said. She was a nosy thing. After she got the message and disappeared, I got back to the conversation. "You think the killer is a vampire?" It wasn't exactly a far-fetched idea. Not around here. But I was getting tired of having vamps come after me. For God's sake, I ran a vampire-friendly business and advocated for vampire rights in this town.

"It's possible, but the other blood didn't come from a vampire. So, either this vampire brought the blood with him for some kind of ritual, or the killer is working with a vampire and they killed Fawny together."

"Were you able to at least track the blood?"

"The trail stopped at the lake." Samuel gazed at me for a moment. "But there was something about that blood. The only way I can describe it is that it was like an element or an essence."

"You mean like a smell?"

His gaze went blank for a moment like he was deep in thought. "It was more like a taste. It rolled over my tongue and filled my mind with something very familiar." Then his eyes finally refocused on mine. "This is going to sound strange, but it tasted like you, Charley. It led me straight to your house. That's the real reason I came back last night."

None of what Samuel was saying made sense. "I can assure you it wasn't my blood up at the lake. We've been spending a lot of time together lately, so maybe you've got too much of me on your mind." And as much sex as we'd been having, my scent was probably all over him.

I suddenly remembered Sebastian. "I almost forgot. Your cat is in the back room."

"Is that so? Little shit. I should leave him in the alley."

"No, you shouldn't. He looks a little rough, so you need to take him home and feed him."

We went to the back, but when I opened the door, there was no sign of the cat.

"Sebastian?" Not a peep.

Samuel looked under the desk and then up at the ceiling. "Well, he's not up there."

"I'm not losing my mind, Samuel. He was in here a few minutes ago."

He glanced at the back door. "Maybe he let himself out."

"Either that or he's in the bar somewhere."

Samuel pulled me against him. "Well, if you find him, bring him with you tonight?"

"I'll do that. But if he does show up at your door, keep him in the house until I get there. I have a few questions for that cat."

The first thing I saw when I went back up front was Lucy's brother Wes walking in, and he'd been banned from the bar since the night he and his brother, Wyatt, got drunk and turned the place into a fighting ring. I didn't care who they were related to. If you trashed the Stag, it was the last time you got the opportunity.

"Lucy," I said, nodding to the door. "What's Wes doing in here?"

She looked up at him and scrunched her brow. "How should I know?"

When he glanced at me from across the room, probably testing the waters thinking maybe I'd had a change of heart, I shook my head at him to let him know he was mistaken. "Get him out of here before I do."

"It's your bar," she grumbled. "Why should I have to do it? I'll never hear the end of it when I get home tonight."

If I had to go over there, it would get ugly. And if Dog saw him, it would get even uglier.

She set the empty glasses she was carrying in the sink and started to walk down the bar toward him. But then I realized I was about to pass up an opportunity. "Wait a minute," I said. "Is Wes still hanging out down at the Beast?" He'd been going down there ever since former management, a.k.a. Victor Steele, had added strippers to the entertainment roster. I had no idea if Ian Masterson had put an end to it since taking over the place, but if it made him money, I doubted it.

"Yeah. Why?"

My mind started to work. If a vampire was involved in Fawny's murder, the first place I'd look was down at the Beast where the worst of them usually ended up. "I want to have a word with Wes, so I'll take care of it."

She squinted at me. "About what?"

"Never mind." When I headed for him, he made a beeline for the exit. "Hold it, Wes!"

He stopped but didn't turn around. "I got the message, Charley. I'm leaving."

"How about we have a chat first?" I said when he continued toward the door. "I'll even buy you a beer."

He finally looked over his shoulder at me. "What's the catch?"

"Like I said, I want to talk to you about something." A suspicious look crossed his face, but it eased up when I reached over the bar and grabbed a bottle from the cooler. "Follow me."

When we got to the back room, I handed him the beer and got straight to the questions. "When's the last time you were down at the Beast?"

"Last night." He took a swig of beer and narrowed his bloodshot eyes. "Why?"

"Because I'm looking for someone, and you might be able to help me. There's a good chance this particular person has been hanging out down there."

"You banned me from your bar." He huffed and turned the

bottle up, drinking half of it before leaning closer. "Why would I tell you shit?"

"Because it might gain you re-entry to the Stag." As much as I hated to do that, I needed to get information out of him. Find out if he'd heard anything down there about this vampire who'd either killed Fawny or took part in it. Bad actors tended to run their mouths.

After thinking about it for a few seconds, he finished his beer and tossed the empty bottle into the trash. "Buy me a few more of those and I might get chatty."

I was losing my patience with the moron. "I'll buy you one more and let you back in here. If you give me something useful," I added.

"All right, ask."

"Has anyone down at the Beast been talking about a murder up at Blood Lake?"

His cocky smirk quickly faded. "I don't know nothing about a murder."

"How about anyone acting strange or suspicious?"

"Strange?" He snorted a laugh. "That whole club is strange. If you want normal, you come to the Stag."

Well, I wouldn't call my bar *normal*, but it sure as hell wasn't a cesspit like the Beast.

I groaned and realized talking to Wes Wyatt was a dead end. I don't know why I wasted my time or a perfectly good beer on him. "Just get out of here."

He frowned. "What about that second beer?"

"You didn't give me anything useful," I said as I started to go back up front.

"How about stupid?" he said. "Does that qualify as strange?"

I stopped in the doorway and looked back at him. "Go on."

"A vampire was flashing a wad of cash around down there last night. That's a good way to get yourself rolled and killed."

He eyed me slyly to see if he'd whetted my curiosity before getting to the good part. "He was bragging about pulling a fast one on some witch, and getting paid for it."

Bingo.

I stepped back in the room as my pulse started to race. "What's his name?"

"How the hell should I know. I've never seen the guy before."

"What did he look like?"

He shrugged. "Like a vampire. Pale with long, stringy black hair."

Talk about stereotyping. "You do know that not all vampires look like that." Just like not all wolves were sleazebags like him and his brother. "What else do you remember about him?"

He scratched his head as he thought about it. "He had a weird tattoo on the back of his neck."

Okay, that was something. But then again, half the clientele down there had tattoos. "What kind of tattoo?"

"A snake running up his spine and disappearing into his hair."

Again, half the vampires down there had *snake* tattoos, including that bartender I'd killed. But it was a lead and something to pass on to Ian Masterson.

"His hair was covering it up," he continued. "The only reason I saw it was because the idiot dropped his roll of cash on the floor. When he bent down to pick it up, his hair fell away."

"Anything else?"

"I had better things to do than check out a dude." He got a disgusting grin on his face. "Like watch them titties working the stage."

I pointed to the back door. "Just leave."

You would have thought I'd slapped him, the way he looked at me. "That's bullshit! You just told me I could come in the bar if I talked."

"Your reinstatement starts tomorrow." I couldn't believe I was saying that, but I was a woman of my word. I just couldn't stand to look at him right now.

I opened the door to the alley and couldn't get him out of the room fast enough because I had more important things to do than listen to him whine. He'd just confirmed my suspicions that the vampire involved in the murder had shown up at the Beast. I was ninety-nine percent sure of that. Now I just needed to convince Ian Masterson that Fawny's killer was in his midst.

THIRTEEN

Dog stuck his head into the room as I was locking the back door behind Wes. "Murphy just showed up. He's waiting for you at the bar."

Not Murphy again.

"Just send him back here so we don't have to get into it in front of customers."

Dog looked over his shoulder. "He must have read your mind. Here he comes."

"Figures."

Murphy brushed past Dog and came into the room. "Charley."

I sat down and picked up the ace of spades I'd tossed on the desk earlier, absently tapping it on the surface. "What can I do for you, Tom?"

He looked at the card. "What's that?"

"Nothing." I shoved it in the top drawer.

Dog pointed his thumb over his shoulder. "I'll be in the kitchen if you need me."

"Might as well stay," Murphy said. "This pertains to you too."

Dog leaned against the wall and crossed his arms. "Is that right?"

Murphy gave him his best authoritative look, which was wasted on Dog. "We need to continue the conversation we started the other day. One of you can start by telling me about this Mr. Steele who supposedly has been taken care of."

Dog was right. Murphy wasn't about to ignore what we'd told him. "There's nothing to tell. Why can't you just let it go?" I said.

He came closer and narrowed his eyes. "Because another woman went missing."

"Who?" I said.

"A woman who lives alone up at Blood Lake. Fawny Goodman." He eyed me for a moment as if gauging my reaction. "She doesn't fit the profile of the other victims, but she's still missing."

I glanced at Dog before looking back at Murphy. "It's pretty remote up there. You just said she lives alone, so how do you know she's missing?"

"A guy from the Forestry Service comes up here every few months to check on work being done in some of the wilderness areas. He knows her and checks in when he's up here. He went by her house and said she wasn't there. Said the place didn't look right."

From what I'd been told, Fawny didn't seem like the type that needed to be checked up on. He was probably just an acquaintance, and it was just our luck that this guy decided to pass through now.

"Sounds like she lives out there in the middle of nowhere for a reason," I said. "Maybe she went on a hike." Murphy was getting impatient with me. I could see it in the way his lips were tightening. "Just because the woman wasn't home doesn't mean she's missing."

He smirked. "A woman doesn't go on a hike and leave her front door wide open. At least not one with half a brain.

Besides, he went back twice over the weekend, and she hadn't been back. And then there was the blood."

Dog and I locked eyes again, but I quickly pulled mine away when Murphy caught it.

"Blood?" Dog said, distracting him.

He nodded. "The guy found it all over the fire pit next to her house. That's what spooked him and prompted him to call it in."

Dog shrugged. "It could have been animal blood. Living alone up there, I'm sure she's a hunter."

"I suppose that's possible. We won't know for sure until we get the analysis back."

"You went up there?" I said.

He shot me an incredulous look. "What do you think? Rick and I went up there to take samples and investigate. Found a lot of fresh shoe tracks around that fire pit. Based on the size, it looks like at least two males were up there recently."

This was bad, and I found myself trying to recall what kind of shoes Samuel was wearing last night. His clothes weren't cheap, and I had a feeling no other man in Crimson had shoes like his. Except maybe Ian Masterson.

"You need to tell me where I can find this Victor Steele."

I took a step back when he came closer. "I already told you. He's been taken care of. It's impossible for him to have done anything to Fawny Goodman."

"All I know is we've got another missing woman and no one in custody for the others. Where is he?"

"He's dead," Dog said.

Murphy gave him a cold stare. "I ought to take you in."

"For what?" I said. "A crime that doesn't exist?"

A grin slid up Dog's face. "Victor Steele was a vampire, and we all know what happens to vampires when they get offed. You grab a dustpan." He pushed away from the wall and took a step closer to Murphy. "Now back the fuck off."

"Dog..." I warned. He was just fueling the fire.

Murphy glared back at him. "I could take you in just for that."

"But you won't."

"That's enough," I said, getting between them before Dog got his ass thrown in jail. "I need to get back to my bar, so either arrest *me*, or leave."

Murphy pulled his eyes away from Dog's and turned them on me. "This isn't over, Charley."

"It never is."

I waited for Murphy to walk out of the room before looking at my cook. "Don't do that to me, Dog. Trying to get Beau out of jail was hard enough."

He settled down and let out a heavy sigh. "It was either that or chew his head off—literally."

"As entertaining as that would have been, we have bigger things to deal with right now. Like making sure Crimson PD doesn't go all Cinderella and try to match those shoe prints from the lake. One of those sets belongs to Samuel."

Dog frowned. "He went up to the lake?"

"Last night. He traced the blood back to that house and found more left by someone else." I didn't want to get into my conversation with Samuel or Wes Wyatt. Not yet. "Some of the other footprints must be from when the Squad found Fawny up there." I thought about it for a moment. "Come to think of it, maybe Samuel doesn't have anything to worry about. Have you seen the size of Desiree Dubois's feet?"

Dog chuckled. "I better get back to the kitchen. I'm sure someone needs an order of fries by now."

When I walked back up front, Patrick was sitting at the bar. I took a seat next to him and did something I rarely do while working—I ordered a drink. "I thought you were going to call me today," I said, motioning to Lucy to pour me a beer from the tap.

He pulled his phone out. "Want me to go outside and dial your number?"

"Very funny. I'm glad you stopped by though. I need to talk to you about something."

"Don't tell me you broke up with that fine vampire of yours?" He looked at me over the rim of his sunglasses. "Or did you get another special delivery? A box of eyeballs and fingers this time?"

I shuddered. "Thanks for planting that image in my head."

Lucy set my beer down. "That'll be five bucks."

"Get out of here before I take it out of your tips."

Patrick waited until she walked away. "Now that we got rid of that nosy thing, tell Daddy what's wrong."

"What do you know about blood magic?"

He pulled back to give me a hard look. "I know how to drink the stuff, and I recommend it highly, but this vampire don't know nothing about all that other nonsense."

"I'm serious, Patrick."

He chuckled and sipped his gin and tonic. "So am I. That's some messed-up shit." He set his glass down and looked at me sideways. "Jesus, woman, you are serious."

I tried to blow it off. "It's nothing. This stuff with Fawny Goodman has my head spinning." And I couldn't stop thinking about what Samuel had said about that blood. How he'd sensed my essence. What did that even mean?

When I zipped it, he eyed me suspiciously. "We ain't through talking about this, Charley."

"We are for now." I was about to get up when I heard a phone. It kept ringing. "Where is that coming from?"

Beau glanced at the shelf under the bar. "You left your phone under there."

"Why didn't you tell me sooner?"

He handed it to me. "I just noticed it."

There were three missed calls from Candy. "I better call her back," I said to Patrick. "She's going to read me the riot act for not picking up the first time."

"I need to get out of here anyway," he said, finishing his drink. "I'll call you tomorrow." He stopped on his way to the door. "We've got co-op deliveries this weekend, so get your head straight."

"Yes sir." I saluted him as he walked out the door. Then I dialed Candy's number. "Sorry I missed your calls," I said when she answered.

"You need to meet me at the Squad's house," she said without a greeting. There was urgency in her voice.

"Why? What's wrong?"

"Just get in your truck and drive, Charley. Something bad is happening." She hung up without another word.

I went into the kitchen to let Dog know I was leaving. "Candy just called sounding frantic. I need to get out to the Squad's house. Can you keep an eye on things for me until I get back?"

"Sure. You want me to come with you?"

I shook my head. "I need you here. Something probably happened to Mia Winston." She was essentially comatose when I saw her earlier that day, so I suspected she'd taken a turn for the worse. "Just keep an eye on Beau and Lucy. I'll be back as soon as possible."

My adrenaline was off the charts as I headed for the door. It had to be about Mia. If I walked into the house and found a dead witch sitting in that chair, Katherine Belltower's declaration would come to life—we'd have a war on our hands.

FOURTEEN

As I rounded the bend, the sky was lit up in a glow. There was a fire somewhere. I turned onto the dirt road, feeling sicker by the second as I drove closer. Just beyond the trees, the flames grew brighter. And as the house came into view, I could see a line of fire at the rear of the property.

Candy's Wagoneer was parked a safe distance from the house, but she wasn't in it. She was standing in the yard with the Squad as the inferno approached. Mia was missing. She must have been inside the house, still in her trance-like state.

"Are they crazy?" I whispered.

I parked next to her car and got out, feeling the heat hit my skin as I watched the fire begin to circle the house.

"Hurry, Charley!" Candy yelled, beckoning me as the flames continued to spread.

Hurry where?

I ran toward her without really thinking but came to an abrupt halt when common sense kicked in. "What are you doing?" I yelled back. All the way out here, no one would see that fire, and something told me they hadn't called the fire department. "We have to get out of here!"

"No one's going anywhere!" Katherine said, her eyes fixing on mine as she raised her hand, palm side up, and pointed at me.

With a crook of her finger, I was airborne, hurtling toward them. I flew past the fast-moving flames threatening to seal off the only point of escape. The fire accelerated as I hit the ground next to the witches, and our only chance of getting out alive slipped away. We were trapped.

I climbed to my feet and checked the back side of the house for a break in the wall of flames, but there wasn't one. The fire had formed a perfect ring around us, and the grand Victorian was about to become a witches' pyre.

After running back to the front, panic set in. I grabbed Candy's arm and dug my fingers into her skin. "We're all going to die!"

She yanked her arm free and slapped me across the face, knocking some sense into me. "Sorry, honey, but no one's dying today." Then she grabbed my hand while Katherine took the other. The five of us linked up and formed a circle, moving closer to the house to escape the intense heat.

As the flames snapped at the sky, the witches started to chant. But the language was foreign to me. "I don't know what you're saying. What should I do?"

Candy squeezed my hand tighter. "Focus and pray for rain."

Rain? Rain wasn't going to save us. We'd need a monsoon.

I closed my eyes and tried to push the fear away. To concentrate. The heat was suffocating, and all I could hear was the crackling of approaching death. But as I focused harder on the light within me, a miracle happened—my mind started to calm. The sound of the fire grew quieter, and I began to drift. The chanting trailed off into a hum in the distance as the orange flicker of flames behind my eyelids softened to a blue glow.

Hold the line, Charley.

It was the voice of my mother.

Hold the line! Don't let him win!

A crack of thunder made me flinch, bringing everything roaring back. But as my eyes started to flutter open, the voice came again.

Make it weep!

Hot air filled my lungs as I took a deep breath and visualized the sea around me. A tsunami swallowing the house. I couldn't explain it. I just followed my instincts, and that voice in my head. Manifested something with nothing more than a thought. Like muscle memory.

I looked up as a drop of water hit my face. Then another fell. A moment later, the sky opened up, bringing sweet relief to my hot skin.

"Don't stop!" Katherine ordered as the witches began to chant louder.

Despite the rain, the unbearable heat picked up again. Katherine suddenly dropped my hand, and then Candy's slipped away too. All I could hear were flames popping and that voice in my head again.

Brace yourself, Charley.

The heat came in waves, the fire suddenly reaching my back. The pain spread across my shoulders and down my arms, making me scream as the flames licked at my skin. The water washing over me barely eased the pain as I fought to open my eyes, but it felt like a night terror I couldn't wake up from. Then I collapsed and felt my feet leave the ground as I was carried through the monsoon and into the house.

I fell against the sofa, face down as someone carefully peeled away what was left of my shirt. My eyes finally began to focus as someone gently turned my head to the right.

"Samuel," I whispered, lost in the euphoria of the blood dripping between my lips. Then his face faded away along with any trace of the pain.

* * *

I woke with a start and pushed myself up from the sofa. It took me a moment to remember where I was, but it all came rushing back when I felt a wet strand of hair plastered to my face.

My hair!

I sighed with relief when I felt the back of my head and realized Samuel's blood had saved more than just my life. I had a full head of hair. I could still taste his blood on my lips. Then I glanced down at the awful shirt I was wearing. It looked like something straight out of Desiree Dubois's closet.

Candy was on the other side of the room talking to Samuel while they toweled off. When I looked to my right, I flinched. Mia was sitting in a chair with her eyes fixed on me. They seemed empty yet focused.

Katherine came toward me. "There she is."

A wave of nausea hit me as I sat up. "Where's the bathroom?"

"There's a powder room off the foyer," she said with a frown. "Are you all right?"

I ran out of the living room and made it to the toilet just in time to bring up the half a burger I'd eaten that night.

Samuel squeezed into the small space and hunched down next to me. "I'd hold your hair back, but it looks like I'm too late. Did my blood taste that bad?"

I sat back on my heels and let out a halfhearted laugh. "I think I sat up too fast."

Candy appeared in the doorway with a sympathetic smile. "Well, that was graceful. Feel better?"

"I will if I manage to get off this floor." It was getting crowded in there.

After Samuel helped me to my feet, I reached under the shirt to feel my back. There wasn't a hint of a burn, although I remembered the pain vividly. "That's some powerful blood," I said to him. "I'm starting to think you're my guardian angel." If you believed in that sort of thing.

He smiled. "You do make things interesting for me."

"Let's sit you down just in case," Candy said, leading me back into the living room.

Katherine handed me a towel when we walked in. "Sorry about the sofa," I said, sitting down on the one she'd laid over the cushions.

"It's just a piece of furniture, Charley."

It all happened so fast I still wasn't exactly sure what *had* happened. "Since we're all sitting here, I'm assuming that storm put out the fire before it did any damage." For all I knew, the back of the house was gone.

"It was stopped just in time," Katherine said.

"How did the fire start?" I asked. That was no normal fire. Normal fires didn't spread in a perfect circle. It looked like someone had fueled it with a ring of accelerant—or some powerful magic.

A bitter scowl appeared on Katherine's face. "Not how, but who?" The scowl softened into a calculated stare. "But we'll find out, and then there will be no place to hide."

I pitied whoever did this when the Squad got a hold of them.

Candy sat down next to me and gave me a hug. "You were strong tonight. If it wasn't for you, this house would be a pile of smoldering ash right now."

"Me? What did I do?" All I could recall was closing my eyes and saying a prayer for rain. The next thing I remembered was fire scorching my back and pain like I'd never felt before.

And a voice in my head.

Candy stood up and looked down at me. "Are you serious? You stopped it, Charley. You held the line."

Held the line?

It was starting to come back to me now. "What exactly does that mean?"

"It means that the fire stopped at you. You manifested a bright blue halo around you. And the house too."

"You became the line," Katherine said. "You took the brunt of the fire and held it back until the storm finished the job. I've never seen anything like it."

Candy took my face in her hands and shook her head. "I thought I lost you, but then I realized you were stronger than those flames. Then you hit the ground like dead weight and your shirt ignited like a cinder. That's when Samuel appeared out of nowhere and carried you into the house." She glanced over her shoulder at him. "That man is my hero."

He was mine too. I gazed at him for a few seconds, wondering if he'd felt my pain. I'd never complain again about his ability to sense me.

Katherine went over to the window and looked out. "We'll have our hands full for the next month fixing up the yard."

Candy chuckled. "At least."

"The garden is ruined," Fay said, patting her sister on the shoulder. "Mia will be so upset when she sees it."

I looked at the witch sitting in the chair like a zombie. "Is she getting any better?" She didn't seem much better, other than the fact that her eyes were open and she was sitting up. But that wasn't much of an existence if that's all she had to look forward to for the rest of her days.

"She'll come around eventually," Desiree said. "Probably after the rest of us have done all the work to defeat this monster."

Fay glowered at her. "Are you suggesting my sister is feigning catatonia?"

Catawhat?

"Of course not," Katherine said. "Mia was the victim of a

vicious attack. That kind of magic would have killed a weaker witch."

"You mean like Fawny Goodman?" Samuel said.

"Well, no. Fawny was formidable. She could have held her own with any witch in this room."

Samuel's eyes narrowed. "Then why did she die and Mia end up like that?" He nodded to her in the chair.

I thought I saw a slight twitch in Mia's eye, and I knew she'd been staring at me when I woke up on the sofa. Was it possible that Desiree was right? Or was Mia Winston trapped in her own body by some spell, fully aware of her surroundings but unable to move or say a word? My bet was on the latter.

"Tell them what you told me," I said to Samuel.

Candy shifted her eyes to him. "Tell us what?"

"I went up to Blood Lake last night to see if I could find anything the pack or the Squad missed."

Desiree glared at him. "We don't *miss* things."

"Apparently you did," I said.

The witch looked at me like I'd slapped her. "Take that tone with me again and I'll—"

"You'll what?" I got up and stepped toward her. She was rude and obnoxious, and I was getting tired of tiptoeing around her. I'd just saved the woman's house, for God's sake. At the least, she owed me a little common courtesy.

She was clearly vexed by my failure to wither under her scornful gaze. And then I heard something move. When I turned around, I saw a tall bookcase behind me start to teeter. As it tipped forward, I threw my hand up and shot a beam of light at it, slamming it back against the wall so hard the room shook. Half the books slid off the shelves and fell to the floor.

I turned and glared at the witch, and now she was the one withering. Then I grabbed one of the books and threw it at her. Before I could come to my senses, I was pelting the woman with them.

Candy and Samuel both grabbed an arm to stop me from taking out one of Desiree's eyes.

"I think you made your point," Candy said. "Even if the bitch deserved it," she muttered as she tried to force an encyclopedia out of my hand.

I continued to glare at her. "That witch is demented."

"You're just figuring that out? She's missing a few screws if you ask me, but make nice. We have to work with her."

Nice my ass, but I let go of the book.

Katherine was staring at me while I composed myself. "You really are just like your mother." Then she glanced at Desiree. "Delia would have done the same thing."

Desiree straightened her hair. "Considering the circumstances, I'll forgive your feral behavior." But her eyes told a different story. Desiree Dubois wasn't the forgiving type.

I couldn't have cared less. My healthy fear of the witches had suddenly vanished. We were equals now.

Candy turned back to Samuel. "You were saying?"

"I went to the lake to see the spot where Fawny was killed. There was a lot of blood, and some of it wasn't hers."

Katherine seemed skeptical. "How could you tell?"

"Because he's a vampire," I said, not wanting to go through the whole blood fingerprint conversation again. "He could smell it."

Samuel continued. "Most of it was Fawny's, but the other blood was very different."

"Different how?" Candy asked.

"I detected an essence. An essence I know very well." He held my gaze for a moment and then told them the part that unnerved the hell out of me. The part that didn't make any sense but couldn't be ignored. "I could have sworn it was Charley's blood."

Fay gasped, and Katherine's head snapped in her direction.

"What is it?" I asked.

"It's nothing. Fay hasn't been sleeping well," Katherine replied with her eyes fixed on the other witch. "Her sister's condition has made her jumpy."

"There's something you're not telling me."

"Don't be so paranoid," Candy said. "I think we're all just tired after everything that's happened tonight."

Mia suddenly shifted in her chair. It was the first time I'd seen the woman move since the attack. Her eyes grew wider but remained fixed straight ahead, and I caught a twitch of her hand as it rested in her lap. Then a gurgling sound came from her mouth.

"Is she okay?" I could have sworn she was trying to say something.

Katherine grabbed a towel and dabbed it against Mia's lips as saliva dripped from the corner of her mouth. "She's fine. It's another sign that she's coming back to us."

And then I realized the woman's eyes had shifted to mine. Mia Winston was definitely trying to communicate.

"I don't know about everyone else," Candy said, "but I'm exhausted. I'm going home to get some sleep." She looked back at me on her way to the door. "Are you coming?"

"We'll walk you out, but I'm staying with Samuel tonight."

She smiled. "Good. I won't worry about you then."

It was clear as a bell when we walked outside. Other than the wet ground, there was no sign of the storm. If it wasn't for the scorched earth, you wouldn't have suspected a fire had raged over the property either.

After walking Candy to her car, Samuel and I climbed into the truck. "I think they're lying," I said.

He snickered under his breath. "I know they're lying."

I couldn't for the life of me understand why. All I knew for sure was that Candy was walking on thin ice with me. First the lie about my mother, and now she was keeping more secrets?

"I think it's time to get some answers," I said as I started the truck. It was time to ply Candy with margaritas. Time for a girls' night.

FIFTEEN

I was exhausted by the time we got to Samuel's house. All I wanted to do was sleep, but Samuel was on vampire time and wanted to continue our discussion.

"What would Candy and the other witches be keeping from you?" he asked.

"I have no idea, but I think it has something to do with my mother." Like not telling me they stole her body and left it in the forest. "Maybe someone had a grudge against her and now they're taking it out on me." I didn't really believe that, but I was grasping at straws.

"That wouldn't explain Mia Winston or that fire tonight." He hesitated before asking the next question. "Did your mother dabble in anything dark?"

"You mean black magic?" I guess I understood Samuel asking the question. After all, whoever was attacking witches and sending me body parts had clearly gone to the dark side. I shook my head. "My mother wasn't like that. There was nothing dark about her."

"You told me her death was suspicious. Can you think of anyone who wanted her dead?"

I'd asked myself that question a thousand times over the past two years since her car plunged into the river, but the answer was always the same. My mother didn't have enemies. I couldn't think of anyone who would have wanted her dead. "There's only one person who had animosity toward her. Tom Murphy." I laughed. "He can be an asshole, but he's no murderer."

"Agreed."

Samuel went quiet for moment like he was deep in thought. "There still has to be an explanation for that blood at the lake. What I'm about to ask you is going to sound strange, but I need you to humor me."

"Well, this is a strange situation, so ask."

"Before last night, have you had any strange dreams or blacked out for short periods of time? Even for a moment. Found yourself in a room without remembering how you got there."

I stared at him for a few seconds. "I haven't blacked out since partying too hard during my senior year of high school. A night I'd rather forget," I added under my breath. "As for strange dreams, not really. The usual bad one occasionally, but nothing out of the ordinary."

"I'm a hunter, Charley. A tracker. And I'm very good at what I do. There's no mistaking what I sensed in that blood at the lake. It was you, so there must be a connection. Practitioners of black magic can be very sly. They'll go to great lengths to obtain what they need for a spell.

"You think I was put in a trance or under some kind of spell to get my blood? To be used in a ritual up at the lake?"

He gave me a weak smile. "I don't know, but I don't think we can ignore the possibility. I'm even more concerned about why, because whatever the endgame is, we're not there yet."

It made my skin crawl just to think about being violated like that. But as much as I didn't want to believe it, Samuel was making a very good point. "I guess it's possible."

"If this is a vampire, he or she could have taken some of your blood and you wouldn't even know it. It would only take a moment, and we're very good at glamour." His face hardened. "Although I haven't smelled another vampire on you, other than Masterson."

A laugh snorted out of me. "Even Ian wouldn't go that low." Come to think of it. "Would he?"

Samuel shook his head. "No motive."

And the fact that he would have been killing one of his revenue streams. Fawny was valuable to him.

"Since we're on the subject of Ian," I said. "We need to pay him a visit."

"Deliberately?" Samuel looked at me sideways. "Why would we do that?"

Before I could tell him what Wes told me earlier tonight, I heard something fall in another room. It was the sound of something breaking. "What was that?"

Samuel cocked his head. "It came from the back of the house."

I followed him down the hallway toward the kitchen, flinching when I saw Ian Masterson standing in the middle of the room. "Jesus! Don't you ever knock?" The back door was wide open.

"No." He strolled around the room and stopped near the pantry door. "I always wondered what this place looked like inside. Old man Pullman must have been loaded." He ran his finger along the wainscoting on the wall. "Needs a good dusting, though, doesn't it?"

Samuel crossed his arms and shot Ian an irritated look, like it was no big deal to find an uninvited vampire in his house. "How did you get in here?"

Ian nodded across the room. "He let me in."

I followed his gesture to Sebastian lounging on the kitchen counter. On the floor beneath him was a shattered coffeepot. So much for a fresh cup of brew in the morning.

"There you are, you little tramp," Samuel said to the cat. "How did *you* get in here?"

"I'll shut the door so he doesn't get back out tonight." As soon as I said it, Sebastian leaped off the counter and headed for it.

Ian grabbed Sebastian when he bolted across the room, holding him up by his scruff. "Yummy."

"I'll knock your fangs out if you hurt that cat," I said.

Sebastian skedaddled into the hallway when Ian dropped him on the floor. "Relax. I'm not going to eat your cat. Or whatever he is."

"That wasn't funny," I said. "And here I was starting to think you were a halfway decent vampire."

"Don't insult me, Charley."

The warning in his eyes was jarring. "Okay, you're a decent guy."

He was breathing down my neck a second later. "I said, don't insult me."

Samuel was in his face before I could get out of the way, sandwiching me in the middle. "Do you two mind?" I said, wiggling out from between them.

They broke it up when they heard me opening the cabinets. "What are you looking for?" Samuel asked.

"Something to drink. If I have to watch you two go at it, I'm not doing it sober." I really could have used a drink after this night. "Don't you have any wine or tequila in this kitchen?"

Samuel held up his index finger for me to hold that thought. Then he did some housecleaning. "Ian Masterson, get the hell out of my house."

The vampire moved backward at breakneck speed, nearly

missing the door opening as he was ejected from the house. The kitchen door slammed shut behind him and locked.

"We need to let him back in," I said. "He came here for a reason and might have something important to tell us." And I needed to tell them both what Wes Wyatt had told me tonight.

A ruckus came from the backyard as I said it. "I'm not leaving until we talk!" Ian yelled.

Or at least until dawn.

Then I heard what sounded like a cat in heat. "Is he singing?"

Ian continued with his persuasion. "At this moment, your neighbors are probably petitioning to have you kicked out of the neighborhood!"

Samuel groaned and pulled the door open. "Ian Masterson, get in here!"

Ian stepped up to the door with a smirk. "If you insist." After coming back inside, he walked over to the cabinets. "Where did you say the tequila was?"

"There's a bottle of bourbon in the cabinet over the sink," Samuel said. "Help yourself."

After pouring two glasses, Ian handed one to me. "Now, what have you found out about Fawny Goodman's murder?"

I set my glass down on the counter. "I thought you had information for us?"

"I never said that, but something tells me you have information for me." He took a swig of his drink. "I hear there was a fire."

The Squad's house was in a remote area of the woods, but I assumed by now people had gotten wind of the fire. "Someone tried to incinerate the Squad's house tonight. We stopped it just in time."

He squinted at me. "The fire? How?"

"It was Charley," Samuel said. "*She* stopped it."

Ian's brows hiked. "With magic?"

"Well, I didn't do it with a squirt gun."

He studied me for a moment, probably trying to figure out how to exploit me. "You're getting stronger."

I fought the urge to smile because to be honest, I was kind of impressed with myself. I wasn't *getting* stronger—I was already there. No longer a haywire mess.

Samuel got back to business, starting with a question. "You said you worked with Fawny Goodman?"

"Right. I supplied her with product."

"Did she work with other vampires?" Samuel asked.

There was a slight flash of anger in Ian's eyes. "Not that I'm aware of. Unless she lied to me." When Samuel didn't elaborate, Ian looked at him sideways. "Why do you ask?"

"Because I went up to the lake last night, and I detected a vampire had been there."

Ian shrugged. "It was probably me."

"I know what you smell like," Samuel said, looking him up and down.

He grinned. "Fresh as a morning breeze?"

Samuel snickered. "More like a whiff of a septic tank."

The smile on Ian's face vanished. "Now you've hurt my feelings."

"Just tell him about the blood," I said before they started in on each other again. "I'm sure he'll share information with us in return, won't you, Ian?"

A trace of a smile returned to his face. "That depends."

"On what?"

"On what it's worth to me."

I should have known better than to think Ian Masterson had gained some integrity. He was the same old opportunist he'd always been. There was no giving and taking with him—it was all take. But he was invested in what happened to Fawny because it affected his bottom line. It wasn't just an attack on her, it was a direct attack on him too. I had a feeling he wanted to find her killer almost as much as we did.

"There was a lot of blood up there," Samuel continued, "and it didn't all come from Fawny or a vampire. If I didn't know better, I'd swear some of it was Charley's blood."

Ian stared at him for a moment. Then he looked at me. "Is he serious?"

"Does he look like he's joking? But obviously it wasn't my blood, so the plot just thickened." Unless Samuel was right about the killer using magic or glamour on me to get his hands on a vial without me even knowing it.

"All I know," Samuel said, "is that Charley seems to be at the center of everything that's happening, so we need to find Fawny Goodman's killer and put an end to it. I suspect he's a vampire or he's working with one."

"And you need to look at your clientele at the Beast," I said to Ian.

An amused expression came over his face. "So, I'm taking orders from you now?"

"I thought we were on the same team?"

"Yes, and I'm the team captain."

"Well, captain, apparently you don't know what's happening right under your nose."

His amusement vanished. "What are you talking about?"

Samuel crossed his arms. "Yes, what are you talking about?"

"I was trying to tell you just before we walked in on Ian. I had a conversation with one of Lucy's brothers right before I got that call from Candy tonight. Wes Wyatt has been a regular at the Beast lately."

Samuel chuckled. "Why doesn't that surprise me?"

"He said a vampire showed up there last night waving a bunch of cash around. Said he got paid for pulling a fast one on some witch. I don't know about you two, but that sounds like a lot more than just a coincidence to me."

Samuel turned his eyes to Ian. "It certainly does."

"Wes said the vampire had long black hair and a tattoo of a snake running down the back of his neck," I said to Ian. "You need to check your customers."

Ian's lips curled. "The fastest way to lose my customers is to start searching them for tattoos based on the word of your bartender's brother."

"So, it doesn't bother you that a murderer might be drinking at your club?" Or an accomplice to a murder.

He laughed. "Half of my clientele are murderers. I don't ask questions, Charley. I just take their money."

Samuel's annoyance with Ian was growing by the second. "Then I guess we'll investigate your customers for you."

"Put a rein on it, vampire," he said to Samuel. "My club, my responsibility."

Samuel met his glare. "It's time for you to leave."

Surprisingly, Ian kept his cool. "I see I've outworn my welcome."

"You mean your trespassing?" I said.

"Charming as usual." He turned to leave but looked back at me before walking out the door. "Watch your back, Charley."

The warning did nothing to calm my nerves. I had two of the most powerful vampires I'd ever met standing in the room with me, and yet somehow, I felt completely vulnerable to the monster who had ripped Fawny Goodman's heart from her chest.

"I'll watch her back," Samuel said.

Ian stopped in the doorway. "Well, I feel much better now. Nighty night."

After he left, I scowled at the darkness where he'd disappeared. "That vampire drives me crazy."

"In a bad way, I hope," Samuel muttered.

My eyes shot to his. "What other way would there be?"

Ignoring the comment, he grabbed the bottle of bourbon

from the counter and poured himself a drink. "Would you like another?"

"No, thank you." I hadn't even finished the one Ian had poured me. "I'm dead tired, Samuel. Would you mind if I just went upstairs and got some sleep?"

He set the bottle down and pulled me against him. "Of course not. This has been a rough night for you." He kissed the top of my head and released me. "Go to bed."

The moment I walked into the bedroom, I kicked my shoes off and got undressed. I was so tired I didn't even have the energy to brush my teeth, which I'd regret in the middle of the night.

As I slipped into bed, something moved against my leg. I almost screamed as I threw the comforter back. It was Sebastian. He was lying under the covers at the foot of the mattress. "There you are." I moved my legs to accommodate him and curled up in the fetal position, eventually falling asleep to the steady sound of his soothing purr.

SIXTEEN

"What is your problem?" Tucker said. Lucy had nearly knocked her over rushing past her with a bin full of glasses.

Lucy shot her a dirty look and kept moving. "You're in my way."

We weren't even open yet, and they were already going at it. "See? This is why I hate to put the two of you together on the schedule." Lucy was like a horse carrying an inexperienced rider. She could smell timidness a mile away and would take full advantage of you if she knew she could get away with it. And Tucker had a bad habit of letting her do it.

Not today though.

Tucker glared back at her. "You wouldn't have to worry about it if Lucy had an ounce of manners."

It was good to see her stand up to Lucy for a change. It must have been Mag's influence.

Beau had the night off, and I'd come in to help out while I waited until Candy closed the Cauldron. I was cooking dinner for her at my house, hoping I could get her to talk. We hadn't shared a meal together in ages, so it wouldn't be a total waste of time if she zipped up tight and pleaded the fifth. But I intended to get some answers tonight, one way or another.

Dog was looking through the order window when I walked to the end of the bar. "You sure you want to leave me alone with those two?" he asked. "I might have to kill one of them before the night's up."

"I need to ply Candy with tequila tonight to get her to talk to me, so I'll take my chances." After thinking about it for a few seconds, I looked back at him. "You aren't hiding anything else from me, are you?" He'd been complicit with the others about my mother's remains, so I figured I'd ask.

"I learned my lesson, Charley. No more secrets. I should have told you about your mother from the start."

"Yeah, you should have." I wasn't over it completely, but Dog and Candy were family. I loved them both, and I couldn't imagine my life without them. It wasn't worth letting anger drive a wedge between us.

I heard a noise coming from the back. "What is that?"

"I don't know." Dog dropped his dishrag in the sink and headed for the kitchen door. When I met him in the hallway, I was nearly bowled over by Diablo. Beau was right behind him.

"Whoa, boy!" Beau stumbled, trying to pull back on the leash.

Diablo ran into the bar with his red eyes glowing brightly and a case of the zoomies. Then he came back around to me with his entire butt wagging. I'd say he had a happy tail, but he didn't have much of one. It was just a cropped stub.

"You're such a good boy," I said an octave lower than my normal voice. "Did you miss me?" Before I knew it, his front paws were on my shoulders, and I hit the wall behind me. I swear he'd grown since I handed him off to Beau just a few days ago.

When Tucker saw him, she almost dropped the twelve-pack of beer she was carrying. Diablo had been a very different dog when we first encountered him in the basement of the Beast, so she must have been having a PTSD moment.

"It's okay, Tucker. He doesn't have a mean bone in his body." Unless someone tried to hurt me. I hoped he was just as protective of Beau.

She let out a nervous laugh. "If you say so." Then she scurried behind the bar.

"Sorry about that," Beau said, scratching the back of his head. "I'm trying to train him, but it ain't going so well." For once, Beau looked mostly normal. His eyes were back to their usual green, and there wasn't a fang in sight. But he was still sporting that spray tan.

"It's going to take a while," I said, "but you need to learn how to control him in public." I got the dog's paws off my shoulders before he could leave a trail of slobber down my shirt. "I guess he's gotten used to your... you know."

"You can say it." He thumped his chest. "My beast. We're all one big happy family now."

"Thank God for that."

"Why? Were you nervous?"

I held my thumb and index finger about an inch apart. "Just a little bit."

He patted Diablo roughly on his side. "Well, don't be. Me and Diablo's come to an understanding." The dog leaned into him, pressing him to the wall.

"Just let me know if you need any help with dog food or anything." I planned to grab a bag once a week whether he asked for it or not, because Beau wasn't rich like his father.

Dog nodded to Diablo. "That hound needs a good run every now and then to get all that energy worked off. It helps wind the pack down when things get rowdy."

Up here in the mountains, we had plenty of trails to do it. But Beau needed to run the dog at night so hikers from other parts didn't report a cryptid with glowing red eyes.

Diablo planted his hind end on the floor and cocked his head at Dog.

"I think he likes you," I said.

Dog stared back at him. "He just knows who the boss is. A hellhound is no match for a wolf."

"We don't know what he is," I said. "How do you know he isn't a match for a wolf?" I'd seen that dog in action, and I had a feeling he could give a wolf a run for its money.

Without dignifying the question with a response, Dog snickered and walked back into the kitchen.

"What are you doing here anyway?" I asked Beau. Most people didn't show up at their place of employment on their day off.

He shrugged. "We were on our way over to the dog park, and I thought you might want to say hi to him."

"We don't have a dog park, Beau."

"Really? Then I guess we'll take Dog's advice and hit the trails."

The front door opened, and Candy walked into the Stag. As she was setting her bag on the bar, Diablo padded over to her. She froze when he stuck his nose against her pants and started sniffing. But when it traveled toward her crotch, she gave him some serious side-eye. "Don't even think about it."

"Diablo!" Beau yelled. "No!"

He sat obediently and cocked his head. I didn't know whether it was Beau's command or Candy's warning that got the dog in line.

"Good Lord," Candy said. "How much does that thing eat?" She looked down at Diablo as Beau grabbed the end of the leash off the floor. "You two look like a match made in heaven."

"I'm glad you brought him by," I said to Beau, "but we're about to open. You better take him out the back way."

Beau got a goofy grin on his face as he bent down to look Diablo in the eyes. "You ready for a hike? Come on, D."

"I think that dog is good for Beau," Candy said as they disappeared down the hallway. "That boy needs something to keep him in check until he figures out how to deal with his inner Hollerwhatever."

"Hollerwolf, and I hope you're right."

"It's the pack mentality," she said. "They just need to figure out which one's in charge."

I got a visual of the hellhound battling it out with the Hollerwolf in the backyard. "I didn't think about that."

She grabbed her bag off the bar. "You ready?"

I glanced at Lucy on our way out. "Be civil tonight, or you're fired."

"Promises promises," she replied without looking up from what she was doing.

She was the worst employee I'd ever had, but she was a keeper.

* * *

Candy looked over my shoulder at the frying pan I was attempting to make dinner in. "Can I help with anything?"

I nodded to the drawer. "You can see if I have any tongs in there."

She found a pair and handed them to me. "Looks good."

"Cross your fingers that it tastes as good as it looks." It was my mother's fried chicken recipe. I'd watched her make it all my life, but this was my first attempt at cooking it myself.

After setting the chicken pieces on a plate, I reached for the bottle of tequila. "Ready for a margarita?"

"Honey, I've been ready."

I should have gotten her started on one the second we walked into the house, while the chicken drained and the casserole finished baking. Cooking wasn't my forte, but I knew my way around liquor. If owning a bar hadn't taught me how to make a decent margarita, I was useless.

I quickly whipped up a couple of drinks and handed her one. "Enjoy."

She took a sip and smacked her lips. "Now, that's a damn good margarita. What's that I'm tasting?"

"It's a spicy margarita. It's got a little jalapeño in there." Candy liked things spicy.

After taking a few more sips, she glanced toward the kitchen. "Is that casserole done yet? I'm getting hungry."

"Should be. Feel like eating on the porch?" It was a beautiful night, so why not?

"Sounds good to me."

After fixing us some plates, we took them outside and sat at the table I rarely used anymore. I think I'd only eaten out there once or twice since my mother died.

Candy looked at her chicken. "Is this your mama's recipe?"

"Sure is, but I got the casserole recipe off the internet." I waited for her to dig in first and tell me if it was any good.

She picked up her chicken thigh and took a bite. "Mmm..."

"Good or bad?"

A funny smile crossed her face. "It's... good."

I was relieved and went to take a bite of mine, but Candy grabbed my arm. "I don't think you should eat that."

"You just said it was good."

"And I'm sure it would be if it was cooked all the way through."

I cut the chicken open and cringed at the sight of pink juices running out of it. "Why didn't you spit it out?" Food poisoning wasn't what I had in mind for the evening.

"Honey, I've got a cast-iron stomach and something that'll fix me up right as rain when I get home."

Of course she did. I don't know why I was worried about it.

"I'm a lousy cook. Sorry to spoil dinner."

She took a bite of the casserole. "Now, this is delicious."

After finishing what was salvageable of the meal, we settled back in our chairs and sipped margaritas. Before ambushing her with questions, I wanted to get a little more tequila in her to loosen her up.

"Let me make you another drink," I said before her glass was even half empty. "Hell, I'll bring the bottle out so we can do shots."

The glass went still at her lips for a second before she downed the rest of her margarita. "You don't have to cook me dinner and get me drunk, Charley. Why don't you just cut the bullshit and say what's on your mind?"

I hated when she saw right through me. I hated it even more that I was stupid enough to think she wouldn't.

"Okay." I set my glass down on the table, running my finger around the salty edge. "What was that all about at the Squad's house last night?"

"You'll have to be more specific."

"The gasps and the funny looks when Samuel told you about the blood. When you got up and left so fast when Mia Winston looked at me, I knew you were hiding something. I'm not stupid, Candy."

She slid her glass toward me. "I think I'll have that second drink now."

"I don't know if I can handle another secret," I said without looking at her. "You get a pass on one heart-shattering lie per lifetime." I brought my eyes to hers. "Anything after that might blow us up for good."

"You don't mean that, Charley."

"Yes, I do." I felt sick. Like a wall was about to crack. "I'm a grown woman, Candy. You can't keep treating me like I'm sixteen. Can't protect me from anything that might hurt."

She took a deep breath before speaking. "There are things that are best left alone. Secrets that should remain buried." She leaned over the table. "You listen to me, Charley. If I ever lie to you, there's a damn good reason for it. And if I have to tell one of those lies to keep you safe, you better believe I will, even if it does blow us up for good."

My heart hurt from the things she was saying, her words leaving a lump in my throat. I didn't know whether to get up and walk away or accept it and live in blissful ignorance. If there was ever a time that I needed to hear my mother's voice in my head, it was at that moment.

"I love you, Charley. I don't want to fight with you."

"I want to see where she's buried," I said. It just came out of nowhere.

Candy gazed at me for a moment and then nodded. "Okay. I think that's a good idea. Maybe it'll bring you some closure."

Oddly, I felt better. I thought she'd argue about it, but Candy always seemed to know what I needed, even when our relationship was at risk of falling into the abyss.

"But I have to warn you," she said. "There won't be anything left of her. The forest has taken her by now."

I shook my head. "I don't care. I just want to feel her."

"Then we'll go tomorrow morning. First thing." She picked up her glass and gave me a tentative smile. "Now, how about that margarita?"

SEVENTEEN

When we got out of the truck, there were nothing but trees in every direction. The road we drove in on wasn't really a road at all. If it hadn't been for the truck, I doubt we would have made it this far into the woods.

"Where are we?" I asked Candy.

"You were the one driving. And by the way, remember how you got here. If you're the last witch standing, you'll need to know where to take the bodies someday."

Take the bodies?

I let out a nervous laugh. "I don't think I could do that."

"Sure you could. The pack will help you."

She stepped over a mangled tree root as I gawked at her. "Watch your step. Those roots are just waiting to twist an ankle."

"I'm coming. Slow down." For a fifty-seven-year-old woman, she was awfully fast. Working a stripper pole all those years had given her eternal cat-like agility.

We walked for what seemed like an hour, but the scenery never changed. It was forest for miles. When Candy finally stopped, I leaned against a tree to catch my breath. "Are you sure you know where we're going?"

"You better hope I do so we can find our way back to the truck."

A touch of panic hit me. "You're joking, right?"

Above us, a shadow caught my eye. When I looked up, I saw a crow flying overhead, and thought I spotted a single white feather in the middle of one of its wings. "Rex?" All the way out here? It couldn't have been.

Candy glanced up. "Could be. They don't call this the Forest of Crows for nothing."

I recalled the torture session the Squad had put me through not too long ago in the woods behind their house. Those woods had been filled with crows. "Is this forest connected to the one near the Squad's house?" I could have sworn we'd driven in the opposite direction.

She shrugged. "Up here it's all one big forest. It's the hidden spots that are special. Sacred. That's where we're going."

We kept hiking and eventually came to a small clearing. The broad tree canopy filtered out the sun and made it feel more like dusk than just before noon. "Is this it?" I asked, suddenly feeling a lump forming in my throat and a sense of deep loss.

"This is it." Candy walked to the center of the clearing where a configuration of stones had been placed. "Right here."

I was overcome with emotions. The feeling of both butterflies and dread filling my chest as I walked toward the spot. This was where my mother was laid to rest. Like Candy had said, I didn't see anything on the ground other than those large stones. But I could have sworn I felt her. I didn't even care if it was my imagination.

"She really is gone, isn't she?" I finally said after taking it all in for a moment.

"Yes, honey."

I was still having a hard time understanding why they did it. Why it had been necessary to take such drastic measures with my mother's body. With any witch's body. "Help me understand this, Candy."

She took a deep breath and sat down on the ground, patting the spot next to her. "Have a seat."

I sat down and pressed my palm to the earth, feeling for vibrations or anything to indicate that this was *sacred* ground, as Candy had said. But all I could feel was cold grass, leaves, and dirt.

"Like Katherine said," Candy began, "you don't just stick a witch in the ground. Especially one as powerful as Delia Underwood. The magic will disappear into the earth right along with them, and magic is too precious to lose hold of. It's also dangerous. You don't want a vein of magic running through the ground for some amateur to tap into."

"Katherine said you harness the magic first, and then the body is left to the forest." I couldn't wrap my head around how that worked, and I wasn't sure I wanted to. But I did remember those crows carrying off the bones of the creature that had attacked me in the woods during that ritual. I supposed the crows came for my mother too. "How exactly is the magic harnessed?"

Candy pulled her amulet out from under her shirt. "We take the energy and keep it for ourselves. Think of it as an heirloom. Something precious that needs to be preserved."

I nodded to the amulet. "Is it in there?"

"Some of it. We all have a little."

"So every one of you is walking around with my mother's magic hanging around your neck?" Every one of them but me.

She stuffed the amulet back under her shirt. "Every witch has her own way of storing her energy. Katherine keeps hers in the walls of that big house—another reason to be thankful for saving it last night. And Desiree keeps hers—"

"I don't even want to know." The thought of my mother's energy co-mingling with Desiree Dubois's made me cringe. "I guess I just wish I had some for myself. If you'd told me the truth at the time, I could have been a part of all this and had some of her magic too."

Candy's eyes filled with sympathy. "Honey, when are you going to realize you *are* Delia? No amount of the magic we took from her could come close to what you already have inside you."

It sounded nice, and I knew she was trying to make me feel better, but it wasn't the same.

Her tone suddenly firmed up. "And you weren't ready."

"Well, I'm ready now." I stood up and walked over to the stones. "Miss you," I whispered. Then I looked back at Candy as she was climbing to her feet. "Let's go."

"That's a good idea. My legs are about to give out."

As I turned around to follow her, praying we'd find our way back to the truck, I caught a glimpse of something on the ground. A glint coming from under the leaves. I couldn't believe my eyes when I bent down to see what it was.

"What is it?" Candy said.

I cradled it in the palm of my hand. "I think it's a sapphire."

Candy stared at it. She seemed more surprised than I was. "It sure is." Then a smile slid up her face as she pulled her eyes away from it to look at me. "I think you just got that piece of your mama you were looking for."

* * *

I went straight for my bedroom as soon as we got back to the house and pulled that silver necklace from my drawer. The one Rex had dropped from the tree a few days ago. The one with the missing stone in the center.

"Tell me I'm not crazy," I said to Candy as I walked back into the living room and handed it to her.

She held the sapphire to the center of the necklace where a stone had once been. "Looks like a perfect fit."

The necklace—or amulet—was like Candy's but shaped differently. Candy's was oval, but this one was round.

"Did you know she had this?" Candy rarely took hers off, but I'd never seen my mother wearing this one. I didn't even know it existed.

"Of course. It was around her neck when we laid her to rest in the forest."

I shook my head. "I don't understand. Why give me the ring and not this?"

"Because it was Delia's. Some things are not meant to be passed down." She clutched her own amulet under her shirt. "Just like this will be laid to rest with me someday. Besides, all the energy has been taken out of that stone. It's just a rock now." As she rubbed the sapphire between her fingers, it started to sparkle, and it wasn't from the light hitting it. "Well, I'll be damned." She studied the stone for a moment and looked at the silver necklace. "You said Rex brought this to you?"

"That's what Samuel said. He was waiting for me outside the other night, and Rex dropped it on the ground next to him."

"Well, isn't that something. I guess your mama wanted you to have it after all, and she found a clever way to get it to you." She seemed to drift off in thought for a moment. "Where'd that bird come from again?"

"You know where he came from." Rex had been orphaned up in that huge tree in my front yard when some idiot used his parents for target practice. I'd had the privilege of raising him and living with him ever since. But Rex was no ordinary bird. "Can I ask you a strange question?"

"My favorite kind. Shoot."

"I asked you a while back if you had a familiar, and you said no. If I asked now, after everything that's happened, would you give me the same answer?"

Her lips curled into a playful smile. "Not that I need one, but..."

"I knew it! It's Odin, isn't it?"

"You don't think I keep that fat old cat around for nothing."

She didn't fool me. She loved that cat.

"Although he isn't earning his keep very well lately. The lazy beast should have warned me about the break-in." Her mood shifted. "It just goes to show you how dangerous this killer is, getting past both of us sleeping right upstairs."

Just when I was feeling some peace, she had to bring that up.

I looked at the necklace in her hand. "It's interesting that Rex found it and personally delivered it to me. No ordinary animal does something like that." I don't know why I found it awkward to ask the next questions. It seemed kinda out there, but then again, I was talking to a witch who'd just admitted to having a familiar of her own. "I'm wondering if Rex might be my Odin."

"You mean your familiar?"

"Ah... yeah."

"Honey, I can't tell you that. You need to figure that out on your own."

"How did you know Odin was yours?"

She chuckled. "Trust me. If Rex is your familiar, you'll eventually know."

Out of the blue, my hand started to heat up. When I looked at it, my ring was glowing. "What's happening?"

Candy gazed at it and then looked at the sapphire she was still holding. "I don't know, but we're about to find out."

The glow coming from the ring grew brighter, and my entire hand lit up in blue. The light shot from my ring straight into Candy's hand, the sapphire resting in her palm absorbing it like a sponge. The transfer of energy took less than a few seconds. When it was over, the stone in the ring dulled, and the blue color of the sapphire turned black. It felt cold and lifeless on my finger, and I knew the magic was gone.

"I think you can take that ring off now," Candy said, looking down at the stone in her hand. The color was brilliant. It was giving off the most beautiful light. "Looks like it was temporary until you found this. The big guns," she added with a grin.

I wanted to cry, but it was out of pure joy.

Candy stuck the sapphire and the silver necklace in her purse and walked toward the door. "You need to drive me back to the Cauldron so I can open the shop for what's left of the afternoon."

"Can I have my necklace and stone back first?" I felt a little panicky.

Seeing the concern on my face, she stopped and shook her head. "Sometimes I don't think straight. I'm just taking the necklace back to the shop to set the stone. I'll bring it to the Stag later this evening."

For a second, I thought she and the Squad were going to make me jump through hoops to earn that necklace. Eat another spider or something. "You know how to do that?"

"Set a stone? You'd be surprised at what I can do."

Come to think of it, it didn't surprise me at all.

I grabbed my keys and followed her out. Rex swooped down and landed on the porch railing as I was walking down the steps. When he cocked his head at me, I knew I was looking into a pair of eyes that had intelligence far beyond animal or human. "Candy's going to fix the necklace for me," I said to him.

Candy turned and put her hand on her hip. "If you're done talking to your bird."

"Why are you in such a hurry?" I said as I caught up to her and climbed into the truck.

"Because this witch needs to eat. Every hour that the shop is closed puts me one step closer to the poorhouse."

That was ridiculous. Candy's real money came from her

private sessions, and I was convinced the Cauldron was nothing but a front. A source for petty cash. "Fine." I hit the gas pedal. "I'll get a speeding ticket for you."

When we pulled up to the Cauldron ten minutes later, Adelle Spencer was standing at the front door. "Well, what do you know," I said. "Looks like you're not going to starve to death after all."

Candy shot me a look as she got out of the truck. "Don't forget who's holding that necklace in her bag, smart aleck."

I grinned as she shut the door, listening through the window as Adelle yapped about that weight loss potion Candy had given her last week. It didn't look like it was working. Then I headed back home to get some cleaning done around the house before going to the Stag. Maybe catch a nap. Lord knew I was tired, and I needed to be sharp. I had a feeling things were about to get worse. Much worse.

EIGHTEEN

Dig, Charley!

I woke with a start and looked around the living room. After dropping Candy off, I'd done a load of laundry, changed the sheets on my bed, and vacuumed the house. By then, I was too worn out to make myself a late lunch, so I lay down on the couch to catch a quick nap before going to the Stag.

Dig!

What the hell was happening to me? I was wide awake now, and I could still hear that voice in my head.

I got up to grab something to eat before leaving for the bar, but I couldn't shake the thought that I was missing something, and it was right under my feet—literally. The other night, Katherine Belltower seemed awfully interested in where those dogs had been digging, and she thought she'd fooled me by brushing it off. But it had been nagging at me ever since, and it was time to get to the bottom of it. Either unearth something in that spot or put it to rest once and for all.

After slipping my shoes on, I went outside and headed for the shed to get a shovel. Then I went to the spot where I'd ripped off half my fingernails and started digging.

After fifteen minutes, I managed to excavate a hole about a foot deep and wide, and I was already worn out. Georgia clay was no joke. I was about to jab the shovel into the hole again, when I spotted something sticking out from the bottom. It was barely visible. A piece of fabric.

I dropped the shovel and stared into the hole for a moment, imagining a body wrapped in a sheet buried down there. It would explain those dogs digging. But since neither me nor my mother was a serial killer, it had to be something else. I retrieved the shovel and carefully started working the earth around it, but when I tore the cloth with the tip of the spade and saw what looked like a bone, I reconsidered everything I thought I knew about Delia Underwood.

After thinking of all the reasons I should call Murphy, I ignored the voice of reason in my head and kept digging around it until it was obvious I wasn't about to unearth a body. At least not an entire one. It was definitely a bone wrapped in a piece of white fabric, but it didn't look human, and it had symbols carved into it. At each end, there were additional markings drawn on the bone in either paint or blood.

I took it into the house and laid it on the coffee table, debating about what to do with it. Someone had put it there, and *something* wanted it dug up either by me or those dogs. Candy and the Squad had some explaining to do.

I dialed Candy's number, but it kept ringing and went to voicemail. She was probably with a client. But the next client would have to wait, because I wanted answers.

After wrapping the bone back up in the fabric, I got ready to drive over to the Cauldron. As I opened the front door to leave, my heart nearly stopped. There was a box on the porch and a kid pedaling his bike down the driveway.

"Hey!" I yelled, but he disappeared down the road.

It was a plain box with no label, just like the one left on the back steps at the Stag. All I could do was stare at it as a chill ran down my spine. Then I snapped out of it and pulled my phone out to call Dog.

* * *

Dog looked at the box that was still sitting on the porch. "You said a kid delivered it?"

"Yeah. He took off before I opened the door."

He groaned and picked it up. "I guess we better open the damn thing."

We went inside and took a seat. Something rattled when Dog gently shook the box before setting it on the coffee table. Then we both eased back on the couch and stared at it for a moment. It was small. Not much bigger than a shoebox. But you could fit a lot of things in a shoebox, and I was too nervous to even touch it.

"You going to open it?" Dog asked.

I licked my lips. "Well, it isn't going to open itself." My hands trembled as I finally got up the nerve to reach for it.

"Hell, I'll do it," he said, beating me to it. "You look like you're about to fall apart." He reached for the knife in his pocket and sliced through the tape sealing the flaps, but before opening it, he got a whiff of something and went still.

"What is it?" If there was another heart in that box, I didn't think I could take it.

Without answering me, Dog slowly opened it and pulled out some of the crumpled paper cushioning whatever was inside. But he hesitated after he looked at the contents.

"Don't do that, Dog. What's in the box?"

"I'm not touching it with my bare hands this time. Got any gloves?"

My heart was racing. "What are you talking about?" He tilted the box so I could see inside. "What is that?"

He swallowed hard. "It's a tongue."

For some reason, his words didn't register. Probably because they sounded so absurd. "A what?"

"A fucking tongue!" he growled.

That drove it home. After what happened to him when he put his bare hands on Fawny Goodman's heart, I understood why he was hesitant this time.

The box rattled again when he set it back on the table. "There's something else in there." He removed the remaining paper inside, careful not to touch the tongue, and used a piece of it to retrieve the object that was making the noise.

My heart sank into my stomach when he pulled it out. It was Candy's amulet, with a lock of her red hair wrapped around it.

I stood up when I felt the world start to spin around me. "We have to get to the Cauldron." Dog dropped the amulet on the table and reached for his phone, but I shook my head. "I already tried that. She's not answering."

He got up. "I'll drive."

I shoved the amulet into my pocket and grabbed the wrapped-up bone. "I'll follow you."

After Dog got in his truck and pulled out in front of me, I climbed into mine and called Katherine Belltower.

She answered immediately. "Charley? What's wrong?"

"Candy's in trouble. You need to get to the Cauldron now." The fact that someone or something had gotten close enough to snatch that amulet from Candy's neck terrified me. And what about that tongue? I couldn't bear the thoughts that were going through my mind.

Dog didn't even stop for the one red light on the way back to town, and I followed him straight through it. He got us to the Cauldron in just under ten minutes. I mumbled a few expletives when I saw Adelle Spencer standing outside knocking on the door, so it must have been locked. Thank God for that spare key I had.

Dog got out of his truck and came around to mine. "What does she want?"

"She's one of Candy's clients. We need to get rid of her before we open the door."

Adelle narrowed her eyes at me when I walked up to her. "Where is she?"

"Candy?" I said with an accusatory glare. "I left her with you earlier today, so I should be asking you that question."

She stepped closer and lowered her voice. "I need to have a word with her about something she sold me this afternoon."

I didn't have time for the woman. "I'll let her know you came by."

Her lips curled downward. "It can't wait. You need to let me into the shop."

"Actually, I don't," I said as I pulled out my keys.

"Adelle," Dog said as he came up behind me. He looked her up and down with a roguish grin and got a little too close to her. "That's a nice dress you're wearing." Then he sniffed. "You smell good too."

She stepped back and pulled her lapels together. "What are you looking at, wolf?" A low growl snaked up his throat, and without further ado, she headed back to her car. "You tell Candy I'll be back in the morning for a refund."

As soon as she started to pull away from the shop, I slid my key into the lock and pushed the door open. "Candy?"

Dog locked the door behind him and glanced around the room. "Something doesn't smell right in here."

I ran upstairs and looked in every room, but the second floor was empty. "Check the back room," I said as I started to run back down the stairs.

Dog disappeared through the doorway. When I followed him, he stepped in my path to stop me. I looked over his shoulder and nearly lost it when I saw Candy suspended from the ceiling. Her mouth was sealed with duct tape, and her hands were tied together over her head. But there was no rope holding her up. She was dangling by some invisible cord. But what really terrified me was what I saw on the floor. All the furniture—the bed, the table near the infamous closet, a chair—had been turned sideways and pressed to the walls, making space for a black hole in the center of the room. It was no more than four feet in diameter, and directly underneath her, and her feet were dangling a mere foot above it. When I looked closer, it appeared hollow. Bottomless. Similar to that hole in the basement at the Squad's house.

"We have to get her down from there."

Candy flinched when I stepped closer. She dropped an inch or two, her eyes filling with terror. The tattoo of Hecate in the hollow of her neck shifted slightly when she swallowed. Then she closed her eyes, reopening them a few seconds later with a calm, steady gaze directed at me.

"I called Katherine," I said to her. "They're on the way."

She barely nodded, but it was enough to make her drop another inch.

"Be still," Dog said to her. "Whatever this is, it's sensing your movements."

There was a knock at the back door leading to the alley, and Dog went to let the witches in. Katherine walked into the room a moment later. "Oh dear. This is bad."

"You think? Every time she moves, she drops an inch."

Desiree walked up behind her and looked at the black hole. "It's a portal. One wrong move and it will swallow her up, and that will be the last we see of Candy Cane."

When Candy's eyes flared, I glared at Desiree. "Would you shut it."

You tactless twat.

Katherine let out a deep sigh. "Desiree is right. I'm afraid our options are limited."

"What do you mean limited?" They had a portal in their own basement, for God's sake. "What are we supposed to do?"

"The only thing we can. I was hoping it wouldn't come to this, but we have no choice." She reached into her bag and pulled out a gun. "I'm afraid Candy will have to die."

NINETEEN

"You're all crazy," I said. Dog wasn't even arguing with them.

Katherine's stoic gaze leveled on mine. "It's the only way to break the spell."

"Well, that's just great," I said. "Candy will be dead, but at least the spell will be broken." I shook my head at her. "You're certifiable."

"Hear her out," Dog said. "If something rational doesn't come out of her mouth in the next two minutes, I'll take that gun away from her myself."

Katherine huffed. "You'll be missing a leg, if you try."

There was nothing the witch could say to convince me to let her put a bullet in Candy, but the clock was ticking, and we needed to get the absurd conversation over with so we could come up with a real plan.

"It's a classic existential incantation," Katherine said. "It's designed to bring about demise through one's own weakness." She looked up at Candy's hands. "Note the absence of rope. She's suspended by a mental umbilical cord."

I had no idea what the witch was talking about. "Can you dumb it down for me please?"

She groaned and closed her eyes for a second, muttering something about patience under her breath. "That spell is fueled by Candy's own fear. If she panics and squirms enough, she'll lower herself right into the portal beneath her. But... if she dies, so does the spell. The portal will vanish before she hits the ground."

"But Candy will be dead," I reminded her.

"That's where the vampire blood comes into play. The part with no margin for error."

I was beginning to follow where she was going with all this. "Are you saying you want to kill her and then bring her back with the blood?" Even vampire blood had its limits, and bringing someone back from the dead with it didn't always work. It was essentially reanimation, and there was no guarantee the person you brought back would be the same as before. It was dangerous.

Desiree grinned. "Exactly. A bullet to the heart will do the job nicely."

"You're out of your mind." Dog grabbed the gun from Katherine's hand, growling when she took a step toward him intending to make good on her threat. "I'll rip your throat out, witch."

"Dog!"

His head snapped in my direction. "Have you lost your mind too? A minute ago, you were the one trying to stop this horseshit. There's another way, so start thinking."

I looked back at Candy. "Can't we just grab her and yank her down from there?"

Katherine motioned to the black hole. "The moment you cross over the edge, it'll pull you in." She grabbed a book from the floor that must have fallen off the table and tossed it at Candy. The second it flew past the boundaries of the portal, it vanished. It was sucked downward into the hole so fast my eyes could barely track it. "Believe me, I've seen these spells before.

It's toying with her. Feeding off her fear." She glanced at Candy's dangling feet. "I'd say she has about six more inches before the game comes to an abrupt end."

My heart was breaking from even considering it. "I'm with Dog. There has to be another way."

Katherine seemed to mull something over and then looked at Desiree. "There is one other way."

Desiree's eyes lit up like a kid on Christmas morning. "A soul-snatching spell? We haven't done one of those in..." She drummed her fingers against her chin. "... well, never."

"What are you talking about?" I said.

A grin slowly worked its way across Katherine's face. "We could attempt to evict her soul. Force it out of her body, which would essentially render it lifeless and kill the spell."

Dog cocked his head. "Evict it to where?"

"*That* we don't know, but it should be temporary until we can lure it back."

"You mean back into her body?" I said.

"Yes. But a snatching can be tricky," she quickly added. "If Candy's soul fights us, it could trigger the portal spell."

Both plans were risky, but a bullet was out of the question, so I was game for the latter.

"Why don't we let Candy decide?" Dog said.

I agreed, but nodding or shaking her head would send her crashing into the abyss. "How do we do that?"

"She can blink," Katherine said.

Dog looked at Candy who was listening to every word. "Once for yes and twice for no. Is it going to be a bullet?"

She responded with two definitive blinks.

I was relieved, but we weren't out of the woods yet. Not by a long shot. Candy was a fighter, and that could throw a deadly wrench into the plan. I prayed she'd let the Squad take the wheel and relinquish her soul without a struggle.

"It's decided," I said. "Let's do this."

"We still need vampire blood," Katherine said. "And it needs to be fresh for maximum potency. Straight from the vein. We'll entice her soul back into her body by feeding it to her the moment she passes. Before she can slip through the veil. If that happens, it could get very dark. Just as dark as if we'd used that gun."

It was barely dusk outside, so Samuel was out of the question. Patrick was our second option, so I dialed his number. The third option was Ian Masterson, but Candy would kill me.

"Where're you at, girl?" he said the moment he picked up. "I'm at the Stag waiting for you."

Thank God.

"I need a vampire," I said without wasting time with pleasantries. "I need you at the Cauldron now. And tell Lucy and Beau that Dog is with me."

"One vampire coming up."

That's what I loved about Patrick. No questions asked.

After hanging up, I asked Katherine to wait for Patrick with me up front. "I got another box delivered to my house this afternoon," I said, pulling the amulet out of my pocket. "This was inside. It's how Dog and I knew Candy was in trouble."

She took it from my hand. "It must have frightened you."

Not as much as the other thing we found in that box, and I needed to warn Katherine.

"There something you need to know before you pull that duct tape off Candy's mouth. There was something else in the box." A lump started to form in my throat. "It was a tongue. A human tongue."

Katherine stared at me for a moment, and then a knowing look came over her face. "You think it's Candy's?"

"Who else would it belong to?"

She gave me a commiserative smile. "You don't really think Candy would be so calm with her tongue cut out? She would have gotten herself obliterated by now."

"Then whose is it?"

"Fawny Goodman. In addition to her heart, her tongue was taken. It was meant to scare you, Charley."

I sagged with relief, and then my anger started to swell. "When I find the person who's doing this—"

Patrick knocked on the door, taking my anger down a notch. After I let him in, he glanced at Katherine and back at me. "Where's the fire?"

"In the back room," I said.

"Well, all right. Lead the way." He followed me but stopped at the door to the room. After seeing Candy tied up and dangling from the ceiling, he stepped back. "What kind of kinky shit is going on in here?"

"The kind that's going to get Candy killed if we don't break the spell that has that portal ready to swallow her up."

He looked down at the black hole. "Portal? You mean like a portal to hell? Because I don't mess with—"

"I don't have time to explain," I said, cutting him off. "Here's what's going to happen. The Squad is going to perform a ritual to force Candy's soul out of her body. As soon as that happens and the spell breaks, you're going to give her your blood to pull her back in. Got it?"

You would have thought I was speaking a foreign language, the way he was looking at me. "Girl, are you out of your mind?" Then he looked at Dog. "Both of you."

Dog growled back at him. "If I recall, you owe Candy. So shut up and cooperate. We're running out of time."

That was an understatement. She'd saved Patrick's ass on more than one occasion in this very room, and he was going to return the favor.

"If everything goes as planned," Katherine said, "Candy will be caught in transition. That's when time will be of the essence. When I give the order, Patrick needs to get his blood into her mouth quickly. As much as possible." She held Patrick's gaze for a moment. "Do you understand?"

"Got it." He pointed his thumb over his shoulder. "I'll just wait back here in the corner while the rest of you perform your hocus pocus shit."

"No, you won't. We need a fifth body to form the circle."

Fay must have been back at the house keeping an eye on Mia.

Katherine approached the portal and stood dangerously close. "Everyone, join hands. And remember, not so much as a stray hair wanders beyond the edge of that hole." She glared at Patrick when he refused to come forward.

"If you haven't noticed," he said to her, "I'm a vampire, not a witch. I don't know nothing about casting no spells." He grumbled and finally took my hand, but he drew the line when Desiree tried to take the other. To avoid wasting time with bickering, I switched places with him and joined hands with the witch.

Patrick looked up at Candy as she dangled like a deer carcass. "What do you want me to do?"

"You and Dog just stand there and look pretty," Katherine replied. "But whatever happens, don't break the circle." Then she looked at me. "I need you to focus very hard, Charley. Focus on Candy standing right next to you. Desiree and I will do the rest."

Nothing happened immediately as the two witches started to speak in that same language I'd heard the other night when the fire struck. In fact, the room seemed oddly calm. But after a minute or two, my eyelids started to grow heavy, and I suddenly felt dizzy and had to catch myself before I tipped and fell sideways. Things were definitely getting strange. Dog's wolf kept morphing in and out, and Patrick was grinning at me like a fool. But what had me wondering if I was hallucinating was seeing what was happening to Candy. Her body didn't move an inch, but something was fighting to break free from her. A semi-corporeal mist or a shadow.

I closed my eyes and tried to focus, but I reopened them when the chanting picked up. And then either the room started to move, or I did. I felt like I was riding a merry-go-round, gradually picking up speed until I thought I was going to vomit from motion sickness. But then the spinning abruptly stopped, and Candy was floating outside of her body, staring at me with a blank gaze.

My eyes wandered around the circle, landing on Dog. He had the head of a wolf, but from the neck down he was all human.

Am I high?

Patrick gripped my hand tighter. *No, honey. This is all real.*

It wasn't his voice in my head. When I looked to my right, Candy was standing in his place with the duct tape gone from her mouth. *Where's Patrick?* I heard myself say, but my lips weren't moving.

She leaned closer and grinned. *Who gives a fuck.*

When I tried to speak again, the room exploded. I flew backward and hit the wall, sliding down to the floor as a freight train seemed to slam into my chest.

When the smoke cleared, I looked across the room. The portal had vanished, and Candy was lying on the floor motionless. Then I looked at my hands. They were held out in front of me with my fingers splayed, but I wasn't the one moving them.

These nails look awful, honey. We need a manicure.

"What?" I backpedaled and hit the wall, scrambling to my feet. Then I shook my arms out trying to gain control of my limbs again, and to get rid of the haywire energy that had me buzzing like I'd overdosed on caffeine.

Patrick dropped to his knees next to Candy and bit into his wrist. "What about the duct tape?" he asked the witches as blood started to flow down his arm.

Desiree bent down and ripped the tape off her mouth. "Hurry!"

When I get a hold of the bastard who did this to me, I'm going to duct tape his balls to his asshole.

"Candy?" I looked in the mirror on the wall. It was my reflection, but it was someone else running my hands down my waist.

Feels nice having a young body again.

Dog grabbed my chin to look me in the eyes. "Charley? Are you okay?" At least the wolf was gone.

"Right as rain, baby."

I cupped my hand over my mouth.

He cocked his head curiously. "What's going on with you?"

"I think I know where Candy is," I said, glancing at the mirror again. Some serious anxiety was welling up inside me because as much as I loved the woman, there wasn't room for both of us in here.

My body suddenly jolted forward as I slammed into Dog's chest. I felt her leave. A second later, Candy gasped on the floor as oxygen filled her lungs.

"Is she okay?" I asked.

Dog looked over his shoulder. "Looks like it. I think you did it, Charley."

It took all of two or three minutes for Candy to take a few breaths and push herself up. She'd come through it in one piece and seemed to be fine.

After helping her to her feet, Patrick ran his hand over the top of his head looking seriously shaken. "I don't know what the *hell* just happened, but that was messed up."

Candy pushed her disheveled hair out of her face and straightened her shirt. "I owe you, Patrick. Free tarot readings for life." Then she rubbed her sore mouth where the tape had been torn off and glared at Desiree. "You enjoyed that, didn't you?"

I stood there for a moment staring at her, astonished at what had just happened between us. I felt Candy's life force inside me, and it was overwhelming. I doubt I could have taken it much longer. The woman was a beast.

Seeing me looking at her from across the room, she walked toward me with a wicked grin on her face. "That was fun, wasn't it, honey?"

Fun for who?

"But I think I prefer this old body after all," she said with a wink.

When I turned around, Samuel was standing in the doorway. By the look on his face, he'd felt some of Candy's energy too. I could only imagine what he was thinking.

"I'll leave you two alone," she said, slipping past Samuel to go up front.

He glanced around the room and brought his eyes back to mine. "What happened here?"

"Chaos. I'll tell you about it on the way back to my house."

"I'll meet you back at the Stag," Dog said on his way out of the room.

I was done. "I think I'll take the rest of the night off. Unless you need me?"

Dog threw his hand up without looking back. "Go home, Charley. I've got the bar."

Patrick followed him out. "I'll go with you. I need a drink."

Candy was putting her amulet back on when Samuel and I walked up front. "Katherine told me about the delivery you got today." She clutched the sapphire tightly. "I don't know what I would have done without this."

That amulet was a part of her because it held so much of her magic. It would have been like losing a limb. "Now we can be twins when I wear mine," I said, noticing an uncomfortable look falling over her face. "What's wrong?"

She let out a heavy sigh. "I've got some good news and some bad news for you."

Did it ever end? "Just give me the bad news first."

"Your necklace is gone. But the good news is I intend to get it back for you."

My heart sank. "No!"

She cupped my cheek with her hand. "I'm sorry, Charley."

After letting the news sink in, I looked at the sapphire around her neck. "Why would he take mine and send yours to my house in that box? Your amulet is just as powerful."

Candy glanced at Katherine. "Who knows. But like I said. We're going to get it back. That's a promise."

My phone rang a moment later. It was Ian Masterson.

"Hello," I said tentatively, wondering why he would be calling me. He usually just showed up.

"Where are you?" he asked.

"At the Cauldron. Why? What's going on?"

"Stay put. I'm on my way."

Before I could say another word, he hung up. "That was Ian," I said to Candy. "He's on his way over. I think something's happened."

TWENTY

The front door flew open and Ian Masterson walked inside. He was with some guy I'd never seen before, and since he was gripping the stranger by his neck, I doubted the man was here by choice.

Desiree gave Ian a contemptuous once-over. "May we help you?"

"No, you may not, but I believe I can help you." Ian looked back to me. "I decided to do some investigating at the Beast and found this."

So now it was his idea?

He shoved the man into the center of the room. "I think I just found our missing link."

The man had long, stringy hair, just like Wes Wyatt had described, and I caught a glimpse of the tattoo on the back of his neck when he nearly face-planted in the middle of the shop. His fangs clicked into place as he got his footing and darted his eyes around the room.

"This is the garbage who conspired to kill Fawny Goodman up at the lake." Ian brought his eyes to mine. "He has quite a story."

"Start talking," I said.

The vampire glared at me. "I'm not in a talking mood."

"Really?" I glanced at Samuel for some backup.

Samuel leaned against the counter and folded his arms. "This is your show. You don't need me."

"I'd suggest you get in the mood," Ian smacked the vampire in the back of the head.

I stepped closer to him. "Someone hired you to kill Fawny Goodman. Who?"

He laughed. "I don't do hits. I just made it easy for the guy to take a shot at her."

I nodded slowly. "I see. So, you were just an accomplice to the murder?"

The vampire suddenly shut his mouth and stopped talking.

Candy let out a frustrated sigh. "This is getting boring. Why don't you let me and the Squad have a crack at him. He'll be sharing his ATM PIN number with us when we're done with him."

I stepped back and held my hand out, focusing until a ball of light appeared in my palm. "How about if I sever your head while Ian holds you in place?" I nodded to Ian to grab him. "You wouldn't be the first vampire I've killed." I didn't take pleasure in killing, and my hand was trembling slightly from the thought of how far I'd have to go if the conversation went in the wrong direction. If I couldn't convince him to talk.

When Ian yanked the vampire violently by his hair, he winced and gritted out between clenched teeth, "You're going to kill me one way or the other, so why would I talk to you?"

"Well, maybe not. I haven't decided yet. If you cooperate, who knows. I'd say you have a fifty-fifty chance, so the ball's in your court."

"All right!" he said when Ian yanked so hard a clump of the vampire's stringy hair came out. "I'll talk!"

Ian let go of him. "Start by telling us what happened at Blood Lake."

"What's your name?" I asked when he got a hesitant look in his eyes. I knew a little psychology.

He still seemed suspicious but relented. "Russell."

"Russell...?" Not that I cared what his last name was, but anything to keep him engaged.

"That's all you're getting."

Ian smacked him again. "Get to the lake."

He scowled and rubbed the back of his head. "A guy hired me to go up to Blood Lake with him. He said there was a conjure woman up there, and he needed her to do something for him."

"Do what?" I asked.

"I don't know."

I held my hand up, willing the sphere of magic to flare up again. This time even brighter. "Think harder, Russell."

"I said I don't know! Some kind of ritual." He calmed down when I backed off. "All I was supposed to do was glamour the witch. Make her see a different face on the guy so she didn't recognize him."

Katherine gasped. "Fawny knew him?"

"I guess. I didn't ask. I think he was trying to trick her into doing the ritual. But that's all I know. When he pulled out a knife and started cutting himself, I left."

"The man who hired you?" I said, realizing it must have been his blood Samuel found all over the fire pit.

The vampire snickered. "He sliced both his wrists open. That's when I decided to get the hell out of there, and he didn't try to stop me. That woman was alive when I left, so don't even think about pointing a finger at me."

Samuel straightened up and came over to us. "He's telling the truth."

I believed him, but there was still one other detail we needed to know. "What's the name of the man who hired you?"

"He never told me." His eyes were all over the place. Everywhere but on mine.

Samuel dropped his chin and stared at the vampire. "Now you're lying."

"Russell..." I said in a friendly voice. "I will kill you right here in this room if you don't tell us the name of the man who hired you." In that moment, I believed I could actually do it. But it wouldn't serve any purpose to kill the pawn. "But if you do tell us, I promise to let you walk out that door."

He considered it for a moment. "I can leave?"

"You have my word."

The heel of his shoe nervously tapped against the floor. "The guy's name was Richard Wilder... something."

Katherine's face paled. "Was it Wilderbrandt?"

"Yeah, that's it. Wilderbrandt."

For a moment, I couldn't breathe. Unlike Smith or Jones, Wilderbrandt wasn't a name you heard often. Some people would never hear that name in a lifetime. Unless you were from Crimson and knew something about the history of this town.

"You can go now," I said.

The vampire didn't need to be told twice, but as he hurried out the door, Ian started to follow him.

"Where are you going?" I asked.

"He's a loose end, Charley."

I shook my head. "I told him we'd let him leave, and I keep my word."

Ian held my gaze. "Yes, you did. But you made no promises after he walked out."

"He gave us everything we asked him for, so let him go." If this Richard Wilderbrandt found out Russell the vampire had talked, he was dead anyway. And I couldn't have cared less if the monster found out we were on to him. Maybe it would flush him out.

Ian stayed put. "Yes ma'am."

Then I looked at the witches. "What are the odds that the killer is related to the late Victoria Wilderbrandt?" It wasn't actually a question. More of an accusation. A talking point to get their confessions started. But the three of them stood there mute. "And by the way, I found something interesting this afternoon. I was about to drive over to show it to Candy when that package was delivered to my house. Something I dug up in the yard."

Candy seemed kind of nervous, the way her lips quirked into a funny little smile. "Oh yeah? What did you find?"

"A bone. It was buried in the yard right where I was digging the other night. The same place those dogs were digging too." I studied their reactions, knowing damn well they were covering something up.

"Well, you know dogs with their bones," Katherine said. "They bury them in the oddest places."

Without a word, I went out to the truck and grabbed the bone. I was so angry when I walked back inside that I pulled it out and threw it across the floor at them. It came to a stop at Katherine's feet.

"That ain't no dog bone." One by one I looked at their faces, daring each one of them to lie to me again. "Which one of you is going to tell me the truth?"

Candy looked at Katherine. "I'm done with secrets. Either you tell her, or I will."

"We didn't know for sure," Katherine said. "Not until tonight when that vampire confirmed it."

"Confirmed what?" I started to shake from all the adrenaline racing through me. Hell, the floor was vibrating under my feet. If one of them didn't come clean, the place was going to cave in.

Sensing catastrophe, Samuel laid his hand on my arm. "Easy, Charley."

Katherine finally came up to me and had the guts to look me in the eye. "There's someone you need to meet. Go home and pack an overnight bag. We're going on a road trip."

* * *

Samuel barely said a word on the drive back to my place, which was probably wise because my emotions were a powder keg. Katherine refused to tell me who we were driving to Savannah to meet, and Candy was tight-lipped also. I just wanted to get it over with, so we got into my truck and left, agreeing to meet back at the Cauldron in an hour.

We pulled up to the garage and sat there in silence. I needed a moment to close my eyes and just breathe. Something life-changing was about to happen when we got to Savannah, I could feel it in my bones, but I wasn't sure I was ready for it.

"Do you want me to come with you?" Samuel eventually asked.

I turned to look at him. "You would come to Savannah with me?"

He took my hand and brought it to his lips, kissing my palm. "I would go anywhere with you, Charley. All you have to do is ask."

"Thank you for that." It felt like my heart was swelling in my chest. "But I think this is something I have to do on my own."

He gazed at me with a faint smile. Then he pulled his eyes away from mine and grabbed the door handle. "Let's go bury this thing."

We went to the spot where I'd dug it up. I'd been given explicit instructions to wrap the bone back in the cloth and return it to the same place where I found it, with the assurance that everything would be explained when we got to Savannah. I didn't question those instructions because it wouldn't do me any good.

Samuel took the bone from me to examine it. "It's some kind of power object," he said, which was more than Candy or Katherine had told me. And I didn't expect squat from Desiree Dubois. He handed it back to me. "Probably for protection, which explains why they told you to put it back in the ground."

I chuckled. "Well, I hope they didn't spend a lot of money on it because it's doing a lousy job." There'd been a shitstorm of dangerous activity around my house lately.

Since I hadn't shoveled the dirt back into the hole, it took less than five minutes to stick the bone in the ground and cover it up. Then we went into the house so I could pack a few things for the mystery trip. All I knew was that we'd be back late tomorrow night. And thanks to Dog, I didn't have to close the bar and listen to Lucy bitch about how I owed her a night's worth of tips.

I went into the bedroom and looked around, feeling overwhelmed by the simple task of picking out a change of clothes for a day trip. I finally stuffed a few things in a duffel bag and grabbed my toothbrush on my way back to the living room.

My nerves must have been written all over my face because Samuel took the bag out of my hand. "You don't have to do this."

My gut said otherwise. "Yes, I do." I grabbed it back and headed for the door. "Let's go."

Without another word, he followed me out. But halfway to the truck, he took my arm to stop me, his eyes scanning the yard before landing on the garage.

"What is it?" I said as his head cocked slightly like he was listening for something. It was dead quiet. Unnaturally quiet, as if all the insects had left. And the stagnant air felt thicker.

He raised his index finger to his lips and then pointed up at the sky. To the ominous cloud of black wings circling above us.

And then I caught a fleeting glimpse of a shadow moving between the giant oak tree and the garage wall.

Samuel followed my gaze and let go of my arm. "Get inside the house," he said in a low voice. When I just stood there staring at him, he growled, "Run!"

I dropped my bag and almost tripped over my own feet when a massive figure stepped out from behind the tree. Then the circling crows blocked out the moon, and it went so dark, all I could see were Samuel's silhouette and his glowing red eyes as he took off toward it.

Instinctively, I ran for the house, feeling for my keys but remembering I'd stuffed them into the pocket of the duffel bag. I detoured around the corner and pressed my back to the side wall as my shaking hand began to heat up. The energy continued to build until a ball of light whirled in my palm. Then I stepped around the house and took aim, but Samuel and the figure were gone. There was no sign of either of them.

A twig snapped behind me, followed by a grunt. Even with that ball of energy ready in my hand, my heart was beating out of my chest. I slowly peered over my shoulder and saw a massive shadow looming over me, the stench of something foul filling my nose as the heat from its breath hit my back.

I spun around, but the creature knocked me to the ground as I released the light. The magic shot across the yard, taking any hope of getting out of there alive with it. The shadow stalked toward me as I backpedaled in the opposite direction, pumping my fist in vain. When it reached for me, I rolled, scrambling to my feet before taking off toward the woods.

It was so dark, I couldn't see the ground in front of me as I ran deeper into the trees. I could hear it grunting and growling in the distance, the sounds of breaking branches growing louder telling me it was getting closer. Then I spotted light up ahead. A break in the canopy. A clearing. I could finally see the ground under my feet.

As I was running toward the light, I heard my name. I thought it was Samuel, but when I heard it again, I realized it wasn't his voice. It was dark and gruff, like something from the bowels of hell.

I glanced over my shoulder and saw the black shadow bearing down on me. When I looked straight ahead again, Samuel was standing in the middle of the clearing.

"Charley! It's me!"

The voice was coming from my rear. From that thing chasing me.

I nearly collided with Samuel when I looked back at the beast that was now illuminated by the moonlight. A beast I recognized. It was Beau.

Samuel shoved me aside and took on the Hollerwolf, slamming into it when it came to a halt in front of him. The two of them hit the forest floor and rolled, Beau's beast dwarfing Samuel with its massive size.

"Samuel, stop!" I yelled when I saw his fangs sink into the fur of the Hollerwolf's neck. He was about to kill my bartender.

Panicked, I willed my magic, feeling it spread through my fingers and build into a frenetic ball in my hand. Then I hurled the sphere at the ground several feet away but close enough to get their attention. The two of them flew apart, and Samuel shot me an incredulous look.

"It's Beau!" I said.

"Beau?" he repeated, looking back at the huge, scruffy beast.

Beau's face began to fade in and out. The Hollerwolf suddenly seemed paralyzed. Confused. It dropped to the ground, and a moment later, my bartender was lying naked in its place. After a minute or so, Beau sat up and stared at the two of us. Then he felt the blood on his neck and glared at Samuel. "You bit me? What the hell?"

I helped him to his feet. "You were chasing me. And what

was that all about back at the house when you knocked me down?"

"You mean right before you tried to fry me with that ball of light?" Embarrassment washed over his face. "Did I hurt you?"

"No, you didn't hurt me. Scared the hell out of me though." It suddenly occurred to me that he was supposed to be working tonight. "Why aren't you at the Stag?"

He shot me a look like I was stupid. "Isn't it obvious?" Then he looked down at his body. "I'm naked!"

"That you are," Samuel said. "And you stink."

I tried not to glance below his waist, but it was kind of hard not to, with his giant erection staring back at me. "Can you cover that up please."

"Shit!" He flustered, cupping his privates with both hands. "Will you quit looking at it."

I gladly complied and started walking back toward the house. When we got there, I handed Beau my bathrobe. The one I decided to designate as a guest robe for shifters. Then I texted Candy to let her know I was running a few minutes late.

"Why don't you start by telling us why you were prowling around Charley's house?" Samuel said.

Beau's face tightened. "I didn't know where else to go. I guess I panicked when it happened."

"This isn't the first time you shifted," I said. The first time was at the Stag when he and Dog got into it, and he'd partially shifted the day we went to his father's house. I figured he'd be getting used to it by now. "So why did you panic?"

"I don't know. It was different this time. Worse." He scratched his head as his face scrunched up tighter. "I was whipping up an omelet for Diablo, and suddenly I couldn't remember how to cook. My claws came out, and I couldn't figure out how to use a spatula. Next thing I knew, D was sticking his nose up my ass and growling at me."

It wasn't funny, but it kinda was. "I'm sorry you had to go

through that, but you're going to have to figure out this shifting stuff, Beau. It's who you are."

"You think I don't know that?" He let out a frustrated sigh. "I couldn't figure out how to shift back. The last time it happened, I shifted back naturally, but this time I was stuck. I ran over here hoping you could help me figure it out. If you hadn't zapped me back there in the woods, I'd probably still be covered with fur."

That was going to be a problem, especially if he planned to keep working at the Stag. "Maybe Dog can help you figure it out. He can shift on a dime."

"Yeah." His face brightened up as he nodded. "That's a good idea."

It was the obvious idea, now that the Hollerwolf and Dog's wolf tolerated each other.

"We can talk more about this later," I said, looking at the time. "I need to get out of here. Come on, Beau. I'll give you a ride home."

When we got to the truck, Samuel didn't get in. "Three's a crowd in there, especially with Beau wearing that." He nodded to the fluffy blue robe. "I'll see you when you get back from your trip." He came around to the driver's side and leaned onto the window. "Be careful down there."

I shot him a nervous grin. "What could go wrong?"

"Where are you going?" Beau asked.

"To Savannah." It was a five-hour drive, and we needed to get going so I could drop him off and get back to the Cauldron. "It's just a day trip. I'll be back late tomorrow night."

Beau bobbed his head. "Huh. Whatcha doing down there?"

"That's a good question, but I'm not really sure." All I did know was that by morning, I was going to finally get some answers, and I was ready to get in that car and drive.

TWENTY-ONE

I woke with a start, and for a moment I forgot where I was. But the sight of Desiree Dubois sitting next to me jogged my memory quickly. She was asleep, leaning her head back against the seat with her mouth wide open. Candy was riding shotgun because Desiree had refused to sit in the front seat of the old Buick, so I was stuck back here with the obnoxious witch. But I could tell we were getting close to our destination because it was hot as Hades inside the car, and Savannah was known for its sweltering heat and humidity.

"Doesn't this thing have air conditioning?" I should talk. The only air conditioning my truck had was a rolled-down window.

Katherine glanced at me in the rearview mirror. "Yes. It's on."

I cracked the window to circulate the stagnant air, and Desiree's head snapped forward. Strange sounds came from her mouth as she came to life.

It was around three a.m. when I looked at my phone, and the night air smelled of the sea mixed with sulfur from the decaying marshlands, a familiar aroma in this part of the state that was hard to forget. "Where are we?"

Candy looked over the seat at me. "We're about to pull into Savannah." Then she reached into her bag and handed me something. "Here, honey."

"Ooh, snacks." It was a granola bar and bag of pretzels, which I gladly accepted because I was starving. A cup of coffee to go with it would have been nice.

"Never go on a road trip without supplies," she said, looking at Desiree. "You want something?"

"Only if you have croissants hidden in there."

Candy turned around to face the road. "I guess you're out of luck."

I hadn't been to Savannah in years. It was a beautiful city, with spectacular houses and Spanish moss covering the live oaks. When I was younger, my mother and I used to drive down to Tybee Island occasionally to spend a weekend at the beach. It brought back some strong memories.

We finally pulled up to a house in the Historic District, of all places. And it was big. The kind of house the average person could only dream of living in, which made me even more curious. "Now that we're here, you want to tell me who I'm about to meet?"

Katherine parked in the garage behind the house and looked back at me. "You'll find out in the morning."

"It is morning," I reminded her.

The three of them ignored me and got out. After popping the trunk, we grabbed our bags and walked up a flight of steep steps at the rear of the house. I assumed it led to the main level. But before Katherine could ring the bell, the door opened.

"Hilda," Katherine said.

The woman standing on the other side was wearing a long nightgown that looked like a throwback to another time. Her white hair hung at her side in a long braid. I'd say she was in her late sixties or early seventies, and she didn't look happy to be greeting guests this early in the morning.

"She knew we were coming, didn't she?" I whispered to Candy.

"You're not here to meet Hilda. She's the housekeeper."

Of course she was. Anyone who lived in a house like this had staff to open their doors at three a.m.

I followed them inside, feeling the woman's eyes on me as I walked down a long hallway.

Hilda stopped at the kitchen. "Would you like something to eat?"

"A Danish, if you have any in the house," Desiree said with a strange smile that somehow looked like a frown.

Hilda beckoned us to follow her into the kitchen, instructing us to have a seat at a large table to the right. A few minutes later, she returned with a platter of the most decadent-looking pastries I'd ever seen.

Bless you, Desiree Dubois.

That granola bar and pretzels had barely made a dent in my hunger, so I was eager to dive in. When Hilda walked away and returned with a French press full of coffee, I wanted to kiss her. But the woman never even cracked a smile.

I glanced around the room, trying to gather clues about whose kitchen we were sitting in, but I was getting nothing. It could have been any rich person's house.

After we'd eaten and I'd finished my coffee, Katherine stood up. "We should get a few hours of sleep."

That was fine with me. I had no problem falling asleep with a little caffeine in my system. I also wanted to be sharp and alert for this meeting in the morning.

We followed Hilda up a staircase to our rooms. There were four stories from what I could tell when we drove up, and probably twice as many bedrooms. And somewhere in the big house there was a stranger waiting to meet me. I caught myself glancing into rooms as we continued down the hallway, wondering if I'd catch a glimpse of our mystery host. But they were all empty.

Candy's room was next to mine. She stopped at the door before going in. "Are you okay, Charley?"

"I guess." I was growing more anxious about tomorrow. "I'd feel better if I knew what I was walking into in the morning though."

"You're going to have to trust me on that, Charley." With that, she disappeared into her room.

I dropped my duffel bag on the bed and went over to the window. The room had a view to one of Savannah's famous squares. I noticed a man standing next to one of the benches, and it looked like he was staring back at me. But that was ridiculous. He could have been looking at anything.

When it started to make me uneasy, I closed the drapes and stripped down to my T-shirt and underwear. Then I climbed into bed, my mind racing before I eventually drifted off to sleep.

* * *

I woke up to the distant sounds of the city outside the window. My phone said 10:15 a.m., so I jumped out of bed to take a quick shower in the bathroom that joined my and Candy's rooms. It felt weird to shower in a stranger's house, but I really needed one. The soap was a lot nicer than what I had at my place, and there was even a new toothbrush sticking out of a glass next to the sink. It was like a hotel.

After throwing on some fresh clothes, I brushed my teeth and made myself look half presentable. Then I went to Candy's room and knocked on the door. She didn't answer. Neither did Katherine, so I went downstairs to find them.

Muffled voices and clanking sounds were coming from down the hallway. There was a room at the foot of the stairs to the right, with two sofas separated by a large coffee table. The living room. I spotted a pillow on a chair with something familiar embroidered across the front, so I went inside to take a look. My mind raced as I picked it up and tried to recall where I'd seen the monogram before. And then I remembered. It was on that envelope in my mother's private room. It matched the stamp with the letters H A W embossed in the wax.

"Breakfast is served."

I looked back at Hilda who was standing in the hallway watching me. "I'm sorry," I said, setting the pillow back on the chair. I felt like I'd been caught snooping through the bathroom medicine cabinet.

Her unwavering gaze lingered on me for a moment. "The others are waiting for you in the dining room."

She led me down the hallway to where Candy and the Squad were eating breakfast. There was an impressive spread on a sideboard against the wall, making my stomach growl just from looking at it.

"Look who decided to join us," Desiree said as she stuffed a sausage into her mouth.

"I would have joined you sooner if someone had bothered to wake me up." I hated being the last one to the table.

"You needed the rest," Candy said, "so we decided to let you sleep in. Besides, apparently Hester doesn't take guests before noon."

"Hester?" There was that name again.

Candy nodded to the sideboard. "Make yourself a plate and sit down."

Lord knew I wanted to eat, and the sounds coming from my stomach confirmed it, but I was too nervous. I also didn't want to be rude, so I put a few pieces of bacon and a slice of tomato on a plate and poured a cup of coffee. Then I sat down next to Candy and took a sip. "So, what's the plan for the day?"

"We enjoy our breakfast and wait," Katherine said. "The nurse will let us know when it's time."

"She's sick, the woman I'm visiting?" I asked.

"Not exactly." It was all she offered before resuming her breakfast.

It was all so strange, but I reminded myself that it would be over soon. But since we had an hour to kill before this *Hester* person would see us, I forced myself to eat something. The bacon was delicious, but a single bite was about all I could stomach under the circumstances.

Another twenty minutes passed, and Hilda came into the dining room. "The nurse said you can see her now."

"Well, what do you know," Candy whispered to me. "A whole thirty minutes early."

"Yeah, lucky us." Suddenly my heart was racing and I was a bundle of nerves. But Candy was here, so I had nothing to worry about. Right?

We followed Hilda to the third floor, to a room that faced the front of the house. When I walked inside, the first thing I noticed was how big and bright it was. Sunlight streamed in through a row of windows along the wall, and there was someone lying in a bed to the right.

I followed the others over to it and looked down at the old woman. Her white hair fanned out over the pillow, and her skin looked as thin as crepe paper. There was an IV running from her arm to a machine next to the bed. She lay so still, I couldn't even detect her breathing.

The nurse gave Katherine a grave look and turned the machine off before walking away.

Were we too late?

"Is she dead?" I whispered to Candy, horrified.

The woman's eyes slowly opened and shifted to mine. "Not yet."

"Oh! I'm sorry!" I wanted to crawl under the bed. "Things just spill out of my mouth sometimes."

The bed near the headboard started to rise up, lifting her into a sitting position. Funny, though. I didn't see anyone push a button on the bed to trigger the mattress.

Katherine leaned over and kissed her on the forehead. "How are you feeling, Aunt Hester?"

The woman was Katherine Belltower's aunt?

"Still breathing," she replied without taking her eyes off mine. "This must be Charlotte."

Like an idiot, I offered her my hand. She laughed quietly and took it. "You look like Delia. The last time I saw you, you were just a child."

"I'm sorry. Have we met before?"

"Not properly, and it's been decades." The cloudiness in her eyes cleared. Sharpened as she studied me.

I glanced at the others, sensing that life-changing event I'd predicted was about to happen. I could taste it coming. "I don't mean to be rude, but why am I here? Why was I brought to meet you?"

Hester slowly turned her eyes to Katherine. "You haven't told her."

Katherine shook her head. "Not yet, but it's time." She smiled at me and took a deep breath before continuing. "Hester is Victoria's granddaughter. The oldest surviving Wilderbrandt. Our matriarch."

"Then why is she here and not in Crimson?" I don't know why I asked. It just seemed odd for the matriarch of the witches of Crimson to live five hours away. The way Katherine talked about that house out in the woods, you would have thought it wouldn't have allowed Hester to leave.

Hester coughed and wheezed as she sank deeper into the pillows. "Because I'm not ready yet."

"Ready for what?"

"Death," Katherine said. "Hester is ninety-six years old. The forest will call her the moment she returns to Crimson, but death doesn't interest her yet."

"You mean the forest where my mother was taken?"

"Where all our witches are taken," Katherine corrected. "But she'll return home someday, when she's had enough of the mortal plane."

I shrugged Candy's hand away when she rested it on my shoulder. They were working up to the reason I was here, and I wasn't interested in being placated. "What does any of this have to do with me?"

"I've wanted to see you for some time now, Charlotte," Hester said. "Before my body fails me." Her eyes roamed over my face as her lips rose into a smile. "I'm your great-aunt, Hester Adelaide Wilderbrandt. I'm pleased to finally meet you properly."

My head was spinning from trying to put everything together. "I don't know what you're talking about. All my mother's family are dead."

"I'm not from your mother's side," she said.

Katherine delivered the final blow. "My maiden name is Wilderbrandt. My brother, Richard, is your father, and I'm your aunt. You're a Wilderbrandt, Charley."

"And Victoria Wilderbrandt was your great-great-grandmother," Desiree added.

I backed away from the bed as the walls started to close in on me. Richard Wilderbrandt was the name of the man who'd hired that vampire to glamour Fawny Goodman up at the lake. The man who'd killed the witch. Ripped her heart out and sent it to me in a box.

"You're crazy. My father disappeared before I was even born." And my mother was happy to see him go. She barely mentioned him while I was growing up.

"It's true," Candy said. She reached for me again, but the look I gave her made her reconsider that.

"My nephew can be quite charming," Hester said with a cough. "He never married your mother. Wisely, Delia refused his proposals, so there was no messy legal business to take care of when he was forced to leave town."

"What do you mean? My mother said he wanted to leave. Said he wasn't interested in having a kid and a family."

Desiree laughed. "Oh, he was interested in you all right."

Katherine shot her a hostile look to shut her up. "We gave my brother no choice. He was told to leave, and we made sure he never came back. Until now. That bone you dug up in your yard was there for a reason, Charley. There are three others buried at the quarters on the property, each laced with magic to keep him away from the house."

I couldn't believe what I was hearing. All this time I thought my father was nothing but a deadbeat. Now they were telling me he was from a powerful family of witches who'd forced him to leave town.

"We believe he's trying to compel you to dig up the bones," Katherine continued. "To destroy them."

"Then why didn't you warn me?" I said.

Candy scoffed. "Because we were foolish and didn't want to believe he was capable of it."

"And we weren't sure until now," Katherine said. "Until you brought us that bone and forced us to believe it." She let out a long breath and continued with her theory. "My brother isn't skilled in blood magic, so he must have tricked Fawny into performing the incantation to get inside your head. But that required your blood."

It was all starting to come together. "And since I share the same blood as my father, he used his own. The bastard."

Katherine shot me a sly smile. "Right. Then he killed Fawny and hijacked the spell for his own purposes."

So that's why Samuel was convinced he'd smelled my blood up at the lake. It was my father's. "Why did you make him leave Crimson? What did my father do?"

"My brother is evil. His mind has never been right." Katherine turned away from me and stared out the window. "Even as a child he was interested in disturbing things. As he grew into a young man, black magic became his obsession." She brought her gaze back to mine. "But the real power in the Wilderbrandt line lies in the women. The men are born with some magic, but we hold the lion's share. When Richard found out Delia was pregnant with you, a girl, he saw an opportunity. He intended to exploit his own daughter for dark purposes, so we got rid of him to save you, Charley."

My mother was as confident as anyone I'd ever known, except when it came to men. She gravitated toward the worst ones. The ones who treated her badly. Sometimes I thought she did it just so she could leave them before they had a chance to leave her. To feel in control. I guess my father was a prime example of that.

Katherine slowly shook her head. "Fawny would have never performed that ritual had she known who he was and that you were his target. That's why he needed that vampire to glamour her."

"But why did he kill her and send me her heart?"

"Revenge, darling. Fawny was one of the witches who helped enchant the bones and build the banishing spell. We all took part in it, and with Hester's blessing, the deed was done."

So that's what that note in my mother's room was all about. Confirmation by the matriarch herself of my father's exile.

"My brother tried to kill Mia too, but she's stronger than he anticipated." Her face turned bitter. "Then he thought he could burn us alive in our own house. I would have loved to have seen his face when he realized it was his own daughter who stopped it."

"I would have buried those bones myself if I'd been in Crimson at the time," Candy said.

"You knew about this all along?" I asked her. I was a teenager when Candy arrived in Crimson, but by her silence, I assumed she was complicit. "Why didn't you tell me the truth sooner?"

She came closer and looked me in the eye. "Because Delia told me not to, for obvious reasons. And I'd lie to you all over again if I thought it would keep you safe. If you want to hate me, that's your choice. But I'll never stop loving you, Charley."

We stared at each other, her gaze unwavering. I was the one who finally looked away.

"As for why he sent you that heart," Katherine said, "my guess is it was part of the spell."

I slowly nodded. "Right. I was supposed to reach inside that box and touch it, not Dog."

Something still didn't make sense to me. "If you banished him all those years ago, how is it possible for him to come back now?"

"Because he's getting stronger." Her brows pulled together. "The fact that Richard was even capable of taking over that spell after killing Fawny means he's coming into his power. Power we didn't even know he had. That should frighten us all."

"What about Charley's house?" Candy said. "Can he get in there?"

Katherine's eyes narrowed. "The bones are still in place, so getting in the house won't be as easy as crossing the Crimson line."

I shot her a demanding glare. "My father isn't just trying to get to me, is he? All he has to do is walk into the Stag for that." They were still keeping secrets. I could see it all over their faces. "There's something else in my house that he wants, so what is it?"

Hester's shrewd eyes zeroed in on mine. "Smart girl." She

managed to lift herself away from the pillow and lean closer to me. "And you're right. There is something else he's after, and it's buried in the basement."

TWENTY-TWO

The Stag was still open when we made it back to Crimson, but I had more important things to do before checking in with Dog. I needed to see for myself what was buried in my basement.

After stopping by the Cauldron to get my truck, the ladies followed me back to the house. Rex was waiting on the porch railing when we got there. When I opened the front door, he flew inside, grazing Desiree's cherry-red hair.

She let out a disdainful huff as she reached for the top of her head. Probably to keep that wig from flying off. "Get that mite-infested thing out of here. It'll leave droppings all over the house."

If she didn't watch her mouth, he'd leave some on her head.

"He lives here," I said, "you don't. There's the door if he makes you uncomfortable."

She scowled at me and headed for the basement door, eyeing Rex as she stomped past the chair he'd perched atop. He eyed her right back.

Good bird.

Katherine descended the steps first, followed by Desiree and Candy. But I hesitated at the door. I hated that basement.

When I was a kid, I used to think someone was watching me from the dark corners down there. I couldn't look for fear of seeing a face staring back at me. When I told my mother I was hearing voices in the basement, she put an end to my playing down there, and now I knew why. We even moved the washer and dryer up to the utility room on the first floor to avoid that cold, dark space. I couldn't remember the last time I walked down those steps.

"Charley?" Candy said when she reached the bottom of the stairs. "Are you coming?"

I groaned and started down, my adrenaline climbing up my throat with each step. When I got to the basement floor, a wave of nausea hit me, and it wasn't just nerves. I felt physically sick.

"Are you okay?" Candy said.

"I will be as soon as we get out of here." I looked down at the concrete floor. "Please don't tell me we're going to need a jack-hammer because I don't have one." Then I felt the strangest pull toward the right side of the basement. Toward a bunch of old furniture my mother refused to part with. Even now, I couldn't bring myself to clean it out. And that would have also required me to spend days down there.

"Can you sense it?" Katherine asked, watching me curiously.

"I don't even know what I'm looking for." But since I was being pulled over to that junk corner, I walked toward it.

She glanced at Desiree and Candy. "Bingo."

I moved a few small chairs away from the wall and looked back at them. "Can I get a little help here?"

Desiree wiggled her ridiculously long fingernails. "I'd hate to break these."

"Of course not," Candy said. "Then you'd have nothing to scratch your ass with." She walked over to an old chest freezer that hadn't worked in over a decade. Another piece of junk my mother refused to trash. "Get the other end," she said to me as she grabbed the side so we could slide it away from the wall.

After moving the freezer, I saw a small wooden panel on the concrete floor. "Is that it?" It had been nailed shut.

"We'll need something to pry it open," Katherine said.

I grabbed a crowbar hanging on the wall. "This will do the job."

As she stuck it between the wood and the concrete, it occurred to me that if this thing was dangerous, maybe releasing it wasn't such a good idea. "Are you sure it's okay to open it?"

"As long as *we* open it," she said as she wedged the bar against the hatch.

"Why don't you let me do that," I said when she seemed to struggle with it.

She held her hand up. "I've got this." Then she put all her weight into it, and the wooden panel popped open.

There was a flash, and the hole exploded with light, a hissing sound coming from the center. When the light started to fade, something slithered out. A snake. A long shiny serpent with eyes the color of emeralds. And the thing was glowing.

I lost my footing and hit the floor, scurrying backward when it rose into the air like a cobra and flared its neck. Candy stumbled too, but Katherine and Desiree just stood there gazing at it. And then as quickly as it reared up with its threatening display, the light went out and the serpent dropped to the floor, its scales replaced by the links of a silver chain.

After climbing to my feet, I approached it. "What is that thing?"

"Well, it sure as hell isn't a snake," Candy said, putting her hands on her hips as she glared at Katherine. "You could have warned us."

Katherine picked up the chain, dangling it from her fingers. There was a shiny black stone set in a pendant hanging from it. "Sorry about that. It's been so long, I forgot about the spell."

"You shouldn't touch it," Desiree said.

Katherine wound the necklace in her palm. "It's not a virus, Desiree."

"What is it?" I asked again. "And what was that snake all about?"

"The serpent was a deterrent in case the wrong person got their hands on it." She offered me the necklace. "Go on. Take a look."

At first, I was hesitant to touch it. But as I stared at the stone, it started to draw me in. It seemed familiar. "It isn't going to bite me, is it?" I chuckled and took it from her hand, holding it up to what little light was coming from the bulb hanging from the ceiling. "What kind of stone is it?" I asked as it began to sparkle and glow.

"Obsidian. It was your father's amulet, until we took it from him. He'll do just about anything to get it back."

I almost dropped it and shoved it at her. "It's all yours."

She took it. "No need to be afraid, Charley. Most of its energy came from your mother anyway. Delia finally realized he'd been siphoning her magic into that stone since the moment they met. Little by little so she wouldn't notice."

So that's why it felt so familiar. "So, he stole his power?"

"Yes, and we took it back. But my brother has clearly found a way to get more of it over the years."

Candy snickered. "Maybe he sold his soul to the devil."

"I wouldn't put it past him," Desiree said.

Katherine stared at the stone. "Well, Richard always was resourceful." Then she gripped it tighter. "I don't care who he sold his soul to. He'll never control his daughter unless he gets his hands on this." She dropped the amulet back into the hole and replaced the wooden cover. "But that will never happen."

"Can't you just suck the energy back out of it?" That's what they did to the departed witches in the forest, like my mother.

"Don't you think we've tried?" Katherine said.

I shrugged. "I don't know."

"Taking the magic from that amulet has proven to be impossible." She looked back at the hole. "That's why we buried it. In hopes that the earth would eventually consume the energy, something we rarely do. But in this case, it was the safest option. Clearly it hasn't worked though."

"Why now?" I said. "Why come for me after all these years?" It would have been so much easier to snatch me when I was a kid. The thought made me shudder, although my mother would have gone Rambo on him if he'd tried.

The question seemed to surprise Katherine. "Because Wilderbrandt witches reach their magical majority at the age of twenty-six. You didn't know that?"

How was I supposed to know? I just found out I was a Wilderbrandt. "Well, he's late. I'm twenty-eight."

"Twenty-six, thirty. Witches only get better with age, Charley."

Two years ago, I wouldn't have known magic from a hole in the ground, so I was proof of that. "So what do we do now?"

"We wait for him to make another move. Only next time we'll be waiting for him." She looked at each one of us. "Until this is over, we all need to have eyes in the back of our head. My brother is getting stronger, and there's no telling how much of Fawny's power he stole during that ritual at the lake."

"And after he stole her body," Desiree added. "What he didn't take then, he certainly has now."

Candy gripped her amulet. "After what the bastard did to me last night, I'll have eyes in the front, back, and sides of my head."

Katherine looked at me. "You're what he's after, Charley, so this house is the safest place for you."

I shook my head. "If you think I'm putting myself under house arrest, you're out of your mind. I'm far from helpless, and you said yourself he can't control me without that amulet.

Besides, I have a bar to run." Which reminded me. "As a matter of fact, I need to get over there right now." Seeing Candy bite her tongue, I tried to put her at ease. "I'll have Dog and a bar full of vampires around me for the rest of the night." Not to mention a Hollerwolf. "And Samuel can escort me home."

"Charley's right," Candy said. "She could probably put all three of us in our places."

"Speak for yourself," Desiree said with a curled lip.

After moving all the junk furniture back on top of the hatch —for what reason I didn't know—we left the house.

On my way to the truck, I looked at Katherine as she was getting into her car. "What are you going to do with my father when we find him?"

She gave me a weak smile. "The only thing we can. We're going to kill him."

There was more than enough evidence that the man who'd fathered me was evil. A murderer. And still I had a lump in my throat from her words. If I could have just met him once under different circumstances. Seen who he was through my own eyes. But then I pictured Fawny Goodman's heart in that box and the pain and terror she must have felt when it was ripped from her chest while she still breathed, and my romanticized notions of my father evaporated. I tried to push the images out of my mind along with the instinct to humanize the man. Richard Wilderbrandt was a monster. What did that make me?

* * *

I was about to walk into the Stag when I heard someone behind me.

"What are you doing here, Ian?" I was jumpy, so the vampire was lucky I didn't have a fistful of magic when I turned around.

"Everything okay?" he asked, standing too close for comfort.

"Is there a reason it wouldn't be?"

"I sensed..." His eyes narrowed. "...danger."

I was really starting to regret drinking his blood. "You've got to be kidding me." And he was a little late. The *danger* was long gone. "I already have a vampire looking out for me. I don't need another one."

He glanced up and down the sidewalk. "Really? I don't see one anywhere."

I'd called Samuel before leaving Savannah to give him the news about my paternity, and to put him at ease about any emotions that might have crept out of my head and into his. This vampire sensing nonsense was becoming invasive.

"Samuel's meeting me here, so you can run along now."

Instead of leaving, he followed me inside. "I'll just have a drink until he shows up."

Did I look like I needed rescuing?

"Suit yourself."

I went around the bar to have a word with Beau. "Any more surprises with your alter ego?" I asked praying he said *no*. The Stag couldn't afford to be short a bartender every time the Hollerwolf decided to make an appearance.

He lowered his voice. "Does a craving for raw meat count?"

"Not unless you kill one of my customers to satisfy it."

His eyes traveled down the bar to Ian. "What's he doing here?"

"Hovering. Apparently, I'm incapable of taking care of myself. But don't worry. He'll leave as soon as Samuel arrives." I noticed Beau was alone. "Where's Lucy?"

"Good question. She went on her break about twenty minutes ago." He looked at the time. "Make that twenty-five."

I was about to go to the back to look for her when Dog motioned to me through the order window. When I walked into the kitchen, he leaned against the sink and crossed his arms. "Well? How'd it go in Savannah?"

I had a question for him first. "Did you know I was a Wilderbrandt?"

He stared at me for a moment with his eyes squinted. "What did you say?"

"Answer the question, Dog."

He straightened back up. "I don't know what the hell you're talking about, Charley."

Dog wasn't playing dumb. He seemed genuinely confused. "Candy and Katherine Belltower took me to Savannah to ambush me with the news that Victoria Wilderbrandt is my..." I had to think about it for a second to get my family tree straight. "...great-great-grandmother." A dull stare fell over his face. "Did you hear what I just said?"

"Yeah, I heard you. I'm just having some trouble wrapping my head around it."

I laughed humorlessly. "You and me both. My mother had an affair with Richard Wilderbrandt, Katherine Belltower's brother. Wilderbrandt is Katherine's maiden name," I said before he could ask.

Dog ran his hand over the top of his head. "Well, *fuck* me."

"Katherine said he's evil. He planned to use me after I was born to further his obsession with dark magic, so they got rid of him."

He looked at me sideways. "Got rid of him how?"

I shook my head. "I don't know. They used some kind of spell. Jesus, Dog, how could you not know?" Dog was extremely close to my mother. He knew everything about her. Or so I thought.

He slowly shook his head. "Charley, you were a kid when I showed up in Crimson. Who your mother slept with before that wasn't something we talked about. Or any of my business. I wouldn't lie to you about that."

"Why? Candy did. At least by omission."

His brows arched. "Candy knew?"

"She said my mother told her not to tell me. Said she was protecting me."

He scratched the back of his neck. "Ouch. But you know she meant it. About protecting you. Candy loves you, Charley, so go easy on her."

Beau stuck his head through the window. "Samuel's here."

"Tell him I'll be out in a minute." I had one more thing to discuss with Dog. "There's something else. Something you and the pack need to know about because we might need your help."

"That's a given."

"I know who killed Fawny Goodman. And the person who attacked Candy last night."

His eyes were questioning when I hesitated. "You want to tell me, or should I guess?"

"It was my father. He's back." My phone rang before I could tell him the rest. "Why is Lucy calling me?" She was supposed to be back from her generous break by now and working the bar. "Where are you?" I said when I answered it, but it was quiet on the other end. "Lucy?"

As the dead silence stretched out, it hit me like a gut punch. "Where is she?"

"Hello, Charlotte. You sound so much like your mother."

I'd never heard my father's voice before, but somehow it sounded eerily familiar. "What did you do to Lucy?"

"Nothing. Yet. Come to the lake. To Fawny Goodman's old place. Bring me my amulet, or your friend will die."

TWENTY-THREE

It was a clear night, with the light from the moon reflecting off the surface of the water. A deceptively peaceful scene concealing the lake's dark history. There were ghosts in that water. Maybe even Fawny's, and I was hoping to add another body to its murky bottom.

We were in the woods surrounding the house, with a view of the front door, trying to agree on the best approach to getting Lucy out of there alive. Ian wouldn't shut up. He kept interjecting with his idea of storming the place and ripping Richard Wilderbrandt's throat out. After what my father had done, I had no problem with that. I'd made peace with killing him because it was the only way to stop him. To keep him from going after every witch in this town. It was the only way to ensure that I wasn't looking over my shoulder for the rest of my life. Any doubt was long gone.

Dog finally had enough of Ian's mouth. "Why are you here again?"

Ian cocked his head. "Am I annoying you?"

"You're annoying me," I said. "No one is storming anything." My father hadn't specifically instructed me to come alone, but it was inferred. I was planning to knock on that door solo. And after I got Lucy out of there, I intended to kill him myself if he tried to stop me from leaving.

"I'm going in there alone." I braced myself for an argument.

"Agreed," Samuel said.

Shocker.

Ian gave him a look. "Fine partner you are."

Samuel threw him an impatient glance. "He won't hurt her, you fool. He needs her. And you haven't answered Dog's question—why are you here? Charley has all the backup she needs."

I didn't need as much backup as they seemed to think, but God forbid they let me come up here without an entourage.

"Feeling threatened?" A salacious grin spread across Ian's face. "Relax. Charley isn't my type."

Samuel snickered. "She's everyone's type."

I narrowed my eyes at him. "What do you mean I'm everyone's type?"

"The drapes just moved," Dog said, nodding to the window.

A text arrived on my phone a moment later. "He's getting antsy. I need to go in there. Alone," I repeated when Dog started to follow me.

"All right," he said, throwing his hands up. "I'm backing off. I hope you know what you're doing, Charley."

I didn't have a clue, but I knew the man wouldn't hurt me. Samuel was right. My father needed me. I was his reason for coming back here. But after getting Lucy out of that house, I planned to fight my way out too. If I was stronger than my father like the Squad seemed to think I was, that wouldn't be a problem. But there was one glaring wrench in the plan—he was expecting the amulet in exchange for Lucy, and I didn't have it with me. There was no way he was getting his hands on my mother's stolen magic.

I approached the house, stopping for a moment to let my adrenaline settle. I didn't want him to see me shaking. See how nervous I was. I reminded myself that I was about to come face-to-face with a stranger because that's all he was. Nothing more.

When I reached the door, I noticed it was ajar. I pushed it open slowly and stepped inside, the moonlight streaming in from one of the windows the only illumination in the room.

"Where are you?" I said, looking around at the cramped space. It was a small house. Barely more than a shack.

A figure stepped through a doorway on the other side of the room. "Charlotte."

I couldn't see his face through the darkness, but I could feel his eyes on me. "Where's Lucy?"

"Safe and sound and all tied up."

I could almost feel him smiling at me. "Get her."

"In a moment."

He reached for a lamp on the table and turned it on. I was surprised at how little I resembled him. But I didn't look like Katherine Belltower either. He was handsome, I'd give him that. Tall with brown hair and a square jaw. I saw nothing of myself in him.

"You look like Delia," he said, as if reading my mind. "In the eyes and cheekbones. And something tells me you're just as impulsive and foolish."

"The only fool here is you." It was strange to look at him and feel nothing. Actually, that wasn't true. I felt contempt for the man.

He held my gaze a moment longer and then wagged his finger at me. "You didn't come alone, did you? Did you think I wouldn't know?" He slowly shook his head. "A wolf is one thing, but vampires? I thought my daughter would have better taste in acquaintances."

The bigoted bastard.

His chin lowered. "Where's my amulet?"

"Where's mine?" I countered. Anger was building in his

eyes. He clearly wasn't used to being defied. "And you haven't shown me any proof that Lucy is still alive."

His lips tightened into a thin line as the tension in the room grew thicker. I needed to do something fast before he erupted. I had a clean shot at him, so I squeezed my fist, feeling my energy come together into a hot sphere in my hand. When he took a step toward me, I focused every ounce of my will into manifesting an even bigger ball of light and then hurled it at him.

In the split second it took to travel across the room, my father threw his hand up, splaying his fingers wide. The sphere slammed into his palm, lighting it up like a torch before spinning and reversing and flying back at me. I stood my ground, instinctively catching it with nothing but a thought. I caught the damn thing with my mind, watching it come to a stop inches from my face. A moment later, it exploded, showering me with light as I absorbed it back into my body. The rush was intoxicating.

"You're powerful, Charlotte."

"I am my mother's daughter," I replied, trying to gauge his next move.

He raised his hand again, and black mist came from his palm and snaked across the room. I had no idea what it was, let alone what to do with it. Some kind of black magic, I assumed. But when it reached me and started to take shape, I recognized it instantly. A spider.

A satisfied grin edged up his face. "You thought the spider came from your mother. No, Charlotte. It's your Wilderbrandt birthright." His lips curled into a snarl. "Meet *my* birthright!"

My breath hitched as the spider started to fade back into mist and spread across my face, seeping into my eyes and nostrils. Into my pores. I backed away, trying to escape it, fighting the instinct to open my tightly closed mouth. But then I gave into the urge and inhaled sharply, euphoria washing over me as the spider filled my lungs.

When it was over, I looked back at my father. "And now it's mine."

His eyes filled with shock. Rage. But instead of lunging for me, his lips slowly rose into a smile as he disappeared into a room to his right. When he came back out, he had Lucy in his grip, and she was bound up tightly.

"Motherfucker!" she spat when he ripped the duct tape off her mouth. "My brothers are going to tear your throat out!" She squirmed, managing to scratch his arm with her bound hands.

He slammed her against the wall, pinning her by her neck. Then he looked back at me. "You force my hand, Charlotte."

"I'll get you the amulet," I said, fearing he was about to kill her out of rage. "Just let her go."

"I'm afraid it's too late for that. You've shattered my trust in you. Taken something very precious from me." The look in his eyes was frightening. Maniacal. "You just stole my birthright."

When another ball of energy started to swirl in my hand, he pulled a knife from his pocket and held the tip of the blade millimeters from Lucy's right eye. "I'll blind the bitch before that sphere of light reaches me!"

Lucy let out a strangled gasp but didn't dare struggle.

"Okay." I threw my hands up, letting the energy dissipate. "What do you want me to do?"

His snarl spread into a grin. "I want you to feel what I just felt." He dropped the knife as his hand began to glow, the light building until it lit up like a torch. Before I could anticipate what he was about to do, he pulled his arm back, splaying his fingers as he aimed the magic at Lucy's chest.

"No!" I frantically summoned my own magic, trembling as a sphere manifested in my hand. But it was too late. By the time I hurled it at him, a beam of silver light shot from his palm and slammed into Lucy's chest, the sound of cracking ribs horrifying me.

The ball of energy broadsided him, knocking him back

against the opposite wall. He winced, gripping his smoldering arm but savoring my reaction as a strangled scream came from Lucy's mouth. Shock rolled over her face as she dropped to the floor. A second later, he was gone. Disappeared into another room.

I fell to my knees next to her and gazed at the gaping wound. Then I started to panic. "Help!" I screamed. "Someone help me!"

Samuel came through the door with Dog and Ian right behind him. Without a word, he dropped down to examine Lucy's chest. "Her heart has been severely damaged."

"Where is he!" Dog growled.

"I don't know." I pointed to a door. "He went through there."

Dog shifted and took off out the window Wilderbrandt had escaped through.

With tears streaming down my face, I forced myself to look back at Lucy. "You have to save her, Samuel." When he just stared at me, I grabbed his shirt. "Give her your blood!"

"My blood won't fix this, Charley. She's gone."

"What?" I let go of him and stood up. "You didn't even try!"

Ian leaned against the wall and folded his arms. "One less cocky little shit, if you ask me."

I was in his face a second later. "That *cocky little shit* is my family! Feed her!" I wanted to grab that knife off the floor and cut him open myself.

"There's a heartbeat," Samuel said. He'd bitten into his wrist and dripped some blood into Lucy's mouth.

Ian looked down at her still form with raised brows. "Seriously?"

"It's faint," Samuel said, "but I sense a beat."

Like a dog listening to a whistle, Ian cocked his head. "I think you're right."

Samuel leaned closer to Lucy's chest. "It's fading. My blood can repair the heart, if she doesn't die first. We need to get it beating again."

Ian nodded. "You mean she needs a kick-start."

"Like a defibrillator?" I said.

"Exactly." Samuel glanced at my hands. "And those are the defibrillator."

I took an involuntary step back. "Wait a minute."

"We don't have a minute, Charley. Lucy is dying."

Samuel's words kicked me into action. I quickly focused on calm healing energy, but what I got a few seconds later was a raging ball of blue fire in my palm. "Is it too much?"

Ian seemed to find it all amusing. "There's only one way to find out."

I got down on my knees next to Lucy before I changed my mind and pressed my hand to the wound. I wasn't terribly squeamish, but the bloody mess squishing between my fingers made me want to gag.

"Concentrate," Samuel said. "Visualize her heart beating."

Focusing, I let my energy flow into Lucy. A few seconds of nothing passed, and then her still chest started to move ever so slightly. Then I could feel it. It wasn't just her heart kicking into gear—I could feel her life force. I'd never felt anything like it before.

Without so much as a warning breath, she suddenly sat straight up and let out a loud gasp as her eyes flew open. A bloodcurdling scream escaped her mouth when she looked down at her chest. Then her eyes rolled back in her head, and she dropped to the floor again.

I jumped up. "I killed her, didn't I?"

Samuel bit into his wrist again and dripped more blood into her mouth. "You did everything right. Give it time."

The three of us watched as Lucy's chest started to rise and fall. Then the wound began to close. Heal before our eyes. A moment later, it was completely gone. If it wasn't for all the blood on her shirt, you would have never known that a minute earlier she looked like a dead woman.

"That was quite entertaining," Ian said.

I snorted. "For someone with a black heart like yours."

"Your boyfriend's heart is just as black, sweetheart."

Dog came back through the window he'd jumped out of earlier and shifted, doing a double take when he saw Lucy all healed up. "Vampire blood?"

"Sort of," I said. Wait until I told him the rest of it. Wait until I told *Lucy*.

He grabbed his clothes off the floor to get dressed. "Why isn't she up?"

"She'll be fine." Samuel checked her pulse. "Her heart was ravaged. It'll take a day and some rest to heal completely."

"The bastard didn't leave a trail," Dog said. "It's like he vanished after jumping out that window."

It wouldn't have surprised me if he did. Katherine was right about my father getting stronger. For a male Wilderbrandt who supposedly didn't have much magic in him, he sure fooled me. But I got the better of him. I just prayed I didn't come to regret swallowing that spider. My father's birthright. One thing was for sure. He was going to try to get it back, and I looked forward to us coming to blows again. For the last time.

TWENTY-FOUR

"Put her upstairs in the guest bedroom," Candy said when we got Lucy to the Cauldron.

"Are you sure you don't want to put her in the back room instead of hauling her all the way up there?" She seemed stable, and she'd probably be fighting us to get out of here before morning.

"No way. I don't want that woman's bad juju messing up my workspace."

I couldn't argue with that. Lucy could definitely be toxic at times.

I'd called her brother Wyatt on the way over and told him she was staying at my place tonight. That we'd had a party after closing the bar, and she'd gotten pretty tipsy. If she wasn't good as new by morning, I'd have to come up with another story.

Candy closed her eyes and took a calming breath before addressing the elephant in the kitchen. "You want to tell me why you went up to that lake tonight alone?"

"I wasn't alone." I pointed my thumb at my entourage. "I had two vampires and a wolf with me."

"Don't get cute with me, Charley. You should have taken me and the Squad with you."

"We didn't have time to wait for them." And I didn't want Candy in the line of fire. My father had already gotten the best of her once.

She shook her head. "The perfect opportunity to take him out just slipped through our hands. You were being foolish, Charley."

I wasn't used to Candy being angry at me. Disappointed, yes, but not angry like she was at that moment. "I screwed up, but there's nothing I can do about it now, so can we please move on?"

She let up on the scolding stare. "I'm just glad you're okay."

As things were finally settling down, the Squad's Buick pulled up to the shop. Candy must have called them to let them know what had happened and that we were on our way over with Lucy.

I was surprised when four witches climbed out of the car. "Is that Mia?"

"In the flesh," Candy said. "She came around a little while ago. Katherine said her eyes just popped open. Then she asked for a shot of absinthe, of all things."

I'd probably need a drink too, if I'd just come out of a spell-induced coma.

The ladies walked into the Cauldron, with Fay helping her sister navigate. Though the color in Mia's face was back to normal, the witch still seemed a little unsteady.

Samuel grabbed one of the folding chairs leaning against the wall and offered it to her. "Have a seat."

"Thank you, but I've been sitting for days." Mia's frosty eyes turned to me. "Where is that monster?"

"I don't know," I said. "He got away after trying to kill my bartender."

Katherine's eyes lit up. "Candy said you used your magic to

save her. To repair her heart. Very impressive, Charley. Unfortunately, you may have just ruined our opportunity to kill him."

She was starting to sound like Candy, and I was dreading telling her what else I'd done. About that black mist I inhaled and how furious my father was after I'd done it. I had a feeling we'd have a second shot at him though.

"I don't know about that," I said. "I think I'll be hearing from my father again very soon."

Candy tilted her head. "Why's that?"

I took an extra deep breath to settle my nerves. "Because I took something from him." Every eye in the room was suddenly trained on me. "I ate his spider."

Ian cocked his brows. "You ate his what?"

"Oh dear." Desiree's face went blank for a moment. "How did you do that?"

"More importantly," Katherine said, "where did he get it?"

"He said it was his birthright."

"Well," she said, "even the Wilderbrandt men are born with some magic. But as I said back in Savannah, it's weak at best."

Didn't look weak to me.

"For Richard to have been able to manifest a spider," she continued, "he must have had help cultivating it. His studies in black magic, no doubt." She looked at me curiously. "How did the spider present to you?"

Present?

"Uh... It started out as black mist coming from his hand. He shot it from across the room, but it stopped in front of me. I didn't know what it was until it started to take shape and I saw those legs." I shuttered from the memory. "When it tried to seep into every orifice of my face, I got this overwhelming urge to breathe it in. So I did."

A laugh burst from Katherine's mouth, trailing into a string of chuckles.

"What's so damn funny?" Candy said.

The witch composed herself. "I just realized my brother is stupider than I thought. He gave away his power. To Charley. No wonder she was able to heal her friend."

"He didn't give me all of it," I said. "He had enough left over to slam it into Lucy's chest and stop her heart. His hand was glowing like a torch."

Katherine's laughter ceased. "Yes, that would require a good bit of magic."

"He tried to kill Lucy to punish me. For not bringing him the amulet. You should have seen the look on his face when I inhaled that mist. He was beyond furious." The more I thought about it, the more I wanted to find him and put an end to this madness. "He'll come after me again. I guarantee it."

"Good," Katherine said. "Then you can use his own spider to kill him."

* * *

The Stag had just closed when Dog and I got back over there. The least I could do was help clean up my own bar, especially after being MIA for the past two nights. After that, I was meeting Samuel back at his house.

Mag was sitting at the bar waiting for Tucker to get off. With Lucy disappearing, she'd come in at the last minute to work the bar with Beau for the remainder of the night.

"You doing all right?" I asked as I grabbed his empty glass.

"Can't complain. You?"

I laughed quietly. "Peachy."

Dog peered through the order window and whistled at Mag. He reached into his pocket and laid a twenty on the bar. "I'm being summoned by my pack leader."

"You're back in?" Dog hadn't mentioned that Mag was officially part of the pack again.

"On a probationary basis." A grin slid up the side of his face. "But not for long."

He locked eyes with Tucker as he got up, and I felt like an interloper caught in the heat radiating between them. That girl was so far gone. I prayed his reputation was in the past, and he didn't eventually manifest into a giant asshole. The last thing I needed was a jilted bag of emotions tending the bar. But for now, she was walking on air.

I handed Tucker the twenty and went down to talk to Beau. "You need to watch your back for the next few days," I said to him.

"Is this about Lucy?"

"Yeah. It's a long story, but someone targeted her tonight to get to me. She's fine," I said, predicting his next question, "but he might try to go after you or Tucker next." I glanced through the window into the kitchen. I was pretty sure Dog was filling Mag in so he could keep an eye on Tucker. "Just keep your eyes open until this is over."

He stared at me for a second. "That's all you're going to tell me?"

I didn't have the time or patience to explain the revelation that I was a Wilderbrandt. That my father was the black sheep of the family who'd come home to claim his daughter for nefarious reasons. That had to wait.

"I don't have time to explain, Beau. Just promise me you'll be careful."

"Whatever." Annoyed, he walked away and started collecting empty glasses.

I began wiping down the bar and heard something break. Tucker was standing halfway between me and Beau, with a shattered glass by her feet. There was red wine all over the floor, and her mouth was hanging open.

"Tucker?" She stared back at me like she was looking at a ghost. "Tucker!"

Mag came out of the kitchen and looked back and forth between us. "What happened to her?"

"I don't know," I said, getting an uncomfortable vibe from the way she was looking at me. More like looking through me.

Beau walked up and waved his hand over her face. "What the hell's wrong with her?"

When Mag growled at him, Beau's eyes flashed amber as he returned a growl of his own. The Hollerwolf was about to make an appearance, so I stepped between them and shot Mag a warning look.

Dog came out of the kitchen. "Back off!" he barked.

Mag obeyed, narrowing his eyes at Beau. "What the fuck are you?"

"Nothing you need to worry about right now," I said, going up to Tucker to inspect her blank eyes. "Can you hear me, Tucker?" It was like she was caught in a trance.

Whatever it was suddenly broke, and she looked down at the mess on the floor. "Oh God! I'm sorry!" Then she bent down and started picking up broken glass.

Mag pulled her back to her feet. "I'll get it. You got a broom, Charley?"

"Don't worry about it," I said. "Let's just sit her down."

"I don't need to sit down," she said. "I dropped a glass, that's all."

Like hell that was all. "You had a vision, didn't you?" It was pretty obvious.

"It's nothing. Just some nonsense image of..."

"Image of what, Tucker?"

Her voice got about two octaves higher as she looked away from me. "Oh... I don't know."

"Tucker?" I wanted to shake her. Threats of death had been off the charts around here lately, so any inkling of trouble needed to be spelled out, even if it was just an image in my bartender's head.

She brought her eyes back to mine. "It was you, Charley. You were falling."

"Falling off what?"

"I don't know." She shook her head. "I saw you fall backward and disappear."

I shrugged. "Maybe I'm going to fall off my front porch or something."

She nodded briskly. "Yeah. That's probably it. And then I saw you again and you were just fine. Not a scratch on you," she added with a plastered-on smile.

After staring at her for a moment and realizing I wasn't going to get anything else out of her, I let it go. "Let's close up and get out of here."

"You want me to follow you home?" Dog asked.

I shook my head. "I'm staying at Samuel's tonight." Samuel's place was a lot closer to the Stag than my house, and I really needed to be with him tonight. To forget about the chaos and what was coming next, even if it was just for a few hours. It would all be waiting for me in the morning.

"Then go on. I'll lock up."

I took him up on his offer, my eyes darting up and down the sidewalk as I headed for my truck and got in. I may have gotten the best of Richard Wilderbrandt tonight, but this wasn't over. It would have been stupid of me to let my guard down now. In fact, on the five-minute drive to Samuel's place, every person or shadow I saw was suspect.

When I got out of the truck at Samuel's house, he walked up behind me. "Jesus, Samuel! Make some noise or something." I nearly jumped out of my skin. "You followed me from the Stag, didn't you?"

He pulled me against him and gave me a light kiss. "Guilty."

When we went inside, I grabbed his hand to stop him from walking past the staircase, running my thumb slowly over his skin. He turned and held my gaze as his lips parted, revealing the tips of his fangs. I'd seen them dozens of times, but all I could think of, crave, was having them nip at my skin. The sweet pain that would come when he sank them into me.

I slid my arms around his waist and kissed the hollow of his neck, bringing my eyes up to his. "Take me upstairs."

His lips pressed against mine as my feet left the ground. Before I could catch my breath, we were up the staircase and in the bedroom with my back pressed to the wall. Samuel's tongue explored my mouth, his scent intensifying as he pulled his lips away and dropped his forehead to mine.

"Fuck, woman."

My breathing grew more rapid. "That's the idea."

A moan escaped my lips when his hands slid under my shirt. And then he pulled it over my shoulders and tossed it on the floor as he stepped back and started to undress. I took the rest of my clothes off as he watched me. Then he moved backward toward the bed, beckoning me with his eyes.

I straddled him when he sat on the edge of the mattress, rocking back and forth. Then he flipped me over and ran his fingers down the center of my chest, moving them lower as he sank his fangs into my breast. I gasped from the sharp pain, but it quickly faded to a warm sensation that traveled down my torso and caressed me to my core.

The soft skin of his lips found the edge of my jaw, the tips of his fangs sending shivers through me as they continued up my face. "Say it, Charley." His eyes bored into mine. "Say you belong to me."

"I'm yours, Samuel," I whispered against his lips. "No one else's."

He parted my thighs with his knee and slid inside me forcefully. There was nothing gentle about it. We were a mass of limbs, our bodies fusing from the raw friction. Samuel knew exactly what I needed, and he gave it to me in waves. Soul-shattering waves.

* * *

The sun was breaking through the curtains when I sat up in bed. It was intensely bright, so it had to be mid-morning. I didn't care how late it was. I'd been running on fumes lately and needed the sleep.

With a smile on my face, I lay back against the pillows while butterflies swarmed in my stomach from the thought of what Samuel had done to me in this bed last night. I couldn't get enough of him, and his scent on the sheets was making me want more.

I rolled over and felt the empty spot next to me. Either we needed to look into options for covering up those windows better, or he needed to make room for me in his chamber below the basement.

After climbing out of bed, I searched for my clothes on the floor. I found them neatly draped over the chair, and I couldn't help but smile. Then I got dressed and went downstairs to see if Sebastian had come home. I hoped Samuel had remembered to pick up some cat food.

When I got down to the kitchen, there was no sign of the cat. He was probably off carousing again. But I was thrilled to see that Samuel had replaced the coffeepot Sebastian had broken the other night.

I started some coffee and grabbed a mug from the cabinet. When I turned around to check the refrigerator for some milk or creamer, I got a look at the back wall. The cup slipped from my hand, but I managed to catch it before it shattered on the floor. Written in large letters on the wall in something that looked like blood were two words.

THE LAKE

TWENTY-FIVE

Candy paced the floor of the shop like a tiger trapped in a cage. "How the hell did Richard Wilderbrandt get inside the house without Samuel knowing it? He's a vampire. He should have been able to smell the bastard the second he crossed the threshold."

Samuel and I had been preoccupied for a good part of the night, but I doubted that was the reason my father had gotten in and out of there undetected. Just the thought of him down in the kitchen while we were tangled in the sheets upstairs was enough to make my stomach turn.

"He must have used magic to cover his tracks," I said. "Samuel's going to lose his shit when he finds out." It was daytime, so he was still in his chamber, oblivious to what had happened.

Candy had called the Squad over, and Katherine was standing near the front window with her arms crossed. "My brother's dabbling on the dark side has paid off with power."

"And stealing Fawny's has only given him more," Desiree added.

"What about the spider?" I said. "It must have weakened him when I took it." It was odd that I couldn't feel it inside me. My own spider had done a number on my stomach and made itself known, but other than the initial euphoria when I inhaled that mist, I felt nothing. "And don't forget, we have his amulet."

Katherine pulled her eyes away from the window to look at me. "And he has yours." She let out a frustrated sigh. "The only way to defeat my brother once and for all is to trick him. Lure him to us so we can trap him with a collective spell."

Candy grinned slyly. "You mean we're going to cast a net and catch us a rat."

"Yes," Mia said. "And I get to take the kill shot once he's trapped."

I'd never seen such viciousness in Mia Winston's eyes.

"Indeed we are," Katherine said. "And Charley is going to be the bait."

* * *

I got to the lake just before dusk. Any later and Samuel would have found that message on his kitchen wall and come after me, possibly ruining the plan. But since the message didn't include a specific time or spot at the lake for me to arrive, I hoped my father was already waiting for me.

A branch snapped somewhere behind me. When I turned around, he was standing several yards away near the edge of the water.

"I'm here," I said. "Now what?"

He scanned the woods behind me. "You came alone this time."

"Wasn't I supposed to?"

"Good girl." A grin slowly climbed up his face. "Did you bring it?"

As I reached into my pocket for the amulet, I hesitated. "Where's mine?"

He opened his hand, and I caught the glint of the sapphire in the light. When he saw me finally pull the obsidian stone from my pocket, his mouth twitched at the corner. "Toss it to me."

Did he think I was stupid? "You first."

His smile vanished. "Don't play games you can't win, Charlotte."

I guess he really did think I was stupid, but he was delusional if he thought he was going to get the upper hand. There was no hostage for leverage this time. I also had his birthright inside me, whatever that meant. But I would have been foolish to underestimate him, and I needed to get him to come after me so I could lead him straight into the trap set by Candy and the Squad who were waiting just beyond the perimeter of the lake. Far enough back that he wouldn't detect them, but close enough to ensnare him with their magic before my running legs gave out.

I dangled the pendant from my index finger. "If you want it, you'll have to come and get it yourself." When he took the bait and came toward me, I threw every ounce of my will into manifesting a ball of energy.

His eyes ignited with anger when he saw my hand begin to glow. "You lying little—"

The light shot toward him before he could finish his insult. I'd aimed for the spot between his eyes. The kill shot, as Mia had called it. If I could take him out swiftly, to hell with the plan.

His hand flew up, bringing the magic to a halt like he'd done the night before. But instead of it reversing and flying back toward me, he opened his arms wide as the light softened and began to flow around him, absorbing into his body.

The bastard stole my move.

"So, this is how you want to play," he said when the last trace of the light vanished. Instead of coming at me again, his eyes wandered around the forest behind me. For a moment, I thought he was on to the plan, but then a wicked grin spread across his face as he looked at the water. His hand slipped into his pocket, and a ripple came from the center of the lake. The sun was just beginning to set, and the last golden rays of light caught the shimmer as the ripple widened.

"I have a present for you, Charlotte. Something to convince you I'm not the monster you think I am."

A knot formed in my stomach as something started to break the surface. It moved under the water toward the edge where he was standing. And then a figure appeared. At first it was just the top of a head, and then a set of eyes. When the rest of the woman emerged, I stumbled and almost dropped the amulet. I had to be hallucinating. It wasn't real.

"We could have been a family," he said, pulling his eyes from mine to gaze at my mother standing at the edge of the lake next to him. She was naked and sopping wet, her eyes sparkling blue.

"Mom?" My brain was telling me it was some kind of illusion, but my heart was saying otherwise.

"Yes, Charlotte, it's me." A mechanical smile slid up her face as she held her hand out. "Give me the amulet."

My mother's voice suddenly filled my head, but it wasn't coming from the figure standing by the lake.

It's a trick, Charley. He's a snake.

The imposter spoke to me again, but while her lips were moving, the words were coming from my father's mouth. And there was something in his hand. A bone. The stolen necromancer's charm. It had to be.

He killed me.

For a moment, I couldn't breathe.

Your father killed me, Charley!

I managed to pull myself together. "You killed my mother?"

That thing standing next to him went still, its eyes suddenly turning cloudy and lifeless. Like spoiled eggs. The head tilted sideways as it collapsed into a heap of bones at my father's feet. One of the many skeletons from the bottom of the lake.

He gazed at me curiously. "I took no pleasure in it. It didn't have to be this way. But now I've come back for you, Charlotte. To teach you."

"No." I shook my head. "You came back to exploit me."

"If that's what you choose to believe." He stuffed the bone back in his pocket along with my amulet. "The truth is, your mother threatened to fill your mind with vicious lies. To deprive me of having a relationship with my own daughter. To stop me from cultivating your magic into something so powerful that nothing could stop us."

And there it was. *Us.*

"I came back here two years ago with every intention of making things right between us, but Delia made it very clear that I would never see you again. So, I waited for her at the Stag the next morning. Confronted her as she was coming in through the alley." His mouth puckered into a grimace. "She dismissed me like a gnat. Then she let her guard down and never saw this *gnat* coming."

I listened as he described how he'd murdered my mother. It took every ounce of my will to remain calm and let him dig his hole deeper. Falling apart would have ruined any chance of delivering justice.

"I used a spell," he continued. "A paralysis spell I'd learned from a conjure woman in New Orleans. The same one I used on Mia." He took a steady breath through his nose before continuing. "Then I drove her to the river and injected her with a dose of alcohol from the bar before sending the car into the water. It was genius really. My sister and the others never suspected."

It felt like someone had punched me in the gut. I always knew my mother didn't drive off the road and into that river. She rarely drank more than an occasional glass of wine. Never during the day, and certainly not on her way to work. It was absurd, but the police closed the case for lack of evidence to substantiate any other possibilities. Now I knew with absolute certainty that Richard Wilderbrandt had to die, and Mia Winston needed to get in line. After we snared him in that trap, my father was going to meet his demise at my hands.

We stared at each other. Neither one of us moving an inch.

"Two years is a long time to wait," he finally said, "and I'm growing impatient." His eyes darkened as his jaw clenched. "Give me my amulet!"

I held it up for him to get a good look at it again. "Like I said, you'll have to come and get it."

When he came toward me, I darted into the trees. As I ran deeper, I could hear the cracking of branches and debris in the distance behind me. The steady sounds of the chase. But then the forest got quiet as if he'd stopped. He was ruining the plan. I needed him to chase me.

I caught a glimpse of black wings through the top of the trees. A crow. It must have been Rex following me through the forest. But when he swooped down and grazed me with his talons, tearing at my shirt, I watched him sail back into the sky. There was no white feather in his wing. It wasn't Rex. Then another crow flew down toward me, leaving a gash in my forehead as it slashed me with its sharp claws.

My father stepped out from behind a tree, a low laugh coming from his mouth. "You think you're the only crow in this forest?" Then he gave a signal to the dozens of birds that had gathered in the canopy above us.

I covered my eyes when they descended, stumbling and hitting my head against a thick tree root on the forest floor. As I tried to push myself up, dazed from the fall, my father's face came into view above me.

"I don't want to hurt you, Charlotte," he said as he raised his glowing hand to deliver a final blow. "But you leave me no choice."

* * *

My head was splitting when I woke up on a cold wooden floor. Between the knot on the back of my head and a blinding headache from my father knocking me out with magic, I could barely think straight. But then it all came rushing back when I reached into my pocket and realized my phone and the amulet were gone.

I was so fucked.

The room was dark, the only light coming from the night sky shining through a tiny window near the ceiling. When I heard noises beyond the door of the room I was in, I climbed to my feet and went over to see if it was locked. When I turned the knob, it opened, the smell of bacon immediately hitting my nose.

The door opened to a larger room with a kitchen on the right and a sparsely furnished sitting area on the left. Based on the wood walls and ceiling, I figured it was a cabin.

My father was standing at the stove with his back to me, cooking. "Have a seat," he said without turning around.

There was a small round table against the wall with two place settings. "What is this?" I said.

"Breakfast." He glanced over his shoulder at me. "You like bacon, don't you? Everyone likes bacon."

I had no idea what time it was or how long I'd been in that room, but it was still dark outside. "Where are we?" He ignored me and continued to cook. "I said, where are we?"

"Sit!" he barked.

I did as he said and took a seat at the table, fisting my hand but barely feeling a tingle of magic.

He set a plate of bacon and eggs down in front of me and took a seat opposite me. "Eat."

"Not until you tell me what's going on. And where the hell are we?"

He took a bite of his eggs and chewed, never taking his eyes off his plate. When I started to stand up, he slammed his fist on the table, shaking it. "I said eat!" After taking a breath to calm down, he finally looked up at me. "We're going to enjoy a nice family meal together, and then we'll discuss your future."

I couldn't tell if he was taunting me or completely delusional, so I sat back down and took a bite of bacon, forcing myself to chew. Under the table, I kept pumping my fist, praying for a spark.

"That won't work," he said as if he could see my hand through the top. He pulled the obsidian amulet out from under his shirt. "Not while I have this."

"Where's mine? Or were you lying when you said you'd give it back to me in exchange for yours?" I didn't actually expect him to give it to me any more than I had planned to uphold my end of the bargain, so I was surprised when he reached into his pocket and tossed it across the table at me.

"I'm a man of my word, Charlotte."

I was even more surprised when he let me grab it. But it wasn't the same. The sapphire looked dull and lifeless. The sparkle had gone out of it, and it appeared almost black. "What did you do?"

He laughed quietly. "I siphoned its power into this." He reached for the obsidian around his neck. "It's quite fortified with your mother's magic. And keeping you in line," he added as I continued to struggle with mine.

Now I understood why the Squad had taken it from him and warded my house. He was controlling me with that damn necklace. Either that or he'd put some kind of spell over me while I was out cold in that room. But spells faded, and he was going to get his when I got my hands on that amulet around his neck.

"You have her power now, so why do you need me?" I asked.

He leaned closer. "Because I haven't figured out how to siphon yours yet. Or how to get my birthright back." A disturbing grin spread across his face as he grabbed his fork and yanked me toward him by my arm. "I would gouge your stomach open with this and take my spider back if I could." Then he shoved me away. "But for now, I'm stuck with you."

Without hesitating, I tried to reach for the amulet around his neck. He grabbed my wrist and twisted it painfully. "You ungrateful little bitch." Then he snatched the sapphire from my hand and got up. "I think it's time for another lesson."

"Wait!" I followed him when he opened the door and walked outside. Drained of magic or not, that necklace was mine. One of the few things I had left of my mother.

When I looked around, there were mountains straight ahead of me. He'd taken me to a cabin somewhere in the Blue Ridge, on top of one of those mountains. I could see the edge of a cliff a stone's throw away from the front door. It was both beautiful and terrifying at the same time.

He strode over to the ledge. "You want your amulet? Then go get it." The necklace left his hand and flew into the air. Into the abyss of whatever was below the mountain.

I ran to the edge and looked down. At the bottom of the steep ravine was a rolling river. The amulet was gone, taken by the fast-moving water. When I turned around, he was standing back at the door, and there was a sphere of light whirling in the palm of his hand.

After glaring back at me for a moment, he took a deep breath and let it out slowly. "You're such a disappointment, Charlotte. So I've decided not to waste any more of my precious time on you. You have a decision to make. Either give me back my birthright or die."

Even if I wanted to give it back, I didn't have a clue how. "I guess you'll have to kill me."

"All right then." His face went cold as he raised his hand to deliver the deadly blow.

There was only one way out—down into that raging river.

And then the voice of my mother confirmed it.

Fall.

"Fall?"

My father hesitated. "What did you say?"

Let go of your fear, Charley. Just fall.

I was caught in the confusion of it all—and terrified. But then Tucker's vision suddenly came to mind.

It was you, Charley. You were falling. And then I saw you again and you were just fine. Not a scratch on you.

Fuck it. I was dead either way.

I spread my arms wide as I prepared to take a leap of faith— literally. As I tilted backward and started to close my eyes, I caught a glimpse of a wing. A white feather. Rex! He flew toward my father, snatching the amulet from his neck. With the stone necklace dangling from his talons, he circled back toward me. But it was too late. My foot had already slipped over the edge.

The world seemed to spin in slow motion as I fell, my hand instinctively grabbing the amulet as Rex sailed past me within inches. Then it all sped up again, and suddenly I was looking down at myself. I was dissolving into black mist, floating like dust in the wind over the water.

I became the spider.

Time seemed to stand still. Freeze for what seemed like an eternity. And then in the blink of an eye, I was standing in the doorway of the cabin, and my father was peering over the edge of the cliff. The obsidian amulet was hanging around my neck, and there was a blinding sphere of light burning a hole in my hand.

"You won't find me down there," I said.

When he turned around, he nearly lost his footing and met the river. "How?"

Samuel suddenly shot from out of nowhere and gripped Richard Wilderbrandt by the neck. He lifted my father off his feet with one hand and squeezed him so tightly I thought he was about to decapitate the man. The hatred in Samuel's eyes was matched only by what I'd seen in them just before he'd killed his maker.

"No, Samuel," I said when his grip grew tighter. "I need to finish this."

As Samuel eased up on the man's neck, he flew sideways, taking my father with him as a blur of black fur slammed into them both. The Hollerwolf stood on the ledge and swung its head in my direction, a steady growl coming from its throat. Then it trained its eyes on my father.

Samuel jumped out of the way when the creature lunged. It wrapped its jaws around my father's shoulder, shaking him violently, tossing him into the air like a weightless feather. When he hit the ground, the Hollerwolf stood up on its hind legs and swept a massive paw out, hooking its claws into my father's back and dragging him toward the cliff.

"Beau!" I yelled. The creature stopped at the edge and looked at me, its lips curling into a snarl as its claws dug deeper into my father's back. "Let him go!"

The Hollerwolf swung its head back to my father and let out an ear-piercing growl that made the man's skin blanch. He was frozen in fear as the beast finally dropped him and backed away from the ledge.

My father pulled himself together and straightened up, wincing from the pain. But still, the bastard showed his arrogance. It was like he had a death wish. "Now that you've come to your senses, we can have a reasonable conversation." He gave Samuel a dismissive glance before looking back at me. "Let's continue this discussion inside."

I slowly shook my head. "It's easier to kill you out here."

He looked at the ball of magic whirling in my palm, growing brighter as my hatred for him intensified. "I'm your father, Charlotte."

I swallowed my rage and chose my words thoughtfully. "My mother was the only father I ever had. This is for her." Then I raised my hand and prepared to send the monster back to hell. "And by the way, it's *Charley*!"

The light flew from my hand, hitting my father dead center between the eyes, flaring up as it penetrated his head and continued down his neck and into his chest. His torso lit up from the inside out as it spread to his limbs. His eyes were filled with shock as he stared at me and stumbled back, slipping over the cliff and disappearing into the river below.

I met Samuel at the edge as he looked down. "You found me," I said.

"Of course."

There was nothing to see but the rolling river that had washed Richard Wilderbrandt's body away. A body that would never see the forest. But all the power that he'd been born with —or stolen—had already been taken from him. I was wearing some of it around my neck. And God only knew what had become of his birthright after what had just happened to me when I slipped and almost met the same fate. But I wasn't sure whose spider had saved me. Mine or his?

I glanced around the woods surrounding the cabin. "What happened to Beau?"

Samuel shrugged. "I don't know, but that collision was completely unnecessary. I don't think you needed either of us."

I didn't, but I wasn't going to tell him that. I was just

thankful that it was me who ended Richard Wilderbrandt's life. Delivered justice for my mother.

I let out a deep sigh, grieving the loss of my sapphire amulet but knowing my mother's magic had been captured in the obsidian stone hanging around my neck. "Let's get out of here."

Samuel grabbed my hand. "Excellent idea."

A sense of peace washed over me as we walked away from the cabin. It was finally over, and now I knew exactly who I was.

TWENTY-SIX

I stood at the end of the alley and eyed my target. With my hands cupped together, I manifested a ball of light between them and let it get good and bright until it was spinning in my palms. Then I pulled my arm back and sent the sphere rolling along the ground toward the empty beer bottle at the other end.

"Damn it!" I said as it raced past the bottle and kept going until it finally fizzled out.

Beau walked out the back door of the Stag as I was manifesting another one. "What are you doing out here?"

"Bowling." It was a surprisingly effective way to practice my aim. Magic had become second nature to me, so I needed to keep honing my skills. Perfecting my precision. Being able to take someone's head off with a sphere of light was no joke, and I intended to use it responsibly.

He cocked his head. "You're bowling with magic?"

"Yep." I sent another one down the alley and missed the target again. "I'm bowling zero though." Which just meant I wouldn't be cleaning up a bunch of broken bottles at the end of the night. "How's the wolf doing?"

"Which one?"

"You, Beau." The Hollerwolf showing up at that cabin the other night was the last thing I had expected. Beau's alter ego had been wilding in the mountains when he'd picked up on my scent and decided to crash the party. It had been a free-for-all up there, sending him deeper into his inner beast, trapping him in a state of limbo where he'd been stuck as half creature and half human for most of the weekend. The Stag had been a bartender short until tonight.

He scratched his head. "My eyes are still a little touch and go, but at least I haven't seen any fur today."

I was just glad he was finally getting back to normal in all other ways. He was wearing his usual clothes again and had shed his sunglasses permanently. Beau Henry was out and proud.

He glanced up and down the dark alley. "It's creepy out here."

I used to think so too, but I wasn't uneasy about it anymore, especially that dumpster, because I was armed and dangerous now.

"Do you need something?" I said, getting back to my game.

"Candy's here. She's looking for you."

I followed him back inside and tripped over the lump lying in front of the desk. After catching myself on the edge of the filing cabinet, I gave Beau a stern look. "Why is he here?" I didn't mind sharing the back room with Diablo, but it would have been nice to have a heads-up.

"You were already out back when I got here." He seemed annoyed by my comment. "So now you know."

I should have been the one irritated since he came in late tonight. But it was Monday evening, and the bar was practically dead. I'd also told him he could bring the dog in whenever he needed to, and lately Diablo had been experiencing separation anxiety. Beau's favorite chair was now a giant chew toy.

Lucy was working up front. She'd been less ornery than

usual since having her near-death experience. Still full of attitude, but slightly humbled.

When I walked behind the bar, she sideswiped me in a less than gentle way. "You want to watch where you're going," I said.

She threw me a glance over her shoulder. "Well, if you paid me for my lost tips the other night, I wouldn't have to hustle to make up for it."

"You mean the other night when I saved your life?" I guess she wasn't as humbled as I thought.

She turned around and looked at me like I was the one with an attitude. "And whose fault was that?" Then she continued over to the tap, grumbling about how she never asked me for my help. Lucy was definitely back.

When I looked at the other end of the bar, Candy was talking to that Decker guy. I was kind of hoping he'd decided to leave town. The man didn't sit right with me. Didn't pass my smell test. But he left good tips and Candy seemed to like him. She was a savvy judge of character, so maybe I was being too hard on the guy.

"I guess I don't need to introduce you two," I said when I walked up to them. He was already showing her a card trick.

Candy was studying the cards fanned out on the bar face down. "It's that one," she said, tapping her finger on one of the cards.

Decker flipped it over. "Sorry. House wins."

"Well, shoot." She stared at the ace of spades in front of her and shook her head. "How did you do that?"

"I guess you haven't gotten sick of this town yet," I said. "I figured you might have moved on by now."

He started to gather the cards. "I have some business in Crimson to finish first."

"Oh yeah? What business is that?" He hadn't mentioned business the other times he'd been in here.

Without answering the question, he grinned and slid the ace across the bar toward me. "Isn't this one yours, Charley?"

How *did* he do that?

I looked at the black skull in the center of the card, recalling how he'd said the deck had been custom-made. I found that interesting, since he'd left the ace of spades from that one-of-a-kind deck on the bar the last time he was in here a week ago. In fact, I'd stuffed it in my pocket.

"Thanks," I said, sliding it back to him, "but I still have the last one you gave me."

But come to think of it, I didn't know where it was now. Damn, he was good.

Candy got up and pointed to the kitchen. "I'm going to go have a word with Dog while you tend to your card shark here."

Beau was back up front with Lucy, so that was my cue to get away from the man. Join Candy and Dog in the kitchen until he was gone.

"I'll have a beer," Decker said as I started to leave.

And I was so close to a clean getaway. "What kind?"

"Whatever you have on tap." His grin had vanished, and his eyes seemed darker.

When I returned with his beer, he took a swallow. As he was setting the glass down, his eyes darted to the front door. "I think it's time for me to leave."

"Hope it wasn't something I said," I muttered, thrilled to see him go.

Decker stood up and looked at the ace of spades on the bar. He tossed a ten down and placed his index finger on the card, sliding it toward me again. Then he leaned closer and gave me a good look at his nearly black eyes. "Give this to Samuel Cain. Tell him an old friend stopped by."

"Samuel? How do you know—?"

I did a double take as he disappeared through the front door at breakneck speed. No human being moved that fast.

Samuel walked in a moment later and came up to the bar. He eyed me curiously when I barely acknowledged him, continuing to stare at the window where Decker had streaked past seconds earlier. "Is everything all right?"

I shook my head. "I don't think so." I had the worst feeling in the pit of my stomach as I handed him the ace of spades.

He seemed curious when he took the card from my hand, but his face went dark when he looked at it closer. "Where did you get this?"

"A new customer that showed up last week. He just left and gave me that card along with a message for you. He said to tell you that an old friend stopped by."

His eyes narrowed as he crushed the card in his hand. "Well, what do you know?"

"Who is this guy, Samuel?"

He tossed the crumpled card on the bar and gazed out the window. "His name is Shane Ronan."

Where did I hear that name before? And then it hit me. Samuel mentioned it the night he'd given me a glimpse into his past. The night he told me about working for his father in Boston.

"You wanted to know more about the man who destroyed my life over a century ago." He brought his eyes to mine. "I think you just met him."

A LETTER FROM LUANNE

It's a scary thing to put your heart into a book and send it out for the world to see, and you've all responded kinder than I could have ever imagined. Thank you so much for that!

And thank you for continuing the journey with Charley and her strange and wonderful found family. But Charley's story is just beginning, now that she's learning to master her magic and knows who she really is.

Stay up to date with my latest releases by signing up at the link below. Your email address will never be shared and you can unsubscribe at any time.

www.secondskybooks.com/luanne_bennett

If you enjoyed *Bloodlust Curse*, please consider leaving a brief review. It's one of the best ways to support an author. It really does make a difference, and I appreciate every one of them.

I love hearing from readers. Get in touch on my social media or website. And don't forget to follow me!

KEEP IN TOUCH WITH LUANNE

www.luannebennett.com

facebook.com/LuanneBennettBooks
x.com/Luanne_Bennett
instagram.com/luannebennettbooks
bookbub.com/authors/luanne-bennett
goodreads.com/lbennett14

ACKNOWLEDGMENTS

First of all, thank you to everyone who read *Bloodlust Curse* and your amazing response to the series. Your emails and comments make me excited to share more of Charley's unusual world. I have some incredible readers out there!

I also want to thank the team at Second Sky and Bookouture, and of course my editor, Jack Renninson, for continuing to believe in the books. Everyone has been exceptionally supportive and patient.

And as always, thank you to my friends and family, especially my perpetual cheerleader, Sharon, who should get royalties just for putting up with my ramblings. Friends don't get any better than that. Here's to a few more decades of listening to story ideas.

PUBLISHING TEAM

Turning a manuscript into a book requires the efforts of many people. The publishing team at Bookouture would like to acknowledge everyone who contributed to this publication.

Audio
Alba Proko
Melissa Tran
Sinead O'Connor

Commercial
Lauren Morrissette
Hannah Richmond
Imogen Allport

Cover design
Damonza.com

Data and analysis
Mark Alder
Mohamed Bussuri

Editorial
Jack Renninson
Melissa Tran

Made in the USA
Middletown, DE
16 February 2025

71368929R00156